Agony

NEW YORK TIMES BESTSELLING AUTHOR

KAYLEE RYAN

Cover Design: Sommer Stein, Perfect Pear Creative Covers
Cover Photography: Braadyn Penrod
Editing: Hot Tree Editing
Proofreading: Deaton Author Services
Formatting: Integrity Formatting

PART ONE

Agony

COOPER

I've heard the saying "you don't know what you've got until it's gone" many times throughout my life. There have been songs written about it, but it never applied to me. I never paid much attention. I didn't need to.

Until I did.

Until the day I realized I was in love with my best friend.

Nine words. That sums up my current situation. I don't know the exact moment that I fell in love with Reese Latham. I can't tell you the day or the time, or even where I was. What I can tell you is that my love, it's absolute. It's a "deep rooted in my chest, chains around my heart" kind of love.

I can tell you that she's been a huge part of my life since we were eight years old. I don't have a single childhood memory without her in it. She is and has always been my person. I just didn't realize what that meant until it was too late.

I lost her to someone else. Someone I'm sure who will never love her like I do. He can't cherish her the way that I would. He can't make her laugh so hard that her cute button nose scrunches up. He can't hold her during scary movies. He can't love her like I can. I could continue to list the reasons, but none of them matter.

Because she's in love with him.

She's agreed to be his wife.

I'm reeling.

I want her.

My heart craves her.

But she's not mine.

There is a hole in my heart, and it has her name on it. Reese Latham will forever be the one that got away. Only, she's still here. I still get to see her. Her smile still lights up the cloudiest of days, and her voice will continue to be my anchor in any storm.

I was wrong. I said nine words summed up my current situation when really all I need is one.

Agony.

COOPER

COLLEGE: FRESHMAN YEAR

"Come on, Reese, you have to go," I say to my best friend. I've been lying here on her bed in her dorm for the last half hour. I'm trying to convince her to go to the team's season kick-off bonfire tonight.

"Nope. Not my scene, Coop. You know that."

"You'll be with me."

"Right." She laughs. "And all the floozies who want to hang all over you all night. Hard pass."

"When have I ever blown you off for a cleat chaser?" I ask, but I already know the answer. Never. I've never put anyone before Reese, including girlfriends. If they can't handle our relationship, they can find themselves a new one. We've been best friends since we were eight. I remember my parents dragging me to her house to welcome them to the neighborhood. I saw her pink bike in the yard and got excited. There were no other kids on our street. That afternoon her parents invited mine over for dinner, and Reese and I rode our bikes until we were practically falling off them from exhaustion. We've been thick as thieves ever since.

"Never." She heaves a heavy sigh, bringing me out of my thoughts. "That's just not me, Coop. Look." She holds up her e-reader that I got her for Christmas last year. "I have a perfectly good book to read, and some mint chocolate chip ice cream in the freezer. I'm all set. You go and have fun. Be safe. Call me if you need a ride," she adds, effectively dismissing me.

I have to go tonight. As a freshman on the football team for Central University, I have to be there to support my team. I have a full-ride scholarship, and as a freshman, Coach is starting me as a running back. That's a big deal. I have to be there. "Please, Reese's Pieces," I say, sticking my bottom lip out. I usually bribe her with candy when I pull out the name, but desperate times and all that.

She rolls her light green eyes and holds her hand out. "Hand them over."

"I don't have them."

"What kind of bribe is this?" she teases.

"We'll stop on the way. I promise." I don't know if it's because it's her name, but this girl loves all things Reese's. Then again, who doesn't?

"Cooper," she whines. "I really don't want to go."

"Too bad. You've been holed up in your dorm room since classes started. This is college, Reese. We're supposed to be living our best life."

"Hello." She holds up her e-reader. "I'm trying to live my best life. You keep interrupting me."

"Coach is going to be pissed," I say, kicking off my shoes.

"What are you doing?"

"I'm getting comfortable."

"On my bed?" she asks, annoyed.

"Yep. I'm not leaving you for another Saturday night alone. You either come with me, or I stay. Oh, and I'll be giving Coach your number when he's reaming my ass about not being there."

"It's not even a school-sanctioned event."

I nod. "It is. It's tradition." Her shoulders deflate, and I know I've got her.

"Fine," she grumbles. "I'll go to your stupid bonfire." I don't hide my grin as she climbs off the bed and stomps toward the bathroom. "But I reserve the right to leave at any time."

"Two hours minimum!" I yell as she disappears into the bathroom. I sit up and put my shoes back on, before stretching back out, keeping my feet hanging over the side of her bed.

"You owe me one, Reeves" is her muffled reply.

"Where's your roommate?" I call out to her.

"Tessa is out with some guy she met at orientation. I guess they hit it off," she says, coming back into the room. Her blonde hair is now hanging down around her shoulders, and I can tell she just ran her hands through it. Doesn't matter though; Reese is naturally beautiful; she doesn't need all the flair to stand out. "What?" she asks when she finds me staring at her.

"Nothing. You two hitting it off okay?"

"We are. I'm so glad. We're a lot alike."

"Except she's out on a Saturday night and you're here."

"I'm going out." She sticks her tongue out at me, causing me to laugh.

"Get used to it. I'm not letting you spend our college years hiding away in your dorm room."

"Hush. It's a nice room," she counters. "Do you know how lucky Tessa and I are to have a room with a bathroom for just the two of us? That's sacred and should be taken advantage of."

"It's the size of a Cracker Jack box."

Another roll of her green eyes. "It's mine."

"What's the point of all this freedom if you're not going to use it?"

She laughs. "You act like we lived sheltered lives before college." I raise my eyebrows, and her laugh grows louder. "Okay, but it was my choice. You, on the other hand, Mr. Social Butterfly."

"Hey, don't hate the player, hate the game."

"You're ridiculous. I hate that you're a player, and I hate that game." She gives me a pointed look.

"But you love football. All the more reason for you to come and hang out with the team tonight."

"I already agreed to go," she reminds me.

"Yes, but can you at least pretend to have a good time?" She's shy, and it's my goal to bring her out of her shell these next four years. She was shy in high school too, and I don't want to say naïve, but she's one of those girls who doesn't know how pretty she is. She doesn't even try. I've lost count of the number of times I've had to warn assholes to stay away from her. I refuse to see her be taken advantage of.

There was a short period of time a couple of months ago when I considered us being more. Then I came to my senses. She's my best friend, and I value her, cherish our relationship. No way am I going to fuck it up like I do all my other relationships.

She exaggerates her smile. "How's this?" she says, talking through her teeth.

"Perfect. Can you hold that for the entire night?"

"I agreed to two hours."

"You're going to have such a good time, you'll be there until the sun comes up."

"Don't hold your breath, Coop. You ready?" She slides her cell phone into the back pocket of her short jean shorts. She's wearing a Central U T-shirt and flip-flops. She couldn't care less about impressing anyone. She is who she is without apologies.

"Finally," I say dramatically. "I'm getting old over here." I hold out my hand and have her pull me from her bed. "This thing is actually quite comfortable for a twin dorm room mattress."

"See." She throws her hand that's not clasped with mine up in the air. "All the more reason to stay in and enjoy it."

"Nice try, Reese. Let's roll." With a tug on her hand, I pull her out into the hallway, only stopping to make sure her door is closed and locked.

"Hey, Cooper," a brunette calls out to me as we pass the common area on the first floor. I toss her a wink and a wave, and I don't have to look over at Reese to know that those green eyes of hers are rolled back in her head.

She doesn't comment until we're in my Jeep and headed toward the bonfire. "We can't even get out of my dorm without your harem calling out to you."

"It's just the hype about the season. Me being a freshman and starting and all that." It was the same for me in high school—something she's all too familiar with. She hated it then too.

"Yeah, yeah. Let's get this night over with."

Reaching over, I tap her thigh, resting my hand there. "Cheer up, Reese's Cup. I got you." She shakes her head, a grin pulling at her lips.

My phone rings in the cupholder. When Reese sees that it's my mom, she grabs it, and answers, "Hey, Ann." She places the call on speaker.

"Hey, sweetie. Did I call you or Cooper?" Mom chuckles.

"Coop. He's forcing me to go to a bonfire. He's driving."

"Hi, Mom," I say.

"Hi, honey."

"What's up?" I ask her.

"I just wanted to call and say hi. The two of you disappear to college and suddenly stop calling your mother."

"I'm sorry, Mom." Guilt washes over me. "Classes and football are taking up a lot of time."

"And the ladies," Reese adds as helpful as ever.

Mom laughs. "I don't want to know. Please tell me you're being safe."

"We are not having this conversation," I tell her.

"Fine. I'll have Dad call you tomorrow."

"No. Please don't. It's all good, Mom. I'm covered, promise."

"Literally." Reese cackles. "He already has a harem of football groupies following him around like a little puppy."

"Keep him grounded, Reese."

"I try my best." She smiles over at me sweetly.

"You kids have fun. Be safe. Cooper, call me tomorrow."

"Will do. Love you."

"Love you," Reese tells her.

"Love you both," Mom says, ending the call.

"Laugh it up," I tell her. "Just wait until I talk to your mom. In fact, I should call her tomorrow. Just to say hello."

"Go right ahead. She's not going to believe anything you tell her. I'm the good one, remember?"

"Oh, I remember. Just like the time we snuck that stray cat into your bedroom. What were we, ten? You had these big tears saying she was lonely and convinced me to help you sneak her into your room."

"Frisky. She was lonely," Reese defends.

"Right. Until she had a litter of kittens that you had me smuggle into my house."

"It's not my fault you weren't watching them," she sasses.

"I was ten!" I counter. "I don't even like cats. I was just doing it for you, and I'm the one who ended up getting busted."

"It's not my fault you didn't tell them it was my idea."

She's right. I never do. I've defended her since day one. My buddies gave me a hard time for being friends with a girl—girls have cooties, or so they said. I defended her then, and I've spent the last ten years doing the same. I've defended not just her, but our friendship countless times, and will continue to do so.

"You're lucky I love you," I tell her.

"Yeah, yeah. You got me here, you can stop with the buttering me up thing."

"Come on," I say, parking my Jeep in the open field. "I promise you're going to have a good time tonight."

"I thought we made a pact. No promises we can't keep."

"I can keep this one. Now, get your ass moving, Latham." Pulling the keys from the ignition and grabbing my phone, I climb out of the Jeep, hitting the lock button on the keyfob once she's out as well.

REESE

My palms are sweaty, and I'm pretty sure it's my shaking knees that have me stumbling, not the uneven ground of the field. I can't believe I let him talk me into this. Then again, I can. Cooper Reeves and his big brown eyes are convincing. So much so, that I rarely tell him no. Well, I tell him no a lot, but he always talks me into some crazy plan and has me tagging along for something that's out of my comfort zone. Case and point, this bonfire.

It's not that I'm anti-social. The opposite, in fact. However, I tend to steer clear of social situations where Coop is the main event, at least in the eyes of the cleat chasers. I have thick skin, but a girl can only take so much. He tries to protect me from it, but there's always one or five that get their digs in. I could fight back, but really, what's the point? They're never going to accept that we're just friends. It's as if a guy and a girl having a platonic relationship is unheard of. We're not abnormal. High school was hard, and I'm hoping college is better. Partly, because I was planning to let Coop do his thing, I'll do mine, and we can meet in the middle as time allows. My best friend apparently didn't get my mental memo, which is why I'm walking through a dark field about fifteen miles from campus.

"You sure this is school-sanctioned?" I ask him as I grab ahold of his arm to keep from tumbling over on this rough terrain.

"I might have stretched the truth just a little. Coach won't be here, but he knows about it. He says it's good team-building. He would have found out if I had bailed, and he needs to know I'm a team player."

"Do you not already show him that when you're out on the field?"

"Loosen up." He throws his arm over my shoulders. "Don't take a drink from anyone but me."

"You lied to me." I ignore his statement about a drink. I'm not stupid, and I'm also not drinking. I'd rather have my wits about me. Besides, I'm sure Cooper will have a few, and one of us needs to make sure we get home safely.

"No, I added elements to the story to convince you to come with me. Come on, Reese. I don't want to be known as the guy on the team who doesn't socialize."

"You don't need me here to do that."

"I would feel guilty all night long. How am I supposed to have fun when I'm worrying about you?"

"It's not your job to worry about me," I say the words, but I don't mean them. I like that I know I have him to lean on, no matter what's going on in my life.

"That's what I do. What kind of best friend would I be if I didn't?"

Right. Best friend. He's more than that to me, but he's never led me to believe we could ever be more. No, that's just my traitorous heart falling for him when he's off-limits. I think I was maybe thirteen when I first felt... something. Something other than friendship with my best friend. We were at the Valentine's Day dance, and I was sitting on the bleachers, just taking it all in. My friends Janie and Beth were with me. Anyway, Janie and Beth were both asked to dance, so I was sitting alone. Cooper and a few of his friends were close by, and I tried to sink into myself. I should have known better. Coop noticed and left his friends standing mid-conversation and came to me.

He held his hand out for me, and I could feel my face heat with embarrassment. Not wanting to make a scene, I took it. He led me out onto the gym floor and put his arms around me. By this point, we'd hugged hundreds of times, but this time, it felt... different.

That was the moment that my heart began to wish he was more than just my best friend. That also triggered the rumors that we were more than just friends. It's a battle we've fought since the day we met, but at thirteen, girls are cruel and full of jealousy. Coop has that tall, dark, and handsome thing going for him. He attracts female attention wherever he goes. However, I'm the only one who gets it unconditionally.

Hence the yearning from my heart. No matter how many times I try to stop it.

"There he is!" a loud voice calls out. "Our freshman running back. Get your ass over here, Reeves," the very large, very loud guy orders.

Cooper, with his arm still around my shoulders, guides us to the group. At first glance it's obvious they're all football players. Tall, large, built guys surround the entire right side of the huge fire. When I say huge, I mean *huge*. It has to be at least fifteen feet wide.

"'Sup, rookie." The large guy who called us over holds his fist out for Cooper.

"He's hardly a rookie," another one adds. He too offers Cooper his fist in greeting.

"This your girl?" the big one asks.

"This is my best friend, Reese. Reese, this is Levi." He points to the big one. He's by far the tallest guy here. "And this is Dustin."

"Hi." I wave awkwardly.

"Just friends, huh?" Levi asks, raking his eyes over my body. I can't help the blush that I feel creeping across my cheeks at his attention.

"Yep. Since we were kids," Cooper offers.

"What are you drinking?" Levi asks me.

"Oh, uh, nothing for me. Thank you."

"Come on. You have to have a drink. We're celebrating the upcoming season. We're going all the way, baby." He cheers, holding his red Solo cup up in the air.

"Does your coach know about the alcohol?" I ask Cooper.

"It's the last hoo-rah of the season where he's not going to scold our asses for drinking," Dustin answers.

I nod. Pulling my gaze from the football players, I take in my surroundings. The fire is huge, and this field is full of college students, who, from the looks of it, are already well on their way to being two red Solo cups past being drunk. I've never been much of a drinker. I don't like not having control or knowing who I might end up with, or worse, where I might end up the next morning. And who likes to wake up with a pounding headache and their mouth tasting like ass? No, I've never tasted ass and have no plans to. However, I could only imagine that the morning-after bender breath is the equivalent.

"Hey, Cooper." A voice that sounds like a toddler purrs as she stops to stand in front of us. "I was hoping you would be here." She sticks out her tits and twirls her hair on her finger.

Did I forget to mention that I'm still standing next to him and that his arm is still around my shoulders? We're freshmen, new on campus by only two weeks. She has no idea who or what I am to him. And she doesn't care. None of them do.

"I'll be right back," I tell him, removing his arm from my shoulders and stepping away.

"Where are you going?" he calls after me.

"Just over here." I point to Levi and with more confidence than I feel make my way over to him. "Hey." I wave awkwardly, and he grins.

"Hey." He reaches into a cooler in the back of the truck he's leaning against, pulls out a bottle of water, and offers it to me.

"Thank you."

"No problem." He winks. "So, your boy found someone else?"

"He's not mine. We're seriously just best friends. We've been neighbors since we were eight. He's more of a brother," I say in explanation. I leave out the part that I love him more than just a brother. Nobody wants or needs to hear that. Besides, that's something I plan to take with me to the grave.

"Hop up here and have a seat." He pats the tailgate next to him.

"Short girl problems," I say, looking at the tall truck and the high tailgate.

He throws his head back and laughs, and before I know it, his hands are on my waist, causing me to squeal loudly in surprise, and he's setting me on the tailgate. He picks up his cup and leans his elbow on the tailgate, his body facing me. He's wearing a shit-eating grin. "Much better."

"How tall are you?" I blurt the question. I'm sitting on the tailgate of this tall truck and we're still almost eye to eye.

"Six six."

I nod before saying again, "Thanks for the water."

"You're welcome. So, you're a freshman too, right? I think I would have remembered seeing you around campus."

"Yes. You?"

"Sophomore." He's looking out over the fire but then turns to face me. "You sure there's nothing going on with the two of you? Coop's giving me the death glare even through the fire. I can see the warning in his gaze."

I don't bother to look. I've seen that look on Cooper's face many times. "He's just protective. Trust me." My gut twists just a little. I wish I was wrong, but that's just not the case.

"All right then. Well, since you're single and I'm single, and quite the catch I might add, we should definitely dance." He sets his drink down on the tailgate and turns to step between my legs that instinctively open for him.

It sounds slutty, even in my head, but it's not. Trust me. He's just a big guy, and well, like I said, it was instinct. "Dance? Here?" My eyes scan the field, and sure enough, there are couples dancing, if that's what you want to call swaying back and forth with their tongues down each other's throats.

"Come on, it'll be fun. We can fuck with Reeves." His eyes dance with mischief.

"He's not going to care that we're dancing." At least not like Levi thinks he's going to.

"Then what's stopping you?" he challenges.

"Get me down from this thing," I tell him, and he smirks.

"I thought you'd never ask." His hands grip my waist, and he lifts me in the air, only he doesn't put me down. Instead, he just holds me suspended in the air, staring up at me.

"What are you doing?" I ask, resting my hands on his shoulders for support.

"Gotta make it look convincing." He winks, then begins to lower me to the ground. However, he holds me close, every inch of my body pressing against his on the way down. Once my feet, attached to wobbly knees, are firmly on the ground, he links his fingers with mine and pulls me a few feet away to where the others are dancing.

His big arms pull me close, and we begin to sway to the music. It's a slow song, one I've heard countless times on the radio. I think it's by Brett Young. "How are you liking CU so far?" Levi asks.

"Well, I've only really seen my dorm room, the library, and the cafeteria outside of my classes."

"You don't get out much, huh?" He chuckles.

"Not much of a partier."

"Yet, here you are."

"Yeah, well, Coop wouldn't leave me alone until I agreed to come with him," I grumble.

"Here we go," he says, adjusting his hold on me as the song changes to Tyga's "Taste."

Levi takes that as an opportunity for us to cut loose. He pulls me impossibly closer and rolls his hips. One hand is resting on the small of my back, and the other hangs at his side as he begins to rock his hips.

Something you don't know about me? I love to dance. It's my jam. I'm not ashamed to admit that I spent hours in my room growing up, just dancing and acting a fool. It wasn't until I started high school that I took it to a whole other level. Janie, Beth, and I all took a hip-hop class. I loved it. We all did. So, yeah, I've never been one who was able to resist moving to the beat.

I move to straddle his leg and do a little grinding and swaying of my hips. Levi moves his hands to rest on my hips, and we quickly find our rhythm.

"There you go. Damn, no wonder Coop's been keeping you all to himself." Levi's smile lights up his face.

I smile at him and roll my eyes. "I've kept myself hidden, thank you."

"Why would you do a thing like that?" he asks as he bends his knees and shimmies down to my level, then back up again.

"It's easier that way. All the football groupies they're mean as hell, and no matter if I argue back or sit around and tell them until I'm blue in the face, they're still catty about our relationship. They say nasty things, and honestly, I would just rather remove myself from it all."

"But he's your best friend?"

I sigh. "Yes. Which is why I'm here tonight instead of sitting at home reading my book and eating my mint chocolate chip ice cream."

He throws his head back and laughs, turning us around to where my back is now to the fire. "I'm a mint chocolate chip fan myself."

"Well, I have a small fridge/freezer in my dorm, and it's as stocked as the tiny appliance allows. If you're ever over in Banner Hall, stop in, and I'll share."

"You might be willing to share, but your boy over there, he doesn't look too happy about us dancing together."

I don't look back, because I've seen the look he's talking about. I used to get my hopes up and think that it meant Coop wanted more. However, time has shown me that his look, although intense, is just him looking out for me. "Nah, he's just protective."

He leans in close, and once his lips are next to my ear, he whispers, "I think you're wrong about that." His hot breath caresses my ear as I struggle to comprehend his words. Then he's gone and talking to someone next to us.

"Reese." I snap out of my fog when I hear my name. I turn to see Coop and some dark-haired girl hanging off his arm. "You okay?" He lifts his hand as if he's going to touch me, and then drops it to his side.

"Why wouldn't I be?" I ask with more snark than he deserves. I can see a small tic in his jaw, and only because I know him well enough to know that my words hurt him. "I'm fine, Coop." I give him a bright smile. "I was just giving Levi here a little lesson in dancing."

"Oh, you think so?" Levi laughs. "I want a rematch."

"You really think you can show me up?" I tease.

"Yo! Dustin, gimme something good," he calls out.

Dustin thrusts his arm in the air giving him a thumbs-up, then bends his head to his phone. The music stops, and then an old school tune blares through the speaker on the back of what I assume is Dustin's truck.

"Color Me Badd? Really?" I laugh as the beginning chords of "I

Wanna Sex You Up" begins to play.

"You backing out? I get it. You're worried you can't hang. It's fine." He slides his arm around my waist. "I understand, Reese. I would be worried too if I were you."

"Oh, that's cute. You think you can out dance me." I turn so that my back is to his front and look at him over my shoulder. "Watch and learn, Levi. Watch and learn." Bending over at the waist, my hands touch the ground. My ass is now firmly pressed against his crotch, and I do a little shaking before standing up and turning to face him.

He's smiling and shaking his head. "You don't play fair."

I shrug. "Show me what you got, footballer."

"Tight end."

"That's yet to be determined," I quip. I know he was talking about his position, but I can't help but mess with him.

"Coop's an idiot," he mumbles.

"What's that?" I ask, even though I heard him loud and clear as if he were shouting the words.

He shakes his head and does this slow sensual sway of his hips against mine that has a cheer breaking out among the group. I let myself get lost in the music and just groove with him. He's got moves, especially for such a large guy. I guess all that time on the field really does help with coordination.

Levi and I hang out the rest of the night. A few members of the team join us, trying to show up our moves, but I must admit he and I killed it. "We make a good team."

"You'll do," I tease.

"All the time busting my balls."

"Well…," I say, and we both laugh. What I thought was going to be a dreadful night, turned into a great time. I'm glad I let Cooper drag me out. Maybe, just maybe, college is going to be different.

COOPER

I t's Saturday. Game day. And I'm stoked. It's the first game of the season, and Coach has me on the roster as starting running back. I knew it was happening, but I'm suited up and ready to take the field. That makes it real. My parents, as well as Reese's, are here. They're all in the stands somewhere. Reese and her roommate, Tessa, are sitting with them. It's nice to have them all here for the first game of my college career.

A loud laugh pulls me out of my thoughts. I look to my left to see Levi, all six foot six of him, staring at his phone with a smile on his face. "What's so funny?"

"She's a goofball," he says, shaking his head.

"Who is?"

"Reese."

"Reese? My Reese?" I ask. I'm shocked by his answer.

That stops his laughter as he turns to look at me. There's a smirk on his face. "I thought she wasn't yours?" His statement is a challenge.

"Of course, she's mine," I say, before adding, "She's been my best friend since I was eight."

"Just your best friend?" His stare is intense.

"Dude. We've talked about this. She's *my* best friend. So why are you texting her?"

He shrugs. "We exchanged numbers last week at the bonfire."

"She's off-limits."

"You just said she wasn't yours."

I inhale sharply. "She's my best friend," I repeat through gritted teeth.

"Okay?" He grins. "Is that what the cool kids are calling it these days?"

"Cut the shit." I'm getting pissed, and that's the last thing I need before taking the field. I need to focus.

He sobers up. "So, are you telling me that I can't talk to her? That she and I can't be friends?"

"She's different," I say, trying to remain calm on the outside while on the inside, I'm a raging bull. This isn't the first time I've had to warn someone away from Reese. Hell, I've been doing it since we started high school. She deserves better than some player who's not going to appreciate her.

"I can see it in your eyes, Reeves. You don't know me, so stop judging me."

"I know you. I am you," I tell him.

"No." He shakes his head, his face void of emotion. "You're not me, rookie. You're in the big leagues now, Reeves. This is college. You might have been able to pull that tough guy shit off back in your hometown, but things are different now. She's not your girl, and you're no longer the big man on campus."

He's right. I fucking hate it, but he's right. "What did the text say?"

He throws his head back and laughs. "You want me to tell you about my private conversation with a friend?"

"My best friend."

He shrugs. "Maybe she's on her way to being my best friend too."

"You've known her a week."

"So, is there a timeline on these things? I mean, come on. If you weren't being such a douche right now, I'd say the same for you." He gives me a pointed look.

"I don't want to see her get hurt. She deserves someone who knows she's wife material."

"Someone like yourself?"

"No. Not like me. But yes, I understand that about her."

He watches me for a few seconds longer than is comfortable and turns his phone to show me his screen.

Reese: Game Day: It's all about the penetration.

Her text is followed with a winking face emoji.

Levi: I'm the master at penetration.

This feeling, I know what it is, but I refuse to name it. It shouldn't bother me that Reese is texting Levi. It shouldn't bother me that I haven't received a text message from her.

It shouldn't, but it does.

I hate feeling this way, and I don't know how to quell it. I don't know how to stop feeling as if I have to protect her from everything and everyone. That's just us. Cooper and Reese. That's who we are, who I am. My phone vibrates on the bench beside me.

Reese: Good luck today, Coop. I know you're going to do great.

It's not a fun, flirty text like the one she sent Levi, but it's mine. Already I can feel my shoulders relax, and the storm inside me begins to calm. She's always had that effect on me. She's the calm to the storm. My best friend. That's one of the main reasons we can never be anything more. I could never risk losing her if we didn't work out romantically. We kill it as best friends. It's what we were meant to be.

"That her?" Levi asks.

Wanting to give him an olive branch, I turn my cell so he can read the screen. He nods, pats me on the back, and stands to walk away. I stare down at my phone, reading her message twice more, letting it calm me.

Me: Thanks, Reese's Pieces. See you after the game.

Tossing my phone into my bag, I follow my team to the hallway. I'm about to take the field for the first time in my college career. My parents, my second parents, who are Reese's, and my best friend are all here to watch me. That's what's important. Closing my eyes, I listen to the sounds of the stadium flow around me. My teammates are pumped, and the crowd is on fire if the noise is any indication. This is my life for the next four years.

Welcome to Central University.

We won by two touchdowns. The rush of winning my first ever college game is real. I'm floating on cloud nine. My high school team always had a winning season, all four years. This, however, this win is on another level. It's heightened. Playing at the college level is the best of the best. At high school, almost anyone can make the team. In college, you have to have the skill, the drive, and the talent. I made three of our four touchdowns. The moment I stepped out on that field, the game was my focus, and my stats are evidence of that.

"Good game, rookie," Levi says, stepping up to his locker that's beside mine. His hair is wet, and he has a towel hanging around his waist.

"Thanks. It was a team effort."

He shakes his head. "Modest. I like it. But you were on fire out there."

"Just love the game."

"You coming to the house tonight?" he asks.

The house, as he refers to it, is a huge old Victorian just off campus. The house is occupied by the football team. Well, not all of them, but the juniors and seniors who don't depend on their scholarship to provide them housing. As a freshman, my scholarship states I will live in the dorms for my entire first year at CU. Grades permitting, I can live off campus after that.

"Yeah, maybe. I need to meet up with my parents and Reese's."

"Her parents came to watch you?"

"Yeah, her parents and mine have been best friends as long as Reese and I."

He nods. "Bring Reese with you. Oh, and tell her Tessa can come too."

I bite back my snide remark about him knowing her roommate as well. "Yeah. We might see you there." I keep my reply vague. While I want to hang out with my teammates, I also want to celebrate with my best friend. I just don't know if I can handle pulling drunk guys off her all night and still manage to have a good time. I'll just have to see what she wants to do. I might not even be able to convince her to go.

Glancing at my phone, I see a text from my mom telling me that everyone is waiting for me just outside the locker room. I rush to get dressed and toss my stuff in my bag, throwing it over my shoulder. I wave to my teammates, bumping fists and slapping a few high-fives with their words of "good game" and "killed it, freshman" as I make my way out of the locker room.

I find my parents, Reese's parents, Garrett, and Eve, as well as Reese and Tessa, right where Mom said they would be. I hear a loud squeal, and I know what's coming. I drop my bag to the floor and brace for impact as Reese rushes toward me. I catch her as she wraps her arms and legs around me. "You killed it!" she exclaims.

I chuckle. Reese has always been my biggest cheerleader. She slowly releases her hold, and I help her to steady herself back on her feet. Her arms go around my waist in a hug. Slinging my arm around her shoulder, I return her embrace. "Thanks."

"Good game, son." My dad steps up and shakes my hand.

"Oh, Coop." Mom has tears in her eyes. Reese sees as well and steps away, letting Mom have her turn. Eve is next, followed by a handshake from Garrett, and a hug from Tessa.

"Do you have time to grab something to eat with us?" Mom asks.

"I've got nowhere to be."

"Oh, Reese said there was a party with your teammates."

"Levi texted me." Reese holds up her phone. "I assumed you'd want to be there to celebrate with your team."

"Are you going?"

"We're going," Tessa answers for her.

"Reese," her dad says. His tone has warning.

"Don't worry, Dad. I won't go if Cooper doesn't."

Her words seal my fate. She wants to go. I don't have to convince her, and I know that if I don't go, she'll stay home, just like she told him she would. I could easily bow out, but I can see it in her eyes. This is what she wants to do. I'll just have to keep a close eye on her, and then I need to get the message out to my teammates that she's off-limits.

How hard could it be?

My "how hard could it be" turns out to be a fucking nightmare. Reese and Tessa went back to their dorm to get ready after dinner, with plans for me to pick them up for the party in an hour. I sent them a text letting them know I was outside their dorm. I wasn't expecting to swallow my tongue when they climbed into my Jeep. Both are wearing short jean shorts, with CU tank tops. It's simple, understated, and unapologetically Reese, but damn, she looks hot. They both do. Tessa, with her long dark hair cascading down her back, and her bright green eyes, could make any man beg for her to be his.

The minute we walked into the house, all eyes were on us. We were instantly surrounded by my teammates, who wanted to talk about the game. Eventually, Tessa disappeared with Dustin, and Reese ended up a few feet away, laughing and talking to Levi. As for me, there's a cute little redhead who has attached herself to me and deemed herself my sidekick for the night. She's cute, tall, much taller than Reese, with red hair and brown eyes. She's got curves for days.

Levi catches my eye and winks with a subtle nod to my new companion. I get his meaning. I understand how this works. Football players are like celebrities on the CU campus. As a player on the starting roster, with stats that helped us win the game today, I could have my pick of women. Too bad I can't focus on Carrie—or was it Cara—to take advantage of that. I'm too busy watching out for Reese, and by association, Tessa.

When Levi slings his arm around Reese's shoulders, and her head tilts back, her laughter ringing out over the loud music, I know I'm in for a long night. "Excuse me." I pull the redhead's arm off mine and walk away. "Sounds like I missed the punchline," I say, stopping to stand next to Reese and Levi.

"Coop." Reese smiles. "You've got to teach Dustin some moves." She points out onto the makeshift dance floor, and it takes me no time to find Dustin. His arms are flailing around, and his hips are jerking, but not in a sexy, "let me seduce you" kind of dancing. It's more... I don't really know. I've never seen anything like it. Poor Tessa is standing about two feet away, just grooving to the beat like the rest of the partygoers, while Dustin is in a world all his own.

"There's no helping that."

"Right?" Levi agrees. "Come on, Reese. Let's show him how it's done."

I stand back against the wall and watch as the two of them let loose just like they did at the bonfire. Reese is smiling and happy. Levi has his hands all over her as he moves to the beat, and it doesn't seem to faze her. That's a good thing. I'm glad she trusts him, but she can do better. I make a mental note to tell her that.

"Hey, Cooper." The redhead appears by my side.

"Hi." I nod, not looking at her, keeping my eyes on everyone dancing.

"Want to dance?" she asks.

Already I can tell that this girl is a stage-five clinger, and I have zero room in my life for that. "Thanks, but I'm beat from the game. I just want to stand here and take it all in."

"We could go upstairs." She licks her ruby-red lips, the same color as her obviously unnatural hair color.

"Cooper, my man." My roommate Nixon holds his fist out for me. "You killed it out there today."

"Thanks." Nixon is a freshman like me, and he's also on the team. However, he didn't get any playing time today. He's a kicker, and his leg has damn good accuracy. The starting kicker is a senior this year, so his time is coming.

"Who's your friend?" he asks, nodding toward the redhead whose name I still can't seem to remember.

"Cara," she purrs, and I fight the urge to roll my eyes.

"Nixon, this is Cara." I remove her hands from me yet again when I see Reese motion for me to join her out on the dance floor. "I'll be right back." I give no other explanation as I go to her. "What's up?"

She grabs my hands and moves them around with hers in some silly dance move. "We're supposed to be celebrating your big win." She smiles up at me. Her green eyes are lit up with happiness.

"Well, we better dance then." I match her move for silly move, making her laugh. This is us; it's what we do. What started out as a night I was dreading, turns into the perfect night, celebrating with my best friend.

Chapter 4

REESE

"I can't believe that freshman year is almost over," Tessa says from her seat on the couch at the house. She and I have pretty much made this our stomping grounds. Tessa and Nixon are dating, and yes, I set them up, and since he and Cooper are always here, so are we. It took a few months of curious looks at me and Coop for everyone to get it through their heads that we are truly just friends. It's not really that hard of a concept to grasp.

"Right? It's hard to believe we're moving into our own place." I can barely contain my excitement. There are two months left of classes, but we signed our lease yesterday for our new place. We get the keys in a month, so that gives us one month to move from the dorms and get settled.

"Are your parents still bummed out that you're not coming home for the summer?" she asks.

"I'll visit."

"You know what I mean."

"Yeah, they were disappointed, but they agree. The apartment is the perfect location, and it's a great price for what we're getting. It doesn't make sense to pass on it, or rent it and not live there. What about yours?"

She shrugs. "Out of sight, out of mind."

Unlike me, Tessa's parents aren't heavily involved in her life. They're both high-powered corporate attorneys and work their lives away. That's why every break we've had this year, she's come home with me instead of going to her folks' place. Not once did they comment on their displeasure of her not coming home. Makes a girl appreciate what she has, that's for sure.

"You sure you don't want another roommate?" Nixon asks Tessa.

She smiles at him. "Like you're not going to be there all the time anyway."

"Exactly. I should just go ahead and move in."

"And miss out on all of this?" she asks, just as Levi, Dustin, Cooper, and a few other guys from the team come into the living room. Dustin and Levi sit next to me on the couch, which leaves Cooper. He reaches down and picks me up, causing me to squeal. He takes my seat, placing me on his lap.

"What's going on?" he asks.

"Oh, you know, Nix is just trying to convince Tessa to let him move in with us in our new apartment."

"What? If anyone should get to move in, it's me," Cooper states confidently.

"Oh, really? Why you?"

"Best friend." He points at his chest.

"Boyfriend." Nix mimics Cooper and points at his own chest.

"Best friend trumps boyfriend all day long," Cooper declares.

"What?" Nixon asks, shocked. "You can't be serious?"

Cooper nods. "Yep."

"How do you figure?" he asks.

"That's just how it goes." Cooper doesn't offer any type of explanation.

"I can give her more than you can," Nixon counters.

"Like what?"

"My dick for one." He holds up his index finger.

"Nixon!" Tessa scolds him. Her face grows crimson with embarrassment.

"You should be used to this bunch by now," I tell her.

Reaching for a pillow on the couch, she covers her face as she starts to laugh. "Uh, Tessa, you don't know where that pillow has been, or what it's seen," I remind her.

"Gah!" She tosses it onto the floor, making us all laugh.

"Don't worry, T," Dustin chimes in. "We don't let any of the good stuff happen outside of the bedrooms."

"You're forgetting that we've been to your parties," I tell him.

He shrugs. "That's partygoers. I'm talking about those of us who live here."

"Speaking of living here, who's on the list for next year?" I turn to look at Cooper over my shoulder.

"Me, Nixon, Levi, Dustin, Trey, and Hank."

"That's it?"

"Yeah, it's only a six-bedroom. Four upstairs and two in the basement."

"Isn't there more than that that live here now?" I ask, confused.

"Yes. But they doubled up. Most are seniors. They're graduating, so we decided to dial back a notch," Cooper explains.

"Makes sense." I look over at Nixon. "Why are you trying so hard to move into our place?" I point at Tessa and then myself.

"Hello? Wake up with my girl or these baboons? I'll take Tessa any day."

"Aw." Tessa leans in and kisses his cheek. "That was sweet, babe, but it's still not happening."

"I don't get it. What, do the two of you have some kind of super-secret society that you're trying to hide from us?"

"Yeah?" Cooper pinches my leg, causing me to yelp and retaliate the same way.

"No. We just want our space. Our time."

"So you don't have room for me?" Nixon asks.

I can hear the hurt in his voice. "It's not that, Nix," I say soothingly. "It's just we want it to be us girls. It's not like you're not allowed to stay over or hang out at our place. We just made the decision no boyfriends moving in.

At least not this year." I wink at him, trying to lighten the mood.

"See. That's why best friends trump boyfriends," Cooper boasts.

"Actually, that rule applies to best friends too. At least those of the opposite sex."

"Come on, Reese's Pieces, you can't kick me out." He bats his eyelashes and puckers his lips into a pout.

"You don't even live there." I laugh at his antics.

"Yeah, but if I needed to?"

"If you needed to," Tessa answers, "Reese and I would discuss the options and get back to you. Besides, we only have a two-bedroom."

"So, I'll just room with Reese," he says, as if it's the simplest answer in the world.

"I'm sure her boyfriend would love that." This from Levi, who has been quiet up to this point, which is unusual for him.

"What boyfriend?" Cooper asks, leaning a little to see my face from where I'm now sitting sideways on his lap.

"There is no boyfriend."

"Not yet, anyway." Tessa wags her eyebrows. "I've been trying to set her up with this guy in my English lit class."

"You didn't tell me that," Cooper says.

"That's because I haven't agreed to go out with him."

"What's his name? We'll check this guy out." It's more of a demand than a request.

"Coop's right," Levi agrees. "If we don't know him, we can find out. It's not hard for us to find answers on this campus."

He's not being conceited, just speaking the truth. Football players are like celebrities at CU. In this college town, football is life. "Nobody is finding anything out about anyone. If I decide to date him, that will be my choice. I don't need you"—I give Cooper a pointed look—"or any of you"—my eyes scan Dustin, Levi, and Nixon—"to investigate him."

"Good luck getting Cooper to agree to that," Levi mumbles under his breath.

I choose to ignore him. "So, are all of you staying here over the summer? Or are you headed home?" I ask, changing the subject. Kind of.

"Trey and Hank are headed home. They'll be back mid-July for football," Dustin tells me.

"I thought football started when classes did?"

"It's not a requirement of freshmen to be here earlier, but it's required of the upperclassmen," Nixon explains.

"Really? I find that odd. Shouldn't it be the same for the entire team?"

He shrugs. "That's just how Coach does it. He works with the veterans for a few weeks, and then when the rookies come into the fold, we're ready for them."

"Huh." I've been best friends with Cooper since I was eight, and just when I think I know everything I need to about the sport he loves, that we both love, I find myself learning yet another new piece of information.

"Not all colleges do it this way. This is Coach's thing. Something about coming to school is overwhelming enough. He says that it gives the veterans on the team time to reconnect, and then we take the newbies under our wings. You know, like I did with these two knuckleheads," Levi says of Nixon and Cooper.

"Here we go." Nixon rolls his eyes. "He can't let it go," he says, pretending to be annoyed, but we can hear the humor in his voice.

"Laugh it up. You assholes would have been lost without me," Levi boasts.

"So, what are we doing tonight?" Tessa asks.

"You see it," Dustin tells her.

"What? No party? Are you all feeling okay?"

"You've got that one locked down." He points to Nixon, who grins, pulling Tessa's hand that's entwined with his to his lips. "The rest of the guys are out at some seniors-only bullshit, which I get. And Reese has this one locked down." He points to Cooper. "So, no, Levi and I are just chilling for the night."

"Hey now. I don't have anyone on lockdown," I correct him.

"This one gets prime pussy vying for his attention on the daily, yet he turns them down." Duston points at Cooper.

"Vultures," Cooper grumbles.

"What's that?" Nixon asks.

"They're all fucking vultures. They want my attention because I'm on the team. Put a girl in front of me that's with me for me, and we'll talk."

"She's sitting on your lap, dude," Dustin says, with a look of disbelief on his face. "Tell me you see that."

"How many times do we have to tell you that we're just friends?" Cooper groans.

Just friends. "Come on, guys, catch up," I tease.

"I've never known you to hook up with anyone," Levi challenges.

"My sex life isn't your concern."

"What about you, Reese? It's not just Cooper here that's been sitting the bench when it comes to the opposite sex," Dustin calls me out.

"My sex life isn't your concern," I repeat Cooper's response.

"Denial," Levi coughs into his hand.

"Just because you're not as cool as us, doesn't mean you have to hate," I sass.

"I'm the king of cool," Levi fires back.

"Well, king of cool, why don't you order us some pizza since we're staying in?"

"Yeah," everyone agrees.

"Cough up some cash." He holds out his hand, and we all pass him some money. Tessa and I both work part-time at the local coffee shop, and Cooper and the guys, well, I'm not sure where the guys get their money. I know that Cooper worked and saved up, plus his parents— like mine—send us a monthly stipend from our college funds. It's none of my business, so I never asked. It's not like they're rolling in cash. I just assume they have the same set up that Coop, Tessa, and I do.

Cooper and I both got scholarships so that extra money our parents saved is now spending money. And my apartment, splitting that cost with Tessa, equals out to be the same as my room and board at CU, so it's a win-win situation for me and my parents.

It's still hard for me to believe that my first year of college is almost over. It flew by, but I admit it's been fun. Tessa and I have become close, and the guys on the team have become more than just Cooper's friends. They're my friends too.

The rest of the night we just hang out watching movies and eating pizza. Tessa and I ran to the store and got some brownie mix to make, and the guys devoured them before they were even cooled. We expected it because they always do, so we cut us both a small piece before we told them they were ready. All in all, a great night with great friends.

COOPER

COLLEGE: SOPHOMORE YEAR

"I'm back, bitches!" Trey yells as he exits the back door of the house.

It's the weekend before classes start, and this is my new home. I'll be living in the house, also known as the football house, with four of my teammates. I didn't mind dorm life, but the freedom of living here is already proving to be better.

My current situation wouldn't be possible in the dorms. We've got a fire going in the fire pit, and everyone is gathered around drinking beer. Yes, we're underage, but we're drinking responsibly. This is college, after all.

Nixon is cuddled up with Tessa in his lap. Those two are going strong. I wasn't sure it would last when Reese first suggested fixing them up, but it turns out my best friend has a knack at matchmaking. Speaking of my best friend, she's sitting next to me in her lawn chair. She's wearing one of my CU hoodies that swallows her. It's a good thing since she's using it as a blanket to also cover her bare legs. She's a tiny thing. At least a foot shorter than my six four. Her blonde hair is pulled up messily on top of her head, and her face is void of makeup. Not that she needs any. Reese is naturally beautiful. She's the girl next door, the one that you take home to introduce to your parents.

Last year was a struggle for me as I had to learn to share her with my teammates. They're my friends too, but Reese, she's my best friend. There isn't anything that I wouldn't do for her. She hit it off with everyone she met, not that I'm surprised. My teammates all adore her, and they've all kind of taken her under their wing.

Speaking of my teammates. Levi, Dustin, and Hank are all sitting around the fire too. Dustin has a girl sitting on his lap. I don't know her name, and I don't care to. She eyed me up and down as soon as she walked through the door earlier tonight. No thanks. Anyone who is here with someone else and gives me that vibe, I'm out. He can have her.

My dating life in college has been dull. Sure, I've dated here and there, group things, but nothing that sticks. Not to sound conceited, but I've made a name for myself here at CU on the field. As a sophomore, there are already rumors that I could go to the big leagues. Me, Cooper Reeves, playing for the professional football league. I can remember Reese and me sitting outside on her back deck or mine, and we would talk about life and what we wanted. I always dreamed of playing professionally. What kid didn't? I just never thought that would be me. I've busted my ass to get where I am, and I don't need the distraction of a girlfriend, and even if I wanted one, how would I know they were with me for me? I'll stick to Reese being my plus one when I need it. We have fun no matter where we are.

"We're going to state again this year," Hank says, plopping down on the grass.

"That's the plan," Nixon agrees with him.

"What's going on here? Is this everyone?" Hank asks. His eyes scan each of us and then the yard.

"Just us. We told you, man, we're laying low this year," Levi explains.

"Why in the hell do you want to do that?"

"Two of our five roommates are married off, and this guy—" Trey points over to Levi. "—he's all about keeping his nose clean," Trey says.

"When Coach tells you scouts are watching, you take the shit to heart," Levi counters. "That's my end game. I don't want to be stuck behind a desk the rest of my life. I want to play football."

"And I'm not married off," I grumble. I do not want to go over this shit all over again this year. Reese and I are close, inseparable even, but we're not together. Why can they not get that through their thick skulls?

"I can't even get her to let me move in." Nixon pouts.

"What? You don't want to live here?" Trey actually sounds offended.

"Wake up in a house smelling like sweaty balls or wake up with my girl? No contest, my man, no contest."

"Yeah, yeah," Trey grumbles.

"Can we at least make this night more interesting? You all are sitting around like you're retired," Hank jests.

"What do you have in mind?" Reese asks him.

"How about some truth or dare?" Hank rubs his hands together in childish glee.

"Sure. I'm in," Reese agrees easily.

"Me too," Tessa says.

"Why not?" I say, tossing my agreement out there. We played this once last year, and there were more dares than truths. We ended it after Samson, a senior who has now graduated, took the dare to drink a gallon of milk in an hour and keep it down. He failed, and he was up all-night puking. I was never so glad to escape to my dorm room.

"I'll go first," Hank says. His eyes skim over each of us, looking for his first victim. "Levi."

"Dare," Levi answers immediately.

"I dare you to drink an entire jar of pickle juice."

"Do we even have pickles?" Nixon asks.

Hank shrugs. "Don't know, but if not, I'll think of something else."

"I got you," Trey says, jogging off to the house to see if we do, in fact, have a jar of pickles. "Score!" he yells a few minutes later, stepping out onto the back deck and holding a jar of pickles in the air.

"Are they cold?" Levi asks.

"Yep."

"Are they expired?" Reese laughs.

"Does juice expire?" Trey asks, squinting to look at the jar by the light of the fire.

"The contents in the juice does. Let me see." Reese holds her hand out, and he gives her the jar. She examines, turning it in her hands. "You're good. They don't expire until December."

"Bottoms up!" Hank cheers.

Levi reaches over and takes the jar from Reese, twists off the lid, and kills it. He downs the jar without stopping. When it's empty, he wipes his mouth on his arm, twists the lid back on it, and places it on the ground next to him. "Let's see." His eyes scan us until he stops on Tessa and Nixon. "Tessa. Truth or dare?"

"Hmm, let's go with dare."

"Babe, you sure about that?" Nixon asks.

She shrugs. "Can't be that bad."

"Tessa, I dare you to… kiss Reese."

"What kind of kiss are we talking? Tongue?" Tessa inquires easily.

"N-No." He chokes with laughter. "Just a kiss. A peck on the lips."

"Reese?"

"Don't keep a girl waiting," Reese quips, making us all laugh.

Tessa stands from her seat on Nixon's lap and saunters over to Reese. She exaggerates the sway of her hips and flips her dark hair over her shoulder. "Ready, gorgeous?" she asks in a low, deep voice that's not even remotely sexy. Reese stands from her chair and clasps her hands behind her back. Leaning forward, sticking out her ass, she puckers her lips and closes her eyes.

We're guys, so we all watch with rapt attention, regardless of the spectacle they're making out of it as Tessa's lips press against Reese's. It's hot as fuck. It happens fast, and when they pull apart, Reese plops down in her chair, tilting her head back and resting her arm across her forehead.

"I'll never wash these lips again," she says dramatically.

Tessa cackles with laughter as she makes her way back to Nixon, where he opens his arms for her, and she once again settles on his lap. "Now, who's my next victim." She taps her index finger to her lips as she ponders who to call on. "Cooper."

"Truth."

"Oh, our boy's feeling like sharing tonight," Trey comments.

"Truth. Okay. Do you masturbate?" Tessa asks with glee.

"Yep," I answer automatically. "There is no shame in a little self-love."

Everyone cracks up at my answer, but I'm being real. A man has needs.

"You're up," Hank reminds me.

"Dustin."

"I'm going dare."

"I dare you to... eat a raw egg."

"Do we have eggs?" Nixon asks.

"Dude? You do live here," Trey reminds him. Nixon shrugs, not the least bit upset that he has no idea what food we have in our kitchen.

"You have eggs," Reese tells him. "We used them for the cookies Tessa and I made yesterday."

"Cookies? What cookies?" Hank asks.

"You missed out," Reese tells him. "They were gone in no time. I think they lasted maybe ten minutes, and it was a double batch."

"Damn it," Hank mutters under his breath.

"You need me to go get the egg for you?" I ask Dustin.

"Nah. Hop up." He taps the girl sitting on his lap on the leg, and she whines but stands. He stands too and heads toward the house.

"Dustin, where are you going?" she calls after him.

"He's just going to the house to get an egg," Reese explains politely.

The girl pulls her eyes from Dustin's retreating form and glares at Reese. "Did I ask you?"

Reese raises her hands in the air. "Hey, I was just trying to help."

"Right." The girl laughs humorlessly. "You can't even nail down your own man." She points at me. "Don't you be worrying about mine."

"Leave." My tone is ice cold. I'll be damned if I'm going to let her talk to Reese that way. Not in my house.

"Excuse me? You can't just tell me to leave. I'm here with Dustin."

"Not anymore," Dustin says, stopping to stand behind her, holding a carton of eggs in his hands. "You heard the man, leave."

"Are you fucking kidding me right now?"

Agony | 37

"Do I look like I'm kidding?" Dustin counters.

"Dustin." The girl stomps her foot.

"Leave." Dustin's voice is composed yet just as cold as mine.

"Guys, it's fine." Reese tries to reason with us.

"It's not fine," Dustin says before I have the chance to. "You see, Reese is one of us. We're tight. You disrespect her, you disrespect all of us. That goes for Tessa too," Dustin says calmly. "I have zero fucks to give about you being sorry. You've been asked to leave."

"Whatever. What a fucking joke." She grabs her purse that's almost bigger than she is from the ground and storms off, disappearing around the side of the house.

"Dude, maybe you should go check your truck, make sure she doesn't fuck with it?" Trey says.

"Nah, she's not got it in her to be like that." Dustin takes his chair and opens the carton of eggs.

"I'm so embarrassed." Reese, with her knees to her chest in the chair next to me, buries her face.

Reaching over, I place my hand on her shoulder. "Hey, there's nothing to be embarrassed about."

"She was a clinger anyway." Dustin shrugs. "Now, Reese, are you going to watch this epic event that's about to happen?" She slowly lifts her head and looks at Dustin. "You know you want to see this." He grabs an egg from the carton and knocks it on the arm of his chair to crack it open. "Bottoms up." He tilts his head back and opens the egg, letting it drop into his mouth. He swallows and reaches for his beer. "That's how it's done," he says after taking a big swig. "My turn." He grins wickedly. "Reese."

"Oh, God." She half laughs, half moans. "Truth."

"All right." Dustin nods. "Let's see. Give me a minute here." He looks off into the distance, lost in thought. "I got it. How old were you when you lost your virginity?" he asks just as I am taking a drink of my beer, and I start to cough.

"Sorry, went down the wrong pipe."

"You okay over there, Coop?" Dustin asks with a shit-eating grin on his face.

"I'm good." I take a drink to clear my throat and open my mouth to tell her that she doesn't have to answer. I don't want her to be even more embarrassed than she already is to tell them she's still a virgin.

"Eighteen. Senior prom," she says before I have a chance to stop her.

"What?" I turn to look at her. "You never told me that."

She shrugs. "It was no big deal. More of a means to an end kind of thing."

"Who?" That single word is the exact demand that it sounds like. It's invasive, but I can't seem to find it in me to care.

"Joey Patrick, my prom date."

"You let her go on a date?" Hank asks, surprised.

"What do you mean by that?" Reese asks him.

"Nothing." He holds his hands up, and I glare at him over her shoulder.

"You didn't tell me that."

"Fine. Cooper. Truth or dare?" Reese asks me.

I can see the challenge in my best friend's eyes. "Truth."

"When did you lose your virginity?"

Fuck me. I don't want to answer this. We don't talk about this stuff, not really, which is why I didn't know. I'd prefer to not have the imagery of her with anyone else in my head. I can't have her, but neither can they. I know my thought process is fucked. I'm fully aware. She's going to hate my answer, but I give it to her anyway. "Janie." I clear my throat. "Senior prom." She nods like she had a good idea, but I can see the hurt in her eyes.

"You're up," she says, standing from her chair. "I'll be right back. I need to use the restroom." Her steps are hurried as she walks away, and I didn't miss the crack in her voice.

"You fucked up," Levi says.

"I wasn't going to lie to her."

"It should have been her," Hank chimes in, ever so helpful.

"She's my best friend."

"Then go after her," Tessa says, none too kindly.

"Yeah, I'm skipping my turn," I say, standing and heading toward the house. I block out anything else they might say as I go in search of Reese.

She's not anywhere downstairs, and her car is still parked out front. Not that I thought she would leave. She's smart enough not to drink and drive. Taking the steps two at a time, I check the bathroom, but she's not there. Slowly, I push open my bedroom door to find her curled up in a ball on my bed. Her legs are hidden under my sweatshirt, as tears from her eyes coat my pillow.

My heart lurches in my chest. I hate that my actions, my truth caused her tears. *Agony.* That's what I feel watching her swipe at her tears.

"Go away, Coop."

"No." I step into the room, close the door, and turn the lock. I don't need anyone coming in here and making this any worse than I've already done on my own. I need some privacy to talk to her about this. No matter how badly I just want to ignore it and wish that we could erase the last fifteen minutes and make it disappear.

I kick off my shoes and climb into the bed beside her. "Reese," I whisper.

"I'm fine, Cooper. Just give me a few minutes."

"No. You're hurting because of me, and I won't leave you like this."

"I was there. I knew that you took her to prom."

"I'm sorry." I don't know what else to say. "It was pretty much like you and Joey." I swallow hard, even thinking about my friend and her together causes me pain. "It was a means to an end. We were both curious and wanted to see what the hype was about. That's it. Joey was my friend," I say was because I'm not sure I can forgive him for this.

When she rolls over, her red-rimmed eyes find mine. "I'm sorry too. I have no right to be upset. I guess I just assumed that it didn't happen. I mean, Janie never said a word about it. She went on her merry way, acting as if life was normal."

"We weren't together. She was my date, Joey was yours. It was just something that happened."

"We all stayed at my house that night. How did I not know?"

"I could ask you the same thing." If I would have known that she and Joey were doing… that, I would have stopped him. Stopped them. I don't know how, but I know that the thought of her with him kills me. Not because Joey's a bad guy. No. In fact, I suggested he ask her. I knew that he would be good to her. If I only knew then what I know now.

"Did he hurt you?"

"What? No. Of course not. Why would you ask me that?"

"Because the thought of him or anyone forcing themselves on you makes me cagey." I give her wide eyes, trying to lighten the mood.

A small smile pulls at her lips. "Yeah, I know the feeling. Janie?" she asks.

"It was nothing."

She nods. "Yeah, that's pretty much how it was with us too. Afterward, we both looked at each other and started laughing. We were both super nervous, but he was... good to me."

"I wish you would have told me," we both say at the same time.

"It's weird, you know? Talking to you about it. That's not really what we do." She gives me a look that I can't describe. If I didn't know better, I would call it yearning.

"Yeah, I guess we can agree to not discuss these things in the future. Just promise me something."

"Okay."

"Don't let anyone take advantage of you, and if he, whoever it might be in your future ever forces you or tries to hurt you...." My words trail off.

"I'm a big girl, Coop."

She is, but she's mine. Not in the intimate sense of the word, but she's my best friend, and it's my job to look out for her. Sometimes I wish things were different between us. I wish that... I could have been her first, that she was not just my best friend cuddled up in my bed, but my girl. I've never done the serious-relationship thing. I'm not a cheater, but I don't know how I would be at it. I'm sure I would fuck it up, and then I'd lose her, and that's just not going to work for me. So, no matter how badly I wish that I was her first and she were mine, that's just not how our story ends.

"You wanna go back out?" I ask her.

"No. I'm tired."

"Okay."

"You go," she says, snuggling in close. I wrap my arms around her and hug her tight.

"Nah, I'm good right here."

"They're going to ask questions."

"Let them. I'll unlock the door. They can check on us, like you know they will, and see that we're just friends. We've got nothing to hide."

"Thanks, Coop."

I kiss her forehead, then release her, rising out of bed to unlock the door. I grab us each a bottle of water and set them on the nightstand. I know she gets thirsty in the middle of the night, especially after she's been drinking. Climbing in beside her, I pull her into my arms and close my eyes.

I wish things were different, but I'll take this moment and cherish it with all the others.

REESE

I'm pretending to be asleep when I hear Nixon and Tessa outside Coop's door. They're debating on if they should come in and check on us. Nixon tells her to leave us alone, and Tessa, being the great friend she is, insists that she make sure I'm okay. I pull the blanket up over my face and lie as still as possible.

"Reese," Tessa whispers. "You awake?"

"Babe, they're sleeping."

"I just... hold on a second." I hear the door creak, and I assume she's pushed it open to get a better look. "Oh," she breathes.

"Oh? What, oh?" Nixon asks, keeping his voice low.

"Look at them."

"Let me see," he tells her.

I can picture him, with his hands on her hips, using any excuse to touch her, and leaning around her to see what she's talking about. "He's an idiot."

"Why do you say that?" Tessa asks.

Their voices are low as I strain to hear them. "He's in love with her."

"They're just friends."

"Tell me you think she's not in love with him," Nixon says.

I wait for Tessa's reply that never comes. Hot tears prick my eyes. I thought I was hiding it better. I thought I was doing a good job of not letting on that I love Cooper, not just as my best friend, but as the gorgeous, tall, dark-haired, brown-eyed man that he is. I know we can never be together. I'm not willing to risk losing my best friend. Besides, I'm not Janie or any of the other girls I've seen him date. I'm not even close to being in their league. They're all tall, long legs, dark hair, exotic-looking beautiful women, much like Tessa.

I'm just me.

Just Reese.

"Is he in love with her?" Tessa questions.

"He'd never admit it," Nixon answers. "Come on, you checked on her. Let's go to bed." There's a soft click followed by the sound of their voices as they carry down the hall.

A tear slides down my cheek as my heart feels more exposed than ever before. No matter how much I wish that life was different, it's not. No amount of wishing is going to change the outcome. Cooper nuzzles closer. His hold on me is tight as he sleeps peacefully beside me. He had no problem falling asleep next to his best friend.

I don't know how long I lie here, listening to him breathe while his hot breath caresses my neck. Minutes, hours, I'm not sure. One thing I do know is when I finally drift off to sleep, it's with the dream of the two of us together, as more than just friends.

The sun shines brightly through the blinds on Cooper's bedroom window. It's silently telling me with its blinding rays of heat that it's time to drag my ass out of bed. I'm awake, but my eyes are still closed. I refuse to open them and face the day. Not after last night. I'm humiliated, and I need a few more minutes to get myself in the right frame of mind to deal with all of this.

I came in to use the restroom.

I was tired so I went to bed.

That's my story, and I'm sticking to it. I need to watch myself around

Coop and make sure that what I do for him, I do for the other guys. That should be reason enough for them to quell their suspicions, right?

I hope so.

I hear Cooper moving around the room, so I know that I need to accept defeat and get moving. Slowly, my eyes flutter open. I blink to bring them into focus and almost gasp at what I see. Cooper is standing in front of his dresser, a towel hanging low on his hips facing me. He's drying his hair with another. His eyes are closed as he runs the towel over his head. Lucky for me, he's not in my direct line of sight. I squint but don't pull my eyes away as he drops the towel he was using on his hair and unties the towel around his waist, letting it drop to the floor.

I slam my eyes closed, but it's too late. I can never un-see what I just saw. Not that I would want to. No, never will I forget getting a full-frontal naked look at my best friend. The same guy I'm secretly in love with. He's… big. Much larger than any others I've been in contact with. Not that there have been a lot. In fact, there has only been one. Just Joey. And that experience lacked any kind of luster for a repeat performance. Granted, it was the first time for both of us, but even so, I've decided not to take part in such activities again. There's been no one, and I promised myself after the Joey incident—that's what I'm calling it—that I would never offer my body to someone again just for the sake of getting it over with.

I feel the bed dip and his hand as he rubs my back. "Hey, sleepyhead."

I count to ten slowly in my head before doing a slow blink with my eyes, which I'm sure looks fake as hell. "What time is it?" I ask, rubbing my eyes. Doesn't matter. I still see his impressive cock before he slides his boxer briefs up over his hips.

"Just after nine. We have practice. I didn't want to leave without telling you. We'll be back in a few hours. You girls stay. We'll grab something to eat when we all get back."

"I have laundry to do and need to start packing."

"I'll help you pack. Stay." His voice is soft, not really pleading, but I can tell by his tone of voice that he really wants me to be here when he gets back. I've never denied Cooper anything, so why start now? "Fine, but you're buying lunch or dinner or whatever we're calling it. And we have to start packing after."

"Deal." He leans in and kisses my temple. "Go back to sleep, Reese's Pieces." He stands and walks out the door, shutting it softly behind him.

I can hear the guys as they clamber up and down the hall, and their heavy footfalls as they march down the stairs. The front door slams, and then silence surrounds me. I close my eyes and will myself to go back to sleep. However, that plan is short-lived when Cooper's bedroom door flies open, and Tessa is standing there, hands on her hips, still wearing one of Nixon's T-shirts that I assume she either slept in or slipped on for this little intervention we're about to have. I don't need her words. I can tell by the look on her face she has questions, and she's going to expect answers.

She doesn't wait for an invitation. She saunters into the room, and slides into the bed, slipping under the covers, then turns on her side. I feel her stare, and I know I'm not getting out of this, so I turn to face her as well.

"Morning."

"Morning. You ready to spill?" She jumps straight in to the good stuff.

"It's too early for an interrogation, Tessa."

Her eyes soften. "It's not so much an interrogation as me being worried about you."

"I'm fine. I had to use the bathroom, and then I was exhausted. I decided to just go to bed." I've delivered my story perfectly.

"You can play that card with the guys, and maybe even Cooper, but I'm not buying it."

Closing my eyes, I take a deep breath. Maybe she'll sense my anguish and decide to leave it alone? Slowly, I open my eyes, and she's still lying next to me with a look of worry on her face. "It took me by surprise, that's all."

"Janie, I assume, was your best friend, Janie?"

"Yeah, I mean, we still talk. She went to college in California, so we don't see each other. She never let on that it happened. Literally, she was his date that night. I went with Joey, the four of us hung out and then stayed up in my parents' basement watching movies and listening to music. I had no idea."

"Sounds like he had no idea either?"

"Yeah. I thought that Janie went up to my room to go to bed, and the guys were staying in the guest room. Joey and I were finishing a movie. We started talking, confessions were made, and it just kind of happened."

"Janie didn't tell you about it?"

"No. And I couldn't tell. Nothing changed in our little group. Joey and I talked before it even happened that it was just us getting it over with with people we trusted. He and I didn't harbor any feelings for each other, and nothing was weird between us. We were friends."

"Best friends?" She raises her eyebrows.

"No. Cooper has always held that title."

"What about Janie?"

"She was my closest girl friend, but still, Cooper and I were closer."

"Yet you didn't tell each other about two monumental moments in your lives? Why do you think that is, Reese?"

"Because I wanted it to be him." My words are barely audible even to me, but the way her eyes widen, I know she heard me.

"You need to tell him."

"No. No way. It's not worth the risk. I can't lose him. He's been the biggest part of my life since I was eight years old. No way am I willing to lose that."

"What happens if you don't lose it? I think he feels the same way."

"Right." I laugh. "Look, I appreciate you trying to cheer me up, but I'm not even close to the girls he dates. You're more his type than I am."

"You're wrong. I see the way he looks at you."

"Like a girl who has been his best friend since childhood?"

"No, like the girl he wants but thinks he can't have."

"We're just going to have to agree to disagree on this one." My mind is already all over the place after last night and this morning. I still can't believe I saw him... all of him. I don't need this to confuse me even more.

"What's that blush about?" Tessa asks.

Damn, my best friend doesn't miss anything.

"Nothing."

"Lies." She pokes me in the arm. "Come on, I need details. Did he kiss you? Did he make a move?" Her eyes sparkle with excitement.

"No, you crazy person, he didn't kiss me or make a move. I just… saw something." A very well-endowed something.

"What?" She's confused.

"He just got out of the shower. He didn't know I was awake."

"You saw him naked?" I nod. "What are we talking here? Like bare chest? Ass? Full frontal? Talk to me, woman," she says enthusiastically.

"Don't you have a boyfriend?" I remind her.

"But I'm not dead. I care about Nixon, but damn, Cooper is hot." She holds up her hand. "No offense, and I'd never go after your man."

"He's not my man."

"Mmhmm. Let's get back to exactly what it is that you saw."

"He dropped the towel," I whisper, as if someone might overhear us.

"Front or back, Reese. You're killing me here."

"Front."

She pretends to fan herself. "Give it to me straight. He's huge, right? I mean, all that confidence he walks around with, he has to be huge. It can't just be his good looks and skills on the field that garner that kind of 'I've got this' attitude."

I nod.

"A nod. That's all I get is a simple nod? Girl, I need more than that. Details, woman. I need details."

"I don't know." Embarrassment flushes my cheeks. "It's not like I whipped out a ruler and took the exact measurement."

"The fact that you need a ruler says it all. Nothing under five inches is worth measuring and you can eyeball that."

"He wasn't hard, Tessa."

"Exactly! And you still needed a ruler."

I can't help it, I burst out laughing. "Thank you. I needed a good laugh."

"Girl, what you need is Cooper to give you some of his inches."

"Is that what works for you? Nixon's inches?"

"Damn straight. I'm not ashamed to admit it."

"You made him wait six months."

"He earned it, now he gets this." She runs her hand up the side of her body. "Anytime he wants."

"You're terrible."

"You ready to go home and start packing?"

I bite down on my bottom lip. "Coop asked me to stay. Said we could all grab lunch when they get home. I made him promise they would come and help us pack if we did."

"Oh, my bestie is a genius."

"Right? Free labor, and he has to pay for lunch."

"So, what do we do now?" she asks. "Go back to sleep?"

"Nah, as much as I'd like to, I'm wide awake."

"Me too. Let's go see what they have to eat in this place."

Together, we make our way to the kitchen and end up eating leftover pizza from last night. Nothing beats cold pizza for breakfast. We lounge around the rest of the morning. We did pick up from the get-together last night, and tossed all the trash, wiped off the counters, before settling in the living room and watching a movie.

"This is nice to come home to," Nixon says about an hour into the movie. He bends to kiss Tessa. "Glad you stayed."

"Thank Reese, or better yet, Cooper. It was his idea."

"See how this could be? I could come home to you every day." Nixon bats his eyelashes at Tessa.

"You're relentless."

"Just when it comes to you," he replies.

"How was practice?" I ask Cooper when he sits on the arm of the couch next to me.

"Good. Team is tight this year. Let me grab a shower, and we can go get some food." He squeezes my shoulder and heads toward the stairs. "Did you all pick up?" he asks.

"Yeah."

"Thank you."

"See," Nixon says, taking a step back from Tessa. "This could be the life."

"Me picking up after you all the time? No, thanks."

"Babe." He clutches his chest. "You wound me."

"Go, you stink. Why didn't you guys shower after practice?"

"We were in a hurry to get home." He blows her a kiss and rushes up the stairs.

"That's Cooper's influence. You know that, right?"

"He probably just felt bad that he asked me to stay and just wanted to get back sooner. That, and I'm sure he's starving."

"Keep telling yourself that, Reese."

That's my story, and I'm sticking to it. I know Cooper, and Tessa is wrong. Too bad my heart can't help but wish that I wasn't.

COOPER

"How is it possible that two tiny little women managed to pack so much shit into a single dorm room?" Nixon asks.

"They have their own bathroom."

He stares at me with a blank expression. "They use a ton of shit they don't need, to get ready every day."

"And the clothes," he says, taping a box shut. "I've been dating Tessa for a year, and haven't seen her wear half of this shit," he grumbles.

"Don't question it, man. Just roll with it."

"I don't understand women." He shakes his head in utter confusion.

"You don't have to understand them, but imagine your life without her."

"I don't want to. Seriously, Coop, she's it for me." His tone is serious, and the grin that's pulling at his lips tells me that his revelation is not something new.

"It?" I ask him.

"Yeah. You know, the forever and ever, all the bathroom shit, and clothes she wants. Marriage and babies forever."

"We're starting our second year of college. We're not even of legal drinking age yet." I don't know why I'm surprised. From the very first meeting, he's been head over heels for Tessa.

He shrugs. "When you know, you know."

"I guess so," I say dismissively. It's not like he's going to propose today or anything.

"Don't knock it until you try it."

"What's that?"

"A girlfriend. The one person you can count on no matter what."

"I have a best friend for that."

He nods. "For now."

"What do you mean for now?"

"What are you going to do when she meets someone? What happens when he gets pissed because she decided to drink and spend the night in your bed, curled up in your arms? What's going to happen then, Cooper?"

"That's not going to happen."

"Keep telling yourself that, buddy."

It's hard for me to imagine a situation where Reese and I aren't close. That's just how it's been and how it will continue to be with us. Our bond is tight.

The dorm room door opens, ending our conversation. "You guys are the best," Tessa says, wrapping her arms around Nixon's waist. He bends to kiss the top of her head.

"What she said." Reese stops to stand next to me. "We got tape." She holds up the shopping bag with a few fresh rolls of packing tape inside.

"Good. I just used the last of this roll." Nixon holds up the tape dispenser that is now indeed empty.

"What's left?" I ask Reese.

"Just the toiletries that we use every day and some clothes, books, and our furniture. I didn't expect us to be done packing this soon. You guys are packing machines. We can't move in for two more weeks."

"Great. Can we go eat now?" Nixon asks. "We've been at this for hours."

"Three hours." Tessa laughs at her boyfriend.

"I'm starving," he tells her.

"We just ate before we got here," Tessa counters.

"It takes fuel for these guns." He flexes his arms, and she playfully rolls her eyes before looking over at me.

"Are you hungry too?"

"I could eat." I turn my attention to Reese. "You know what sounds good? A big bowl of your mom's white chicken chili."

"My mom's not here," Reese replies.

"Come on, Reese. It's been ages."

She looks over at Tessa and Nixon. "You all in the mood for white chicken chili?"

"Never had it, but I'm in," Nixon tells her.

"Looks like we're going grocery shopping," Reese says, and I pull her into a hug.

"Why don't you pack a bag and stay with me tonight?" Nixon asks Tessa.

"You too," I tell Reese. "I'll drive and can bring you both back here tomorrow."

The girls share a look before they both nod and proceed to pack a bag. Once they're ready, we pile into my Jeep and head to the grocery store.

"I don't know where you came up with that, but I'm damn glad that Cooper talked you into it. That was so damn good," Nixon tells Reese.

"Her mom used to make it for me all the time when we were growing up. It's one of my favorites," I say.

"Yeah, so much so that he asked me and my mom no less than a million times if I was sure I knew how to make it before we left for college." Reese laughs.

"Sounds like Momma Latham is a good cook," Nixon comments.

"The best. Reese isn't the only one I begged to learn how to make it. I used to beg my mom too. Instead, she would call Eve, that's Reese's mom, and tell her that her son, meaning Eve's son, which meant me, needed some white chili." I smile thinking about it.

"Was your mom mad?" Tessa asks.

"Nah. She and Eve are best friends."

"So what, your families are super tight?" Nixon asks.

He already knows this, so I'm not sure why he's asking, but I answer him anyway. "Yeah. Neighbors and best friends, all of us for years now."

"So, the two of you are kind of destined to be together?" He points his index finger at me and then at Reese. "Reese is literally the girl next door."

"We're just friends." Reese is quick to squash the idea. "And us being neighbors growing up isn't new news."

"So," Nixon sits up straighter on his spot on the loveseat, "you're telling me that your moms never once suggested that the two of you would end up together?"

I look at Reese to find her looking at me. We both shake our heads. "No." I pull my eyes from hers, and the look I can't explain to Nixon. "They know we're friends."

"Never?" Tessa asks in disbelief.

"What's with the inquisition? Our families are, well, like family. Coop and I being together is more like incest," Reese speaks up.

Tessa gives her a look, but it's gone before I can decipher it. "Yeah, what she said," I agree with her. Just because she's the coolest fucking girl I've ever met, and the most beautiful doesn't mean that we aren't just friends. I wish people could understand that.

"What smells so damn good?" Levi asks, entering the kitchen. Dustin, Hank, and Trey all trail in behind him.

"Reese made white chicken chili," Tessa explains.

"Fuck me. A smoke show, and she cooks?" Levi drops to his knees. "Marry me." He bats his eyelashes dramatically, making Reese laugh as she pushes on his chest to shove him away.

"Get out of here with that nonsense. We both know you can't handle me," she quips.

"Oh, sweetheart, care to wager on that?" he asks her.

My hands are balled into fists at my sides. I don't understand their relationship. They hit it off the first time they met freshman year, and since then, they're this teasing easygoing duo. Hell, she sends him messages that are full-on innuendo before each game. I get messages too, but mine are from my Reese—the sweet, loving cheerleader she's always been with me. I love that Reese, but part of me is jealous that I don't get the flirty Reese either. At least not when she's sober.

"You can't afford me," she teases.

Nixon catches my gaze. I can read the question in his eyes. *You good?* I nod at him, a subtle nod that he returns. "What are you jokers getting into tonight?" Nixon asks them. In this moment, I've never been more grateful for my best friend. He's changing the subject, knowing that my nod was a lie. I'm not okay. I hate seeing the two of them like this. I just wish I knew why.

"Nothing. Everyone is cramming for finals or packing their shit to move back home for the summer."

"That's what we did," Reese says. "Well, but not to move home. We're staying here. Did you decide what you're doing?" she asks Levi.

"Yeah, I'm going to go visit the folks, and will probably come back here."

"What about you three?" she asks the rest of my housemates.

"Going home," they all reply.

"So it's really going to be the four of us all summer?" She looks at me, then over to Nixon and Tessa.

"Oh, the secrets we'll keep," Tessa quips.

"Nope. No secrets. We get all the details." Levi points at Reese. "I'm calling you daily. I want the juicy bits." He stops and seems to think about it, then turns to Tessa. "On second thought, I'll be calling you daily for the real juicy bits," he tells her, making us all laugh.

"Not happening. What happens in the house, stays in the house," Reese jokes.

"I live here," Levi reminds her.

"Yeah, but if you're not here to witness it, it's your loss. This summer stays between the four of us and these walls." She grins at him.

"Whatever," Trey pipes up. "They're all just boring married folk anyway. We're not missing anything."

Reese rolls her beautiful green eyes, and the smile pulling at her lips is one that can brighten the darkest of days. "You want some chili or not?"

"Want," Levi, Trey, Hank, and Dustin all reply at the same time.

"It's on the stove."

The four of them rush off like toddlers being bribed with ice cream. "You'd think it's been days since they've eaten," I say, watching them leave.

"Like you can talk." Reese pokes her finger into my ribs, and I retaliate by pulling her into my lap and tickling her until she's screaming that she's going to piss her pants. I let her go, and she rolls off my lap and darts down the hall to the bathroom. I don't realize that I'm staring after her until I see a hand waving in front of my face. Blinking, I look up to find Nixon standing in front of me. I glance around and see that Tessa is no longer in the room with us.

"What's up?"

"You went from looking like you could murder our roommates to all googly-eyed." Nixon smirks.

"Whatever." I avert my gaze to hide the truth.

"You're a shit actor, Reeves."

"Who's acting?" Levi asks, sitting next to me on the couch, with a huge bowl of chili.

"Do we own bowls that big?" I question him. Partly because it's a huge fucking bowl, and the other part to sway the conversation.

"I think it's Reese's or maybe Tessa's. I know they use it when they cook." He takes a huge bite. "Who's acting?" he asks again. So much for swaying the conversation.

"Reeves here. He needs to work on his acting skills." Nixon not so helpfully points out.

"You changing majors?" Levi asks. There's a twinkle in his eye that tells me he knows better.

"Nix is just being an ass."

"Au contraire, my friend. I'm being anything but. How am I an asshole for speaking the truth?" Nixon raises his eyebrows in question.

Before I can answer, the girls walk back in the room, Tessa following Reese. They've both changed their clothes.

"We're tired," Tessa says, looking at Nixon. "I just wanted to say goodnight."

He rises from his seat, and on autopilot, I do the same. "I'll come with you." He wraps his arms around her waist and leads her back upstairs to his room. He doesn't say goodnight to any of us. His only focus is Tessa. As it should be. I exhale a sigh of relief that our earlier conversation has been squashed.

"You going to bed too?" I ask Reese.

"Yes," she says, covering her yawn with her hand. "It's been a long day."

"I'll grab you a water and be right up," I tell her.

"You don't have to. I just didn't want to be rude and go to sleep without saying goodnight." She steps forward and wraps her arms around my waist, giving me a hug, one I don't hesitate to return. She pulls back and turns to walk away. I watch her as long as I can, just like earlier.

"He's right," Levi says, pointing his spoon at me. "You're a shit actor."

"Stop with the acting nonsense," I say, exasperated.

He shrugs. "You're only lying to yourself. Well, and her. You're lying to her."

"I'm not. You know us. You've seen us together. You and Nix have this romanticized concept that she and I are meant to be together. We're not. She's my best friend."

He nods. Good, maybe he's finally getting it through his thick skull. "I've never doubted that. None of us have. Anyone who sees the two of you together knows that you have a strong connection."

"Then drop this acting and lying bullshit."

Levi's face grows serious, something you don't see from him very often. "You're one of my best friends. I don't want you to wake up one day and realize what you missed out on."

"How am I missing out?"

He shakes his head, clearly disappointed with my answer. "I need more chili." He stands and walks back into the kitchen, dismissing me and our conversation. I follow after him, grabbing two bottles of water from the fridge. Dustin, Trey, and Hank all sit around the table with empty bowls in front of them.

"Thank you," Hank says as I'm ready to walk away.

"For what?"

"For having a girl like Reese that knows her way around the kitchen."

"Tessa helped."

He nods. "Yeah, I should thank Nix too."

"You guys can clean up since we bought and the girls cooked."

"If we keep coming home to meals like this, doing a few dishes is a small concession," Trey agrees.

I leave them to it. Taking the stairs two at a time, I push open my bedroom door to find Reese curled up in my bed. She's already sound asleep if her even breathing is any indication. I place her bottle of water on the nightstand on her side of the bed, then do the same with mine. Stripping out of my clothes, I pull on some basketball shorts and climb into bed.

I lie still, listening to her soft breaths. I wish things were different. I wish I could love her like she deserves to be loved. I wish that I could call her mine, but there are no guarantees in life. Nothing to assure me that if I were to cross that line, that one, she would be receptive to it, and two that she would always be mine. We're safer staying friends. I know that if we were to test those boundaries, there would be no going back. And if things ended, our relationship would be ruined. My lifelong best friend would no longer be there, and the thought of that causes my stomach to sour. That can't happen. I never want to lose her, and this is the only way I know how to do that.

REESE

Tessa and I have been in our new apartment for a little over a month. It's an all-new level of independence. Sure, living in the dorms I was independent, even staying over at the house with Cooper, but this, having my own place not ran by the college, it's an all-new level.

"What are you doing today?" Tessa asks. She's sitting on one end of our second-hand couch, while I'm on the other. It's Saturday morning, and we're both moving slowly today.

"I've got nothing. What about you?"

"Nixon's picking me up and we're going to see a movie. It's such a dreary day there's not much else to do. You should come with us."

"Thank you, but no thanks. I'm just going to hang here. Maybe get caught up on laundry. Read a book or two." I smile and shrug.

"Oh, did I tell you? I finished *Pants on Fire* by Lacey Black. So good."

"That's on my Kindle. Maybe I'll read that one."

"As much as I want you to meet Cricket and Rueben, I want you to come with us even more."

"Go, enjoy the day with your man."

"What's Cooper getting into today?"

"He's with Sasha; at least, I assume he is. She is his girlfriend."

"She's a bitch," Tessa says, not holding any punches.

"She's not my favorite person, but I get it. Coop and I are close; she's intimidated by that. It's nothing new. It's always been like this. The girls get jealous of me for no reason."

"She's a mean girl."

"That seems to be his type."

"I guess." She rolls her eyes. "Anyway, you should really come with us."

"Not happening, Tess. You and Nix don't need a third wheel. Go enjoy your time with him. Football is about to be in full swing, and that time is going to be limited. You should soak it up while you can."

"I hate leaving you here all day by yourself."

"Why?" I laugh. "I'm perfectly fine spending the day in this lovely quiet apartment with my book boyfriends. This is freedom at its best."

"Do you mind if Nix stays over tonight?"

"I told you, you don't have to ask me. He's your boyfriend. Hell, you can move him in for all I care. He can help with the bills," I tell her. "I know you two are growing closer every day. Just because we agreed to live together doesn't mean that plans don't change. If you decide you want out, to live with him, just give a girl some notice." I mean that. I want her to be happy, and anyone and everyone who looks at the two of them together can see that happy is what they are.

"No. I don't want to rush into anything too fast. It's bad enough that my heart is going to be pulverized if this ends between us."

"What makes you think it might end?"

"He's crazy talented, Reese. They're talking possible pros, and he's a sophomore."

"Okay. What's that have to do with the two of you?"

"Hello. Famous football star. He can have anyone he wants." I can see her insecurities shining through. We all have those moments. It's my job as her best friend to make her see she's talking crazy and worrying for nothing.

"You're right. He can have anyone he wants." Her face falls. "He has you. You are who he wants, Tessa. He's crazy about you. Nothing is going to change that. He needs you there by his side to support him through all of this. You were there before the fame, before the talks of the pros. He knows that you're with him for the right reasons. That goes a long way. And if that's not enough, let's talk about how he looks at you. As if you are the only person in the room."

"I love him."

"I know you do."

"I've never felt this way about anyone. It's scary, and we're young, and I just don't want to rush it too much. My heart is already in deep. Us living apart, even though we sleep over at his place or mine most of the time, that gives us some sense of independence. I want to know that if this goes south, and we end things between us, that I have a place to come home to."

"Tessa," I say softly. "You will always have a place to come home to. I am your best friend. You are welcome here with me, no matter what the circumstances. Don't let fear stop you."

She nods. "Thanks, Reese." She stands. "I'm going to grab a shower." She's almost to the hallway when she turns to look at me. "Reese."

"Yeah?" I say, turning my head to look at her. "He's an idiot."

"Who?"

"Cooper. He's letting his fear stop him. In fact, so are you."

"Our story is different. Losing Cooper as a part of my life would be devastating. It's better this way. Besides, I can't compete with the Sashas of the world."

"That's where you're wrong. The Sashas of the world can't compete with you." She turns and leaves me with her words.

There have been many times over the years I've thought about risking it all and telling him how I feel. I love him. Not just the him who's my best friend, but the man he is. Every single time I chicken out. Then he brings home someone like Sasha, and I'm reminded that my choices have been good ones. No way can I compete with the tall leggy brunette.

It's early afternoon. I'm still in my pajamas, and I have no shame. I've enjoyed lying here on the couch, listening to it rain while I get lost between the pages of a good romance. I just finished *Pants on Fire*, and just like Tessa said, I loved it. I'm trying to decide what to eat for lunch before I dive into another book when my phone rings. Glancing at the screen, I see Levi's goofy face.

"Hey," I greet him.

"Reese," he whines. "Where are you?"

"Um, I'm at home. Why?"

"Because I'm starving. It's been forever since you've cooked for us."

"It has not." I laugh. "I was there last week with Tessa. We made chicken stir fry."

"Last week. That's a whole seven days."

He's right. I've been spending less time at the house than usual. Cooper started seeing this Sasha girl a few weeks ago, and I know she's not a fan of mine, so I've been trying to give them space. That, and it's just easier for me. It hurts my heart to see him with someone else. I know that's my issue and I need to get over it. I was hoping a little distance might help with that.

"I think you'll live."

"No. I. Won't," he sighs dramatically. "What are you doing today?"

"Nothing much. Just lounging."

"Come feed us."

"You know you sound pathetic and desperate, right?"

"Can you hear my stomach growling through the phone?"

"Surely between the five of you, one of you can cook." In fact, I know they can.

"We can, but it's not as good as yours. Come on. You're just hanging out by yourself. Come over. Text me what you need and I'll run to the store."

"I'm not alone. I just spent several hours wrapped up in a handsome man named Rueben."

"W-What?" he stutters. "Who is this Rueben? Has Reeves met him yet?"

"Nope," I say, popping the P. I'm barely holding in my laughter.

"Bring him. We need to meet him."

"Yeah, no, that's not happening." Although my Kindle does go with me everywhere I go, so I guess, technically, I am bringing Rueben and all my many other book boyfriends with me.

"Damn it, Reese. He's going to be pissed."

"Who?" I smile to myself. He's too easy to mess with.

"Cooper."

"All right, you're talking crazy. Is that lack of food?" I tease him.

"Yes," he says, deadpan.

"Fine. I need to shower. I'll text you what to get. How many are there?"

"The six of us, Sasha, and Tessa."

"Everyone is there?" I try to hide my disappointment.

"Well, no, but I'm sure they will be."

"Okay. I'll see you soon." I end the call, not waiting for him to say goodbye, and fire off a text. I'm craving tacos. My stomach growls just thinking about it. Tossing my phone on the couch, I rush down the hall to the shower.

An hour later, I'm pulling my car into the driveway. It's full, which means everyone is here. I don't see Coop's Jeep, and I'm thankful. Spending the rest of my day fielding mean girl looks from his new girlfriend isn't exactly my idea of a good time.

"Finally," Hank says when I walk right in without knocking.

"Not you too." I laugh.

"Levi said you were making tacos."

"I'm going to teach you boys how to cook."

"Who are you calling boys?" Dustin asks.

"Well, you're acting like boys. Seriously? You can't make yourself lunch?"

"You spoil us, Reese. Tessa too. We would have asked her, but they're out on some date, and Nixon threatened us to leave them be."

"Aw. He's so good to my bestie."

They all nod their agreement. I have a feeling I could get them to agree to anything about now. "I'm putting you all to work."

"As long as we start cooking now. I might die of malnutrition," Trey says dramatically, holding his stomach as if he's literally in pain.

"Come on." I playfully roll my eyes and offer Trey my hand to pull him off the couch. Four very loud sets of footsteps follow me into the kitchen. "Okay. Hank, you're on tomato duty. Trey, onion duty, Levi, lettuce, and Dustin, you'll help me with the beef and the chicken."

"Yes, ma'am," Hank says in his southern drawl.

I get to work, and we fall into easy conversation. The guys talk about the upcoming season, and I chime in here and there. "I'm really excited for Nixon to get some playing time this year," I say, adding in my two cents.

"Right?" Dustin agrees.

"It sucks he rode the bench most of the year, but that's the hierarchy of being a freshman with an upperclassman who matches your skillset."

"Can I just say it's hot as fuck that you know so much about football?" Hank says, making me blush.

"That—" Levi points at me. "—that little blush ranks up the hotness factor."

"Right? She has no idea she's beautiful," Dustin agrees.

"Stop. If you want dinner, you'll hush."

"Coop's a fucking moron," Hank grumbles under his breath, but we all hear him.

Even Cooper.

"Why exactly am I a fucking moron?" Cooper asks, walking into the kitchen. Sasha is at his side, her hand gripping his tightly. She gives me one of those looks that says "don't fuck with me," before plastering on her fake girl smile. I fight to roll my eyes until my back is turned to them. Then I let it loose, and Dustin chuckles under his breath.

Busted.

Dustin leans his shoulder into mine as we stand side by side at the stove.

"What are you two doing over there?" Cooper asks.

I keep stirring the beef and let Dustin answer for us. "Our girl is trying to teach us how to cook."

I know the "our girl" comment was a dig at Cooper, although he doesn't take the bait.

"It smells great."

"Duh, Reese is cooking." This comes from Tessa. I turn to look over my shoulder, and she gives me an exaggerated wink as she leaves Nixon's side and comes to stand next to me at the stove. "You're making me hungry, and we just had ice cream."

"That's fine," Nixon tells her. "I can eat."

"Told you," Levi says. My back is to him, but I can only imagine that his shoulders are squared, and his chest is puffed out. Proud of himself. "There's plenty," he tells Cooper. "I figured everyone would end up here eventually."

"Done." Hank slides the diced-up tomatoes from the cutting board into a bowl. "Anyone want a beer?" he asks. I hear the refrigerator door open as everyone calls out that they want one. "Tessa?"

"Sure."

"You staying here?" Nixon asks her.

"Yes, dear," she says sweetly.

"What about you, Reese?" Trey asks.

"No. I have to drive home."

"Why don't you just stay here like you always do?" he asks. The room falls silent, other than Trey's muttered, "Shit."

"You can stay with me," Levi says. "I have plenty of room."

"That's okay," I say, the same time Cooper says, "No."

I whip around to look at him. He's watching me. Those brown eyes of his stare me down. His look is almost pleading. I start to soften, then I see Sasha pull on his arm. He ignores her, but the trance is broken. There is nothing wrong with me staying over with a friend. He gets to live his life while I pine away for him. This has to stop. I have to move on. There will never be a great Cooper and Reese romance.

"Are you sure you don't mind, Levi?" I ask him.

"Reese." Cooper's tone is full of warning.

"Hell no. That's the least I can do for you coming over here to cook for us."

"That's what friends are for."

"Bottoms up, Reese's Cup." Trey hands me a beer.

I make a show of placing the bottle to my lips and tilting my head back. I let the cold liquid pour down my throat. "Everything's done. You guys can dig in."

"You first," Hank says.

"I'm just going to run to the restroom." I set my beer on the counter and slip out of the room. There is a half bath just off the kitchen, but I need a little more space than that. I just need to get my head on straight. Instead, I take the stairs to the basement. There is a common area with a pool table, two bedrooms off it, and a bathroom. Luckily, the guys are fairly clean, so I have no worries when I lock myself inside. I take care of business, wash my hands, and stand with my hands on the counter, staring into the mirror. "Get it together, Reese."

Taking a deep breath, I open the door to find Tessa standing there. "You okay?"

"Yes."

"Reese." Her voice is soft, but I can hear the warning for me to be honest with her.

"I'm good. I promise. I just need to… move on, and that hurts my heart a little. I've known for a long time."

She pulls me into a fierce hug, one only a best friend can pull off. "I'm here if you need to talk, or get drunk."

I laugh. "Thanks, Tess. Come on. I'm starving."

The kitchen is noisy when we enter. Everyone is eating, laughing, and having a good time. Tessa and I make our plates, and instead of squeezing in at the table, I place my plate on the counter next to my beer and try to jump up on the counter.

"Hold on, shorty. I've got this." Levi sets his plate down where he was coming back for what I assume is a second helping. He places his hands on my hips and lifts me up to the counter with very little effort. He goes right back to making his plate. My cheeks are flushed as my eyes dart around the room. They land on Cooper as he stares at me.

Once everyone has had their fill, we move to the living room. "Cooper," Sasha whines. Yes, it's a whine, and it's annoying as hell. How does he put up with that? "Let's go to your room."

"No." He doesn't even entertain the idea or try to reason with her. He just flat out turns her down.

She leans over to whisper in his ear. "How about that?" she asks where we can all hear her.

"No." Again, he blatantly dismisses her.

"Anyone need anything from the kitchen?" I ask, standing. I can't sit here and watch her. He can do so much better. I don't know why he doesn't see that. I get a yes to a couple of beers and a bottle of water for Tessa.

"I'll help." Cooper stands to follow me.

"Are you kidding me? Why are you following her?" Sasha says snidely.

"Because that's a lot for one person to carry."

"Why does it have to be you who helps *her*?" She says the word *her* as if I'm a snake that could strike out and bite her at any second.

"The *her* you are referring to is my best friend."

"I'm your girlfriend." She stomps her foot like a toddler.

I know because I'm watching this all unfold like a train wreck that I can't look away from. "Coop, it's fine. I've got this." I turn on my heel and start for the kitchen. I stop just inside the door and listen.

"Come on, let's go upstairs." Sasha tries again.

"No."

"I bet if *she* wanted to go, you would," she sneers.

"You're right. I would. Do you know why?" He doesn't give her time to finish. "She's my best friend. The most important person in my life, and I'll be damned if I'm going to let you treat her like she's anything less than that."

"Are you fucking her?" She gasps.

Cooper heaves a sigh. "No. I'm not fucking her. Not that it's any of your business."

"We're dating."

"We *were* dating. Now we're just acquaintances. If you can't respect Reese, you're not welcome here."

"Are you serious right now? You're never going to meet someone who's going to put up with her place in your life. I was willing to overlook it, but I deserve better."

"How exactly is giving her dirty looks and being a bitch to her overlooking it? And I don't want someone in my life who doesn't accept my family. Reese is family."

"Fuck you, Cooper Reeves. I can have any man I want."

Agony | 67

"Then go find him. Because this one doesn't want you."

"Tell him." I hear Sasha say. "Tell him that I'm better than her. That she's going to hold him back." The room is deathly silent. "Fine, who wants to go get drunk and laid?" Again, she's greeted with more silence. "Fuck all of you." She storms off—if the pounding of heels against the hardwood floor is any indication.

I scurry to the fridge and gather what I need. I feel him before he speaks. I've always been able to tell when he's near.

"Hey. Sorry about all that."

I turn to face him. "It's not a big deal. We knew this would happen, right? People don't understand our friendship."

"I don't need anyone in my life who is not going to accept you."

"You prepared to be a single man for eternity?" I joke, trying to lighten the mood.

"Reese." He reaches out and pushes my hair off my shoulders. "I'm sorry."

I shrug. "I better get these out there."

"Let me help you," he offers.

"No." I spin away out of his reach. "I've got it." I rush back to the living room and pass out drinks, taking a seat on the floor and propping my back against the love seat where Tessa and Nixon are cuddled up. Hank puts on a movie, and we all settle in. I can feel Cooper's eyes on me, but I refuse to look at him. I'm not mad at him, but he confuses me. He'll stand up for me, put me before anyone else. While I appreciate that, my fragile heart, the one that belongs to him, takes it as a mixed message. That's on me, not on him, and I get that. However, it doesn't make it any easier for me to handle.

When the credits roll, Nixon stands. "We're calling it a night." He offers Tessa his hand.

"Come on, party poopers. Watch another one with us," Trey says.

"Nope." Nixon picks Tessa up, tossing her over his shoulder. Her laughter fills the room as he takes her upstairs.

"My room's ready for you whenever you're sleepy," Levi says. "I even put clean sheets on this morning."

"Reese." Cooper says my name reverently. "Can we talk?"

"Sure." I shrug like it's not a big deal. It shouldn't be. My heart just didn't get the memo.

He stands from the couch and offers me his hand. I take it, letting him pull me from the floor. "Let's go to my room." I don't say a word as I allow him to lead me upstairs to his room. "I'm sorry," he says once the door is shut.

"You have nothing to be sorry for."

"I hate that she talked about you, about us like that. I know she wasn't nice to you. I saw the looks."

"It's fine, Coop. We've been defending our friendship for years. I'm used to it."

"No. It's not fine. I should have kicked her ass to the curb a lot sooner."

"You're allowed to date."

"I know, but that person will respect you and who you are in my life, or it's not going to work out."

"Okay."

"Okay? Is that all you have to say?"

"I don't know what you want from me, Cooper."

He sits on the bed next to me. His arm settles around my shoulders, and he pulls me into his chest. "I want you to tell me that we're okay. I can't lose you over this."

"You're not going to lose me."

"Promise."

I hold up my pinky finger. "Pinky promise."

He smiles, linking his pinky with mine as there's a knock at the door. "Come in."

"Hey," Levi says, his eyes only on mine. "You ready for bed?" Cooper tenses beside me.

I look up at Cooper, and he shakes his head. "Stay, we have a lot to talk about."

"Thanks, Levi, but it looks like this one plans on being chatty Kathy tonight."

He nods. I see understanding and maybe… pity in his gaze. "If you change your mind, I'm just down the hall." With that, he closes the door.

"You were going to share a bed with him." It's not so much a question as a statement.

"Yes. He's a good guy."

"I don't like it."

"You got your way."

"This is the bed you sleep in when you're here."

"And the Sashas of the world?"

"They're not you."

My heart flutters in my chest as the butterflies swarm, and I have to remind myself that it's our friendship he's so vigilantly honoring. Not love. Sure, he loves me, but not like I love him. He couldn't possibly. It's a love so deep, I'm scared to death that I'll never love another.

COOPER

COLLEGE: JUNIOR YEAR

We made it to the playoffs. For the third year in a row, Central University is going all the way. Our team is undefeated this year, just like last year, and we're so close to another championship I can taste it. We didn't win it my freshman year, but we made it to the final game. Last year, even with losing the seniors, we rallied and pulled off a win. I want to do it again. Not just because it looks good to scouts to be on a winning team.

But I like to win.

It's hard work to put your heart and soul into a game, practice every day of the week, deprive your body of the delicious foods that surround you, give up beer at parties, and miss out on so much because you're in the gym or traveling to a game. No, you do it for the win. For the high that you and your team are the best.

"This blows," Hank says from beside me.

"The win will be worth it," I tell him.

"This is our party, and we can't even enjoy it," Trey grumbles.

"Do you really need alcohol to have a good time?" Nixon asks them. He's listening to our conversation, but his eyes, like mine, are glued to Tessa and Reese, who are currently shaking what their mommas gave them in the middle of our living room floor.

"No, but it helps," Dustin chimes in.

"Think about the end game," Levi tells him. "We're bringing home another championship for CU, and that looks hella good on your stats."

"Hey, Hank. Wanna dance?" A short redhead saunters up to him, batting her eyelashes.

"Thought you'd never ask," he tells her. She latches onto his arm, and off they go.

"See, his mood brightened. Just go find you a co-ed to hang all over you," I say to the others.

"You're right," Trey agrees. "I think I'll go ask Reese." He takes a step forward, but my hand on his shoulder stops him.

"Fuck off," I grumble, and they all laugh.

"Well, someone needs to because I'm about to grab my girl." Nixon drains his bottle of water, tosses it in a nearby trash can, and heads straight for Tessa.

"Hi, Coop, you look lonely. Want to join me out there?" Lisa—or is it Laura—asks as she approaches me. She has long red fingernails that are pointed at the tip. They look like claws, and they're not attractive. Not to me. She's got a red Solo cup in her hand, and from the smell of her, she's long past tipsy.

"No, thanks. The guys and I are strategizing for the big game."

"Oh, come on. I'll make it worth your while," she slurs.

"Tommy," I call out to the freshman who's walking by. "Lisa needs a dance partner."

"Lori," she corrects me.

Tommy's eyes are wide and unsure. "Tommy here will take good care of you. Show her what you've got," I tell him.

He nods, offers her a grin and his arm. She mumbles something incoherent under her breath, but takes his arm, leaning her weight on him. She's toasted, and sex with drunk girls isn't on my radar.

"You know," Levi says, "if I didn't know any better, I'd think you were either already taken or had your eye on someone."

"She's way passed drunk. I don't want to spend my night taking care of her. Tommy can have that privilege."

"What if it were Reese?" he asks, nodding toward where she stands. Her red Solo cup is poised at her lips, and her head is tilted back.

"Reese is different," I say, turning to look at him.

He nods. "Good, but it looks like you're off the hook."

My head whips around so fast I could have whiplash. Sure enough, Scott Southerland is standing behind her with his hands on her hips. Scott is the brother of one of the seniors, Sam, who is the back-up kicker. He's been to a few of our parties. Tonight, however, he's gone too far. I toss my water bottle in the trash and put one foot in front of the other until I reach her.

"Coop!" she says loudly.

Her eyes are glassy from the cheap beer, and her smile is wide. "I missed you." She throws her arms around my neck, stepping out of his hold. I pull her close, my hand resting possessively on the small of her back.

"I've been with you all night." I say the words to her, but my eyes are on Scott. The look I give him does the trick. He lifts his hands in the air and backs away. Smart man.

"Dance with me." She shuffles in closer and begins to sway her hips.

With her arms still around my neck, she tilts her head back and smiles up at me. Her green eyes, even glassy from her buzz, are beautiful. *She's* beautiful. It's getting harder and harder for me to keep all the assholes away from her.

"Come on, Coop. You can do better than that." She then moves to straddle my leg and begins to rock her hips. My cock hardens, as does my grip on her hips.

Everything around us fades to black. It's just me and her alone in this room. She drops her hands to her sides, brushing my cock as they fall, and I tense up. Closing my eyes, I try to think about anything but how fucking sexy my best friend is and how much I want her. I've been hit on countless times tonight, and not one of those women affected me the way Reese is at this very moment.

My Reese.

My best friend.

I've got to tramp this down. And I can start by stopping her from rubbing her pussy all over my leg. That's all I can think about. My grip tightens further, and my leg, on its own, bends to give her better access.

Reese leans her head back, her hair falling over her back, and the long column of her neck is exposed. I can't help but wonder how she would react if I were to lean in and trace her exposed skin with my tongue. Would she like that?

"Get it, girl!" Hank calls out, pulling me out of my X-rated fantasy about my best friend.

Drunk Reese is on fire tonight. She suddenly drops to the floor and shakes her ass before slowly climbing back to her feet. Her hands roam all over my body. She's lost in the music, riding the buzz the cheap beer has given her.

Me, I'm stone-cold sober. I feel every touch, every sway of her hips, and it's driving me insane. My plan is to stop her as soon as the song ends, but one fast song bleeds into another, and I find myself sticking with her out on the dance floor. I'm protecting her. Keeping all the drunk assholes from taking advantage of her in her inebriated state.

Finally, a slow song comes on. I open my mouth to ask her if she wants to get some air, but I freeze when she wraps her arms around my waist and rests her head against my chest. I wrap my arms around her, holding her close. There have been many times in my life where I wished things were different. Where I wished that she was mine. Not just my best friend but my girl. Tonight, that feeling is strong. That wish is loud and all-consuming.

When the song ends, she steps back and sways on her feet. "Coop."

"Yeah?" I ask, brushing her hair back behind her ear. "I don't feel so good."

I jump into action, sliding my hand around her waist and pushing through the crowd. We reach the steps, and I lift her into my arms and carry her upstairs to the bathroom. As soon as her feet hit the floor, she wobbles to the toilet, dropping to her knees and expels the cheap beer.

Sitting on the edge of the tub, I gather her hair in my hands and hold it out of her face. She groans, and then buries her head in the toilet again.

Reese doesn't let loose like this very often. I'm glad that I stayed sober tonight. Sure, it was because of the upcoming game, but I'm glad I'm here to take care of her. To watch out for her.

"Kill me now," she groans, resting her head on her arms that are lying across the toilet bowl.

"No one's dying on my watch. You good?"

"I think so."

I help her sit back and then grab a washcloth. I run it under cool water and hand it to her. She places it against her forehead and sighs. We sit in silence for a few minutes, nothing but the sound of the water running in the toilet mixed with the sounds of the party downstairs to fill the air.

"You think you can brush your teeth?"

"Maybe. Don't let go of me." She hands me the washcloth, and I toss it in the laundry basket, then offer her my hand. Carefully, I help her stand from her spot on the floor, and together, we move to the sink. I grab her toothbrush that she keeps here and add some toothpaste, running it under the water. I hand it to her.

"Good?" I ask after she rinses out her mouth.

"Yeah."

"Let's get you to bed." With my hand around her waist, I open the bathroom door, and we move down the hall to my room. She flops down on the bed and moans.

"Why did you let me drink so much?"

"Me?" I laugh, grabbing a T-shirt and some sweats for her to sleep in. "I didn't let you do anything."

"You should have stopped me."

"Here." I hand her my clothes.

"I have clothes here."

"I know, but this was easier than me digging through your bag. Put these on. I'm going to go grab you something for that headache and a bottle of water."

"I don't have a headache."

"You will. I'm locking this door," I say, grabbing the lanyard with my room key off my desk. No way am I leaving her in this state in a room unattended. "Be right back." Closing the door, I make sure it's locked before making my way back downstairs. I have to field my way through partygoers to get to the kitchen. I grab three bottles of water. Reese needs to drink one now, and I have one for both of us for later. Then I rummage through the cabinets to find a bottle of headache medicine. Taking off the lid, I tap the bottle letting four tablets fall into my hand. Two for now and two for in the morning. I already know she's going to need them. I also know she's going to be pissed at herself for drinking so much. It's good to see her let loose and have a good time. Even if it makes me think naughty thoughts about her.

"Yo, Reeves. Where did you run off to?" Dustin calls out as I leave the kitchen.

"Calling it a night!" I yell back.

"Where's your girl?" He smirks.

"In my bed." The words are out of my mouth before I can stop them. His eyes widen, but I don't have time to explain. I take the stairs two at a time and quickly unlock my bedroom door, slipping inside. What I see takes the breath from my lungs.

"Coop, is that you?" Reese asks. "I need help. This stupid shirt." She huffs. "Cooper?"

"Sorry, yeah, it's me. Let me help." I jump into action, placing the headache medicine and bottles of water on the nightstand. Somehow, she's managed to twist her arms with her shirt pulled halfway over her head. Her sheer black bra is giving me a full view of her breasts, and her nipples have decided it's also time for a show as the pebbled buds peek through the thin material. I swallow hard and walk toward her. My cock is hard. Not just hard, but steel behind my zipper as I take her in. I've seen her in a swimsuit, but this... did I mention I can see her nipples? Perfect round pebbled buds just begging for my mouth.

She's your best friend.

"Coop, are you going to help me or not?" She huffs again.

"Hold still." I tug on her shirt and, between the two of us, we get it over her head and off.

"Thanks." She throws herself back on the bed dramatically.

Her jeans are unbuttoned, and her boots are lying haphazardly on the floor. Her toned flat belly taunts me as she leaves it out on display. My eyes rake over her, and even though I know it's wrong, I can't seem to stop myself. I'm a guy, she's gorgeous. Of course I'm going to look.

She slides the zipper of her jeans down and lifts her hips, trying to pull them off. "Help me."

I don't speak, but I do lift both legs, grip her jeans, and tug until they slide off. I avert my gaze to the floor where her boots are. I busy myself picking them up, so we don't trip over them tomorrow, and place them by the door. I take my time folding her jeans and putting them neatly on the desk. I count slowly to one hundred, then pretend to be fascinated with my phone and count another hundred just as slowly to be safe. When I turn around, I'm greeted with a sight that I will never be able to forget.

Reese is lying on my bed in nothing but a sheer black bra and panties. If you can even call them that. It's a thong. A very tiny thong. I know because she's curled up, and her ass, her bare ass, is facing me. I swallow hard, but don't look away. I can't look away. It's painful, not just because my cock is pressing against the zipper in my jeans, but because I can't have her. I can't ruin years of friendship over one night in bed. However, I'll have this visual with me for years to come.

I'm lusting after my best friend.

I'm staring at her body.

I'm going to hell.

"Reese." My voice is gravelly. "Let's get you dressed."

"Too hot," she mumbles.

"Come on." I grab the T-shirt I need to get her covered. I know her, and if she wakes up like this in the morning, she's going to be mad at herself. "Let me help you." She groans but holds out her hand, letting me pull her to a sitting position.

"I need this off," she says, reaching behind her back.

"Let's put this shirt on you first."

"No, Coop. I can't. I have to take this off." She grunts and then heaves a heavy sigh as her bra becomes loose.

Closing my eyes, I count slowly to ten. "Where are my jeans? I need to put this with my jeans." My eyes are barely open, and she's climbing off the bed, stumbling across the room to place her bra on top of the jeans I just placed on my desk. When she turns to face me, I get a good look before averting my gaze.

"Here's your shirt." I hold my hand out, eyes closed, head angled toward the wall. I'm trying really fucking hard to respect her privacy right now, but fuck me, she is a vision. Nice pert tits, a handful if I'm guessing, and her nipples are like beacons of light in the night.

I want to taste them.

"Thanks." She takes a step forward and fumbles. I reach out to break her fall, and her tits end up pressed against my arms.

"Fuck," I mutter.

"Sorry." Her reply is meek.

"No. It's not you. It's fine. Are you okay?" I keep my eyes trained on hers.

"Yes. I think I need to sit."

I nod and help her to the bed. "Let's get you dressed." Carefully, I pull the shirt over her head and close my eyes as she slides her arms through each opening. Snatching the sweats, I kneel before her, helping her into them. She stands and supports her weight on my shoulders as I pull them up her creamy thighs. "All set," I say, standing. My voice is gruff, and my throat is parched. I reach for one of the bottles of water and down it.

"Here, drink this and take these."

Thankfully, she does as I ask. When the water bottle is empty, she hands it back to me, and I toss it into the small trash can next to the bed. "You good?"

"I'm good." She moves back on the bed and wiggles her way under the covers. "Are you coming to bed?"

Fuck. I can't lie next to her like this. "I'm just going to grab a quick shower." Grabbing a shirt and some sweats, I snatch my room key from the desk and rush down the hall to take a cold shower. I don't bother letting the water warm up. I strip out of my clothes, before turning on the spray, and stepping underneath it. I don't feel the cold, not while my body is on fire for her.

For Reese.

My best friend.

Taking my cock in my hand, I pump hard and fast. The water is barely warm before I'm spilling my desire down the drain. Reaching for the knob, I turn the water to hot and let it beat down on me. I can't believe I just did that. I jacked off to images of my best friend. What's worse is I don't know how I'll ever be able to see anyone but her ever again.

Finishing my shower, I dry off and get dressed. By the time I make it back to my room, Reese is thankfully sound asleep. I lock the door and climb into the opposite side of the bed from her. I stare up at the shadows dancing across the ceiling as I berate myself for what I just did. For this entire night, I ogled her, and that was wrong. Oh, so wrong, and I know that it is. But, if it's so wrong, why did it feel so right?

REESE

I'm awake, but I don't want to open my eyes. The room is spinning, and I know once I peel my eyes open, it's going to be worse. On instinct, I slip a leg from underneath the covers and throw it over the bed. I've heard that if you can put one foot firmly on the floor, the room will begin to settle. I don't know because I've never drunk like I did last night.

"Ugh, I'm too short," I groan.

A deep chuckle fills the room. I don't have to look to know it's Cooper. "Good thing I cut you off when I did."

"Why?" I moan. "Why did you let me drink so much?"

"Hey, I'm not your keeper."

I manage to lift my finger and point to his side of the bed, my eyes still closed. "Best-friend job description."

Another deep chuckle greets me. "I gave you water and headache medicine."

"Thank you. I could use another round after I relieve my bladder."

"Already got you covered. The second round is waiting for you on the nightstand."

"Can you go to the bathroom for me too?"

"Let me guess. The room is spinning?"

I swallow hard, fighting off nausea. "Yep."

"It's like pulling off a Band-Aid. Get it over with, and then you'll feel better."

"That's easy for you to say. I hate throwing up."

"Come on, drunk girl." I feel the bed dip and hear his feet hit the floor. "I held your hair back last night. What's once more?" I hear from my opposite side.

"I'm sorry." Slowly I peek one eye open. Nothing bad happens, so I peel the other open as well. The room is still spinning, so I try to focus on Cooper.

His eyes are soft as he stares down at me. "Nothing to be sorry for. I've always got you, Reese." With that, he holds out his hand and helps me sit up. "Can you walk? I can carry you."

"Number two, please."

"Up you go," he says as he bends and scoops me in his arms. His long strides carry us to the bathroom, where he gently sets me on my feet. "You need my help?"

I look down at the T-shirt and sweats I'm wearing. I recognize them as his. "Did you give me these?"

He nods. "I helped you change." There's something in his voice that I can't decipher. My head is too foggy, and the nausea is overpowering.

Oh, God. Embarrassment washes over me. I think back to getting ready yesterday. Did my bra and panties match? Not that it matters. Cooper doesn't see me that way, but it would make me feel better if they did. My stomach rolls, and I'm going to be sick. Dropping to my knees, I crawl to the toilet just in time to lose the contents of my stomach.

I keep my eyes closed as I groan and wait for my body to revolt yet again. I feel Cooper gather my hair and hold it off to the side, as his hand soothingly traces up and down my spine. Neither of us says a word, but then again, we don't need to. We know each other well enough that he knows I'm embarrassed. I'm embarrassed, but grateful it's him here with me. Taking care of me like he's always done.

"You good?" he asks.

"I think so. I really need a shower."

"I'll go grab your bag." He releases his grip on my hair, gives my shoulder a gentle squeeze, and leaves me alone.

I manage to fall back on my ass and lift his T-shirt and pull his sweats away from my body. I heave a sigh of relief that my undies not only match but were sexy. Not that it matters to him, but like I said, it makes me feel better.

"Reese," he calls through the closed door. "Okay if I come in?"

"Yeah."

He smiles when he sees me with my back resting against the tub. "Here." He steps into the small bathroom and hands me a bottle of water and two tablets.

"My hero." He just shakes his head.

"Here's your bags." He sets the bag I packed with clothes and the toiletry bag I leave here for nights I stay over.

"Thanks, Coop."

"You good? You need me to help you?"

I wish. "No, I'm good. Thank you for taking such good care of me."

"I'm going to go see what I can wrangle you for breakfast that won't sour your stomach. I'll be downstairs."

"What are we doing today?"

"What do you want to do today?" he counters.

"A whole lot of nothing."

He laughs. "We can make that happen, Reese's Pieces. I'll be downstairs. Oh, I almost forgot." He pulls my phone out of his back pocket. "Here. Call if you need me." With that, he turns and walks out.

I remain where I am on the floor, propped up against the tub until I feel like I can actually move. Slowly, I climb to my feet. Reaching out, I lock the door, and then strip out of his clothes, but not before smelling them. They smell just like him, and well, alcohol, so sadly, they must go.

I wish I could remember more of last night. He's seen me in bathing suits, but what I had on last night left little to the imagination. Did he like what he saw? I mean, he is a guy, but apparently not enough to act on it. Sure, he wouldn't take advantage of me, but today... today he could have acted on it. That's merely wishful thinking on my part.

I spend some time in the shower, just standing under the hot spray. It helps to wake me up and wash away the fog of my hangover. I can't believe I drank that much. Never again. I'm never drinking that much *ever* again. I hate feeling like this. What's worse is what could have happened had Cooper not been here to take care of me. Then again, I wouldn't have even considered it if he weren't. I knew he had me, just like he knows I always have him. That's what best friends are for.

Thirty minutes later, I'm making my way down the stairs to hear the guys and Tessa in the kitchen.

"There she is," Levi calls out.

I wince at his loud voice. "I'm right here," I tell him.

He grins and comes to me, throwing his arm over my shoulders. "How you feeling, slugger?"

"Like death."

"Here." Cooper hands me a plate with a plain bagel with cinnamon cream cheese icing.

My favorite. Both of them. "Thanks, Coop."

"He made a special trip," Tessa speaks up.

I look over at her, then my eyes slide to Cooper. "Thank you."

He nods.

"So, Reese, we were thinking about having another party tonight." Hank grins as he says the words, unable to keep a straight face.

"You do that. I'll be at my apartment, curled up on the couch, far, far away from the alcohol. I can't believe I drank that much."

"If it makes you feel any better, I feel just as bad as you do," Tessa adds.

"It was good to see the two of you let loose for once," Nixon says, kissing her on the cheek.

"Yeah, well, don't get used to it. I hate feeling like ass," I mutter.

"You and me both," Tessa agrees.

"For real, though, what's going on tonight?" Hank asks.

"I have a date." Trey's wink is exaggerated.

"Oh, yeah? Who with?" Dustin asks him.

"Cute little co-ed that was here last night."

"Nice." Dustin holds his fist out for a bump, and Trey knocks his fist in reply.

"I've got nothing," Levi announces.

"There's a party over at that baseball house. You in?" Hank asks.

"Sure." Levi shrugs.

"Me too," Dustin tells them.

"You know, if Coach catches you partying a week before the big game, you're toast, right?" Nixon asks them.

"Who says we're drinking? I'm just going for the ladies." Dustin smirks.

"What about you guys?" Hank asks Nixon.

"No. We're just going to lay low," Nixon says, pulling Tessa close to his side.

"Reeves?" Hank looks over at Cooper.

"Nah, I'm going to stay in and take care of this one." He points toward me. "Her mom and mine would have my ass if I didn't."

"I don't need a sitter. You can go. I won't be drinking again for a long time. A very, very long time," I say, popping the last bite of my bagel into my mouth.

"Nah, I'm good. I'm not willing to risk the wrath of Coach. One night is enough for me."

"Pussy," Hank taunts.

"I'll remember that when Coach lays into your ass." Cooper points at Hank.

"Nah, I'm not going to get into any trouble, unless you know, it's the sexual kind." He gyrates his hips, and I can't help but laugh at him.

"Well, don't be bringing said ladies back here. We don't want to spend our night listening to you and your harem," Nixon tells him.

"Hey." Hank holds his hands out at his sides. "I can't help that the ladies love Hank the Tank."

"Oh, God." Tessa rolls her eyes. "You're calling yourself that now?"

Hank is a defensive lineman for the CU Tigers. The nickname actually suits him. At six foot seven, he stands tall over the rest of the guys in the house, and most of the guys on the football team. He's wide, so wide in fact, that Tessa and I both can stand in front of him, and there are still inches to go. *Inches.* I know this because we've tried it on multiple occasions. He's that big. However, he's not mean. Not like you might think with a nickname like Hank the Tank. It's merely just from his size and his actions on the football field. Off the field, he's a giant teddy bear and a huge flirt.

All three of them, which excludes Nixon and Cooper, are huge flirts. I used to think it was to make Cooper jealous, but as time went on, his threats to kill them for touching me wore off, and they still continue to flirt with me. Just another reminder that he doesn't see me that way. He was just being a good best friend, kind of like a brother, and looking out for me. They know that if any of them were to ever hurt me, he would kill them. Okay, maybe kill is too strong of a word, but he would certainly rough them up. Of that, I am certain.

"Well, if you change your mind, you know where we'll be. I'm going back to bed for a few hours." Hank stands and leaves the room.

"I'm hitting the gym. Levi?" Dustin asks.

"I'm with ya." He downs the rest of his glass of milk and rinses it out before placing it in the sink.

"Look at that. My boy's all grown up," Tessa coos.

I chuckle. The guys always grumble about dishes and especially getting milk out of the bottom of the glass with their big hands. It's taken us years to convince them that if they just take the time to rinse it out, that problem goes away.

Levi bends and kisses Tessa on the cheek. "What would we do without you?"

"You're not going to be alive to find out if you don't get your lips off my girl."

Levi shrugs and comes to stand in front of me. He bends and kisses me on the cheek as well. I feel nothing but friendship and brotherly love from him. "You too," he says, rising. In the past, when he would do this, I would look at Cooper to gauge his reaction. Those days have long since passed. I know his jaw is going to be set, and there will be a warning glare in those brown eyes. I also know that it's for his best friend. No matter how badly I want it to be more, it's not.

"Me too." Dustin shoves a donut in his mouth and stands.

"I'm going to head home, get a few more hours of sleep. I'll be back later," I tell anyone who's listening.

"Just go back upstairs and sleep," Tessa says.

My eyes scan to Cooper. "I don't want to cramp your style today."

"Never." He, too, rinses out his glass and holds his hand out for me. "Come on, drunk girl."

I stick my tongue out at him, and he laughs. Placing my hand in his, I let him lead me upstairs to his room. Once inside, I go to his bed and burrow under the covers. It's a dreary fall day, and sleeping in is just what the doctor ordered to help cure this hangover. Cooper pulls the curtains closed, and I shut my eyes, assuming he's going back downstairs. A few minutes later, I feel the bed dip, and his body moves in settling next to mine.

"You good, Reese? Can I get you anything?"

"I'm fine." I don't turn to look at him. I know he's close because I can feel the heat of his body.

"Get some rest." He places his hand on my hip and doesn't move it. I lie still, waiting to see what happens. Nothing. A few minutes later, his light snores greet me. I relax into the mattress and eventually drift off to sleep, tethered to my best friend. Not just by his hand, but my heart. In more ways than one.

COOPER

I wake with a jolt. My eyes spring open, and I take in my current situation. I'm warm, not unreasonably so, but warmer than usual. I look to the woman lying in my arms and smile.

Reese.

She's sound asleep, but it's her ass, her perfect round, gorgeous, now pink-thong-wearing ass that woke me up. It's currently pressing against my cock. She's covered, fully dressed in her own clothes, but I now know what lies underneath. I saw it in her bag, and I can now after last night get a clear visual in my mind of how she looks in it. I have a clear image in my head. My arms are around her, holding her close to my chest. We've ended up like this a few times; it happens when two people who are as close as we are share a bed. However, this time it's different. This time all I can think about is stripping her out of her clothes and tracing her curves with my tongue.

I've always known that my best friend was gorgeous. Hell, I've warned off plenty of assholes—some of which are my closest friends. She has the kind of beauty that's understated. She's genuinely a nice person. She very rarely has a bad word to say about anyone, and she's loyal to a fault. Her green eyes are captivating, only adding to her beauty.

It's more than just that, though.

She's easy to talk to and a blast to be around. She's not full of drama, and she's one of those people that what you see is what you get. She's real, and that takes her appeal and hotness factor up about a million points. I've always known that, and she deserves a man who notices that about her. Someone who knows she's one of a kind. I'll continue to run them off until he shows himself.

Then last night happened.

Last night, I saw all of her. Sure, she was covered in sheer black fabric, but it left nothing to the imagination. No, my mind is clear, and I can pull up the mental images of her pert nipples and perfectly sized tits, and that ass…. They're all stored away as a moment in life that I will never forget.

I know I should pull away. I'm wide awake. I should slip out of bed and let her sleep, but I can't do that. I physically can't make myself pull away from her. Instead, I'm going to lie here with her in my arms, her perfect ass nestled against my cock, and pretend like this is us. That this is the new us. I'm going to soak up this moment for all it's worth. Then, when it's gone, I'll have the memory of what could have been. When I think about my life, there is not a minute of my future that I don't see Reese in. I need it to stay that way. She's my rock, and I'd like to think that I'm hers as well. As bad as I want her in this moment, I'm not willing to risk losing her, losing what we have just to get my dick wet. Not saying that's all she would be. Even I know that sleeping with Reese would change things. The problem is that it's a risk, one I'm not willing to take. So instead, I'll lie here and soak up her warmth and the feel of her in my arms. Then later, I'll take matters into my own hands, at the vision of my best friend. It's not the first time, and I'm sure it won't be the last. Not when it comes to Reese.

My phone vibrates on the nightstand, and I curse under my breath. Reese stirs. Her arms stretch out above her head, and she rolls over to face me. "Hey."

Has she always looked this beautiful when she first wakes up? "Hi. Feel better?" I ask, faking a yawn. The last thing I need is for her to know that I was being a creeper and holding her close, just because I could.

"Much better. Remind me to never drink like that again."

I nod. Although, I don't know that I'll have the willpower to stop her, knowing how the night might end. My phone vibrates again. Reaching over, I grab it and look at the screen. It's my mom. I show Reese the screen, and she props herself up on her elbow. "Hey, Mom," I greet her.

"Cooper, are you still sleeping? It's one o'clock on Saturday." There's humor in her voice.

"Yep. It was a… long night," I say, glancing at Reese and winking.

"Cooper Reeves, is there a woman in your bed?" Mom scolds me.

"Yep. Want to see her?"

"No. I do not want to see her, Cooper," she sighs.

"Mom, you'll love her. I promise." I switch the call to video chat and hold it between us.

"Hey, Ann," Reese says.

"Reese?"

We both laugh. "Yep."

"Oh," Mom says, and I can hear the excitement in her voice. It's no secret that our mothers think we are just perfect for each other. Their words, not ours. Although they keep them to themselves. I've just happened to overhear them a time or two.

"What are you kids getting into today?"

"Just hanging out."

"You were sleeping?" She tries to keep her question nonchalant, but Reese and I share a look, that ends with us both shaking our heads.

"Yes. We had people over last night. Reese stayed instead of going home late on her own."

"Where's Tessa?"

Have I mentioned that our parents are very involved in our lives? "She stayed here with Nixon."

"Oh, that's right. Well, it's nice that you were there for Reese to stay with you."

I read between the lines. So does Reese. Which is why I assume she changes the subject. "How have you been?" Reese asks.

"Good. Good. Your mom and I are going shopping in a while. It's been too long since I spoke to my son, so I decided to call."

"Cooper," Reese scolds. "You need to call your mother more."

"Me? What about you? When was the last time you called Eve?" I ask, talking about her mom.

"Yesterday," she says smugly.

"See, Cooper, you should follow Reese's lead," Mom says, barely holding in her laughter.

"It's been like three days," I counter.

"Three days without talking to my only son. Just wait, one day when you're a parent, you'll understand where I'm coming from."

I sigh loudly. Dramatically. They both laugh. "Where are you ladies going today?"

"To the mall. Your dads are building a workbench or something in Garrett's garage."

"Dad's sprucing up the mancave again?" Reese asks.

"I guess. You know your mom, and I try not to ask questions," Mom tells her. "That's her. Hold on a sec." We hear her shuffling and then opening the door and greeting Eve. "I'm talking to the kids."

"Hey, kids," Eve says. You can hear the smile in her voice. "What's going on?"

"Oh, they were sleeping," Mom says. Her tone is telling as she makes it out to be a bigger deal than what it is. At least, more than what I want her to think that it is. Even Reese doesn't know what this little nap did for me. Or my thoughts about her.

"We were up late," Reese tells her mom.

"I see. Well, what are you two getting into today?" Eve asks.

"Nothing," Reese answers. "Not a single thing."

Eve chuckles. "Enjoy the break. Cooper, you ready for the big game?"

"You know it. We're bringing home a win," I tell her.

"We're cheering for you. I got my jersey packed and ready," Eve assures me.

"You guys are coming?" I don't know why I'm surprised; they've always supported me.

"Of course, we are."

"No pressure," I say, and all three ladies in my life laugh.

"You know you're going to kill it out there," Reese says. "You've been on fire all season."

"She's right," Mom chimes in.

"Reese, I sent you a package today. Great Aunt Edna made you a sweater," Eve says, barely holding in her laughter.

"I wonder how big this one will be?" I muse.

"She does know I'm an adult now, right?" Reese asks her mom.

"Come on, Reese's Pieces. You should be flattered."

"It was for a toddler, Coop. In fact, I'm not sure even a toddler could fit into that thing."

"She was so mad when you didn't send her a picture of you wearing it," Eve comments.

"Yeah, Reese. You'll have to model it. Eve, I'll take the picture myself," I offer, because it's sure to be a good laugh, but also, seeing Reese in a skimpy state of undress is high on my list of priorities all of a sudden.

"Perfect. Reese, you can take Cooper's too," Eve says, throwing me off guard.

"What does that mean?" I groan.

"Aunt Edna made one for you too."

"Dear God, can we just tell her that it got lost in the mail?" I ask.

"Cooper," Reese scolds me. "Is that any way to treat poor Great Aunt Edna's gift? You will try it on, and I will make sure she gets those pictures."

Our moms laugh. "Let me know when you get it," Eve tells Reese. "You kids have fun. We need to go, or we're going to be late for our pedicures. Love you both," Eve says.

"Love you both," Mom echoes, and the line goes dead.

"This is going to be good." Reese grins.

Reaching over, I tickle her side. "Yeah? You think this is funny? Just wait, I'm framing yours," I say through her laughter.

"S-Stop. I'm g-gonna pee." She laughs. Her cute little button nose is scrunched up just like it always does when she's laughing. It's a look that I've seen often, and one of her best. I love to see her happy.

I move to get a better angle, which has me staring down at her. That's the moment my bedroom door opens. Nixon and Tessa stand there with weird expressions on their faces.

"T-Tess," Reese splutters. "H-Help me."

"You're on your own, girl. I ain't trying to be a part of all that." I look over my shoulder to find Tessa waving her arm in the air toward the bed, where Reese and I are currently having a tickle fest just like we used to when we were kids.

"Mercy?" I ask her.

"Y-Yes."

"And no pictures to send to Aunt Edna."

"Y-Yes. Fine." She gasps for air.

I relent, pulling my hands from her body, and she jolts to action and rushes out the door. Thankfully, Nixon and Tessa jump out of the way to let her through.

Nixon shakes his head while Tessa gives me a knowing look with a smile a mile wide. "We're going downstairs to watch a movie and order pizza. Just wanted to let you guys know."

"Thanks, we'll be right down."

Tessa's eyes sparkle. "Take your time. We can wait." With that, she tugs on Nixon's arm and pulls him out of my room, down the hall. Their footsteps grow faint as they descend the stairs.

A few minutes later, Reese is back. Her face is flushed, her hair is a mess, and her smile is not only wide but genuine. That's just Reese. "Where'd they go?" she asks.

"Downstairs. Movies and pizza?" I ask.

"It's like you read my mind." She walks to my closet and pulls out one of my CU hoodies. It has my last name and number printed on the back. I wait for her to slip it over her head and then follow her downstairs.

As I walk behind her, I can't hide my smile. It's not the first hoodie of mine that she's confiscated, and I'm sure it won't be the last. This time though, it feels different. Seeing her wearing my name and number, it's not new. No, she's done this since we were kids as my biggest cheerleader. It's something that has happened more times than not during our friendship, but this time there is something else. Something that almost feels like want. The last twenty-four hours have been strange, and I'm sure tomorrow things will go back to normal. That's what needs to happen, but the thought leaves pain in the center of my chest. Shaking out of my thoughts, I mentally chastise myself.

She's my best friend.

This is not happening.

Nixon and I let the girls choose the toppings as he and I will eat anything. By the time the pizza arrives, we've convinced them to watch a scary movie.

"You know this is going to suck for us, right?" Tessa asks. I'm not sure if she's asking me and Nixon, or Reese.

"I know," Reese grumbles. "Why in the hell did we let them win?"

"Hey, we watch that sappy romantic shit with you two all the time," Nixon reminds them.

He's not wrong. We usually pretty much give in to whatever they want. Tonight, however, I put up a fight. I've had more sappy thoughts than I can handle with Reese this weekend. I need something that's not going to have me wishing things were different. Something with gore and suspense should do the trick. Something that's not going to tempt me to spill my thoughts and potentially ruin a lifetime of friendship. No, I need scary tonight.

Two large pizzas later, the lights are off, and Nixon cues up the movie. I glance over at the couch, and Tessa is curled up next to him. His arm is around her shoulders, holding her close, and a little bit of envy washes over me. It would be nice to be with someone. To know they're with me for who I am, and not the idea of the fame my future might hold.

"Toss me that pillow," Reese tells Tessa. Somehow, all of the pillows have ended up on the couch. Reese catches it easily and pulls the cover off the back of the couch. She and Reese insisted that we keep covers down here for nights like this. Otherwise, you'd never see a cover in this house. Nixon and I take turns making sure they're clean, because our roommates bring home random girls quite often, and well, that's just nasty to think about Reese or even Tessa wrapped up in… that.

Ten minutes into the movie and the music starts to change. It's not only louder, but it's daunting, warning you, building the intensity that something's about to happen. When a guy in a mask steps out of a hall closet and captures the female lead from behind, the girls scream. Reese jumps into my lap and buries her face in my chest. I wrap my arms around her, comforting her just like I have since we were kids and watched scary movies. She settles against me and doesn't even attempt to move.

I thought a scary movie was the way to go, and although now for a different reason, I know I was right. I'll take these moments with her. I'll bottle them up and keep them close for times when I'm away from her. If I get drafted, like I hope that I do, that's going to change our relationship. Not a day has gone by since I was eight years old that I haven't seen her. The draft, my career is going to change that. Maybe she'll come with me? No, I can't ask her to do that. I can't ask her to give up her life. It took her some time, but she now has her heart set on being a social worker. She wants to make a difference, and I have no doubt in my mind that she will indeed make a difference in so many lives.

Just look at what she's done for mine.

I'm a better person because of her. I find myself doing things that I know will make her smile or be proud of me. She brings that out in me. Hell, she brings it out in my roommates. This house was party central my freshman year. Nixon and I move in, the girls with us, and things calm down. Sure, we still party, but they're tame compared to what they used to be. That's her influence. I strive to be better. For her. I never want her to be embarrassed that I'm the guy she chooses to spend all of her time with. One day when we're older, and we have families of our own, I want her to be proud to introduce me to them as their pseudo uncle and her best friend. Then again, what I really want is to be the man who stands tall next to her, even though I know that can't happen.

Reese jumps in my arms, pulling me out of my thoughts. "I've got you," I whisper in her ear. *I've always got you.*

Chapter 12

REESE

Today is Cooper's last game of the season. It's hard for me to believe that we only have one more year of college, and then it's mundane days of adulting. Well, for me anyway. Cooper is destined for bigger and better things. I can feel it.

It's not just me. There have been scouts coming to his games and trying to convince him to enter the draft this year. I could have told them that they were wasting their time. Cooper promised Ann he would graduate with his degree before pursuing a career in the professional football league. She wanted him to have a safety net to secure his future. I happen to agree with her. It's a career that takes a toll on your body, and you don't know how long you'll be able to play. Having a backup plan as a professional athlete is always a good idea.

There is no doubt in my mind he's going to get drafted. He's too good at what he does. Cooper shines on the field, and the scouts and teams would be blind not to see that. I love it and hate it all at the same time. I'm happy for him. I know he's going to be amazing and kick-ass for whatever team picks him up, but I'm also sad because he's going to be moving away. It will be the first time since we became friends that we've been apart for any period of time, really. Sure, he's gone for his away games, but that's days. This could be weeks and even months at a time before we see each other. It hurts my heart to think about us drifting apart. I know it's inevitable. I'd like to think that even with the distance, we can remain close. I guess only time will tell.

Grabbing my phone, I fire off my game day texts to both Cooper and Levi. Two very different men, and two very different messages. However, they both mean the same thing. I'm thinking about you. Have a good game. My texts with Levi started our freshman year, and it's something I've continued. And, Cooper, well, he's been getting game day texts from me since we got our first cell phones for Christmas when we were twelve.

> **Me:** Game Day: Squeeze into those tight spots.

I laugh out loud as I hit Send. Levi will get a kick out of that one. I try to make them sound as dirty as I can, but still give meaning to his position to the game. It's been a challenge over the last three years, but one I've lived up to.

> **Me:** Kick some ass out there today. We're bringing home the win.

Cooper replies immediately.

> **Cooper:** We're celebrating tonight. Did you pack a bag?

> **Me:** Yep. It's in my car.

> **Cooper:** See you after the game, Reese's Pieces.

I can't help but smile. He's called me that since the day he met me. When I told him what my name was, he said, "Like the candy, Reese's Pieces." I, of course, said yes, and he's been calling me that ever since. My phone pings, and it's Levi.

> **Levi:** It might be tight, but I'm sure I'll be able to fit.

My face flames. His replies are always just as dirty, and sometimes more so than my own. I know he does it to make me uncomfortable, bring me out of my shell as he calls it. I can't be mad, though. I'm the one who started it. Levi is a good guy. He's a goofball, but that's all a part of his charm.

"Where are your and Cooper's parents sitting?" Tessa asks as I slide my phone into my back pocket. She and I just got to our seats—Cooper and Nixon were able to score us tickets on the fifty-yard line, five rows up. Our parents, however, are in a suite. They bought their tickets on their own.

"They have a suite. Coop's dad's work sponsored it, so they got their tickets super cheap."

"That's awesome. We should be up there with them."

"What?" I ask, appalled. "And miss all of this." I wave my hands around the stadium.

"I swear Cooper has made you into a football junkie," she teases.

"Come on now. You know you love it." I lean into her, and she grins.

"Fine. I love it. I love those pants my man wears too." She wags her eyebrows.

"The pants are a bonus," I admit.

"Oh, yeah, you got your eye on someone particular?" She looks at me knowingly.

"All of them." I turn to look out over the field. "With the helmets on, they're all my future husband," I joke.

"Amen to that." She holds up her hand for a high-five.

"Please, you're practically married already." She and Nixon have been going strong since our freshman year.

"Married women can look. Besides, I keep my eyes on Nixon more so than the others anyway. I can't help it if another fine ass just happens to be in my line of sight." She grins, proud of herself for the spin she was able to put on it.

"Right? Well, I can happily look at all the fine asses without shame or regret."

"You might be able to, but we both know which ass you spend the most time looking at." She bumps her shoulder into mine.

"Hey. You're on the screen!" someone yells from behind us. I glance up, and sure enough, Tessa and I are on the jumbotron. We're decked out in our CU gear. I have Cooper's number on my cheek, and she has Nixon's on hers. This isn't the first time the media has put me in the spotlight. Last year after they won the championship, Tessa and I rushed to the field, and Cooper grabbed me and swung me in the air. He had me back on my feet and crushed to his side, already talking to a reporter before I could move away. She asked about us. He told her I was his best friend, then proceeded to kiss the top of my head. He was celebrating, with me, his best friend, but the world saw it as a romantic gesture. It's not just our classmates who we have to continue to remind that we're not together. When he gets drafted, and I know he will, that won't be an issue. Sure, they might ask where I am at first, but once they see I'm not following, the world will know that Cooper Reeves is on the market. He told me it's been nice. That the closer we get to his final year here at CU, the more the vultures come out. Once they run a story on us, it dies down. I guess in a way, I'm his beard. Too bad he can't be mine; of course, my version is a hell of a lot dirtier than his.

Tessa and I smile and wave at the camera. Might as well ham it up. Doesn't matter what we tell them; they are going to talk about us. At least when they talk about Tessa, it's true. She is the love of Nixon's life, and I get to take all the credit for matching them. Something I'll never let Cooper live down. He didn't want me to get involved, but I could see it in the way they looked at each other the first time they met. Maybe I should make a career out of matchmaking.

"What are you thinking about with the goofy grin plastered on your face?" Tessa asks.

"How I helped you find the love of your life."

"That you did." She doesn't even try to deny it. "When are you going to let me fix you up with someone?"

"Never." I chuckle. "I just want to focus on school, and we are about to start our last year of college. Why tie myself down now?" What I don't say is what we both know to be the truth. My heart belongs to my best friend. I know it's crazy, and that he's never going to feel that way about me, but it's my truth. I don't want a relationship to interfere with my last year with him. When he gets drafted, things are going to change. He's no longer going to be an everyday presence in my life. There's plenty of time for my heart to get over him and move on.

"Reese." She whispers my name as if her heart is breaking for me.

"Your man's taking the field," I say to divert the conversation. We both turn to watch as the CU Tigers take the field. Nixon, Cooper, Levi, Trey, Dustin, and Hank lead the pack as they rush out of the tunnel. Nixon and Cooper both look to the stands and give us a casual wave.

Of course, we wave back, but that little stunt will do nothing to keep the reporters from asking about who we are to them. Looks like there will be some more explaining after the win. Yes, the win, because the team is on fire, and I know they're bringing home another title for Central University.

"Come on, come on, come on," I say under my breath. I'm on my feet. Hell, the entire stadium is on their feet. It's the fourth quarter, and CU is up by three. We have the ball with three minutes left on the play clock. A lot can happen in three minutes.

"Gah!" Tessa grabs my arm and pulls me back and forth. "I can't take the stress." She's smiling as she says it. We've been on our feet the entire game. I've loved every single minute of it. I love the sport, and to know that my friends, not just Cooper, but all the guys that I've grown close to are so near to another victory for not only our school but for themselves, it warms my heart. And it makes me nervous for them. Tessa too, apparently.

"We need a touchdown," I tell her.

"Damn right we do, and your man is the one that's going to get it for us." She points to the field where Hank's just launched the ball to Cooper. It's as if I'm watching in slow motion as Cooper jumps up, hands in the air, and the ball lands perfectly in his hands. His feet hit the ground, and he runs. Those long ass legs of his carry him to the end zone.

Touchdown Tigers!

"Yes!" Tessa and I scream at the same time. Her arms fly around my shoulders as we jump up and down and shimmy and shake to the blaring music and the cheers of the crowd that fills the stadium.

The next two and a half minutes, the Tigers hold them off and just like that, after a hard-fought game… hell, a hard-fought season, the Central University Tigers are once again the number one college football team.

"I say we stick around until the crowd dies down," Tessa suggests.

"Good idea. We're supposed to meet up with mine and Cooper's parents at The Hideout. You and Nixon want to join us?"

"Yeah, more than likely. His parents couldn't make the trip, so that will be nice for him to be able to celebrate as well."

"You know our parents, you're all their kids." I laugh as both mine and Tessa's names are called out. Looking down at the field, I see Cooper and Nixon smiling at us. Waving us to the end of the bleachers.

"Looks like we're being summoned." Tessa grabs my hand and pulls me down the five rows of steps until we reach the wall.

"You're going to get your fine ass down here and celebrate with your man?" Nixon smiles up at Tessa like she hung the moon.

She glances over at me. "Go." I give her a gentle shove, and she moves to sit on the edge of the wall, Nixon already standing below to catch her.

"What? You too good to come down on the field and celebrate with your best friend?" Cooper taunts.

"I just assumed with all the rumors last year...." I let my voice trail off.

"Fuck the rumors. I want you down here, Reese."

His brown eyes are lit up like a damn Christmas tree. I'm wavering, not wanting to make this another year of him dodging rumors, of both of us dodging rumors, but when he holds his hand out to me and mouths, "Please," I crumble. Moving, I sit on the edge of the wall just like Tessa did a few minutes before me and jump into Cooper's waiting arms.

"We fucking did it, Reese. Another championship." His deep timbre is in my ear, and my body shudders. I can usually hide my reaction to my best friend. In fact, it's become a talent of mine, but in this moment, with the happiness and joy radiating from both of us, his deep voice just for me in a stadium full of people who want his attention, well, today is not one of those days.

I wrap my arms around his neck, and my feet lift from the ground as he hugs me so tight I lose my breath.

"Cooper Reeves, Natalie James from *The Times*. How do you feel after another win?" she asks, shoving the microphone in his face.

Cooper takes his time to set me back on my feet, and just like before, his arm goes around my shoulders, and he holds me close to his chest. "Like all the hard work paid off. We had a great team all season. The CU Tigers put the work in, and this is our reward," he says dutifully.

"Any word on your going into the draft?" she asks.

"No, ma'am. I'm going all the way with my CU brothers, with my team. We need another championship under our belts." He winks at her, and I swear she blushes.

"Do you have any big plans for celebrating your win?" she asks, her eyes darting to me.

"Celebrating with my team and my loved ones." His arm squeezes my shoulder, and any hope of the reporter missing the action is gone when her eyes dart to where his hand is and then back to Cooper.

"My man!" Trey comes rushing toward us, and to my surprise, picks both me and Cooper up in a hug.

We're all laughing hysterically by the time he puts us down and takes a few steps over and does the same thing to Nixon and Tessa. He's pumped up, as he should be. They all should be. They kicked ass this season. Their hard work and dedication on and off the field are shining through.

Cooper keeps me close to his side throughout the celebration. He even drags me on stage when it's his turn to address his team and the reporters. I try to pull away, but he's not having any of it. One arm is slung over my shoulders while the other hoists the trophy in the air. The cameras flash, and I don't even have to try to remember to smile.

I'm happy for my team.

For my best friend.

For my friends.

They deserve this win, and I couldn't be happier for them.

COOPER

COLLEGE: SENIOR YEAR

In two hours, I could play my last game of football in front of a crowd. I've been playing since I was five years old, and now, it all comes down to this. This one night, in a stadium that will no doubt be packed full of fans. Not just fans, but family. My parents, as well as Eve and Garrett, are both coming. Reese will be here as well. She and Tessa insisted that they sit as close to the field as they can. Nixon and I hooked them up. As seniors, our seat choices are better. Bottom row, right on the fifty-yard line. Of course, it helps that we're both slated to be drafted to the professional football league.

That's what makes this game so bittersweet. It could be my last ever or just the last of my college career. Time will tell, but regardless, I'm staying right here in this moment as long as I can. I want to soak up the feel of the lights, the noise of the crowd, and the rush of the moment when the pigskin falls into my hands, and 1 run into the end zone. I fucking love this game, and all I can do is send up a silent prayer that this one won't be my last.

"Yo, gather round," Trey calls out in the locker room. We amble to our feet and make a circle around our quarterback. "Four fucking years," he says, his voice eerily calm. "We've had each other's backs not just on the field but off. For some of us, tonight is the end. There will be no more running out of the tunnel and waving to the crowds, no more passes, no more plays. For others, this is just a stepping stone. A placeholder in time until you move onto bigger and better things. Here and now, you are my brothers." He closes his fist and bumps it against his chest. "Much love," he says, before his cocky grin that we're all used to slides into place. "Now, let's get our asses out on that field and bring CU another trophy home."

The entire locker room erupts with cheers and words of encouragement and a whole lot of profanity. "Quiet down," Coach says, moving to stand on a chair in the middle of the circle to gain our attention. "I'm damn proud of you. All of you. From the freshmen to those of you leaving this year, every single one of you has brought something to this team. I'm damn proud to be your coach. No matter what happens out there on that field tonight, you are winners. Another undefeated season. That's something to be proud of." He leans over and holds his hand out. "Tigers on three!" he shouts, and we all pile in. Arms flail around while we all join in the huddle. "One. Two. TIGERS!" The sound is deafening and does the trick to get us all pumped up.

As soon as we make it out on the field, the crowd goes crazy. Like always, I glance up and scan, looking for Reese. This year she's easier to find. I give her a wave and then go about my business.

Twenty minutes later, I go stand beside Nixon on the sidelines. "What's up with you? You're quiet."

"I'm going to do it."

"Do what?" I ask, confused.

"I'm going to ask Tessa to marry me." A slow grin tilts his lips.

"Married, huh?" I don't know if he expected me to be shocked, but I'm not. They've been together for four years, and I know without a doubt how much he loves her. We all do. Hell, all you have to do is watch the two of them together, and you can see it.

"Yep. Picked up the ring yesterday."

"When are you popping the question?" I ask him.

"After the game. Win or lose, I walk away a winner. That is as long as she says yes."

"You know she's going to."

"Yeah," he says wistfully. "I know."

"Big steps, my man."

"Yep. I already know it's going to be the best decision I've ever made."

"What about the draft?"

"She's graduating. I'm hoping she'll come with me. I mean, we've talked about it, so that's the plan," he says more confidently.

Leaving. That's the only downside of this new career I hope to be venturing into. It's not the moving that bothers me or the traveling for games. No, what bothers me is that my best friend isn't coming with me. Not that I've asked her to, but how could I do that? She already has a job lined up, and I can't take that away from her. Besides, what's she going to do in a new city? Sit around and wait for me to have time to hang out with her? It's going to suck, and I'm going to miss her like crazy. Every time I think about it, my chest aches. I've been doing good, keeping it in the back of my mind. But this conversation with Nixon brings it front and center.

I have no choice but to leave her behind.

Sure, we'll talk and video chat, but that won't be the same. My biggest fear, which I know is going to be my new reality, is that nothing between us will ever be the same. The thought of Reese not being in my life terrifies me.

"You know if you keep staring at her like that, she's going to get a complex."

Pulling out of my thoughts, I turn to look at Nixon. "What?"

"Reese. You were just staring at her with this lost look on your face. From the look on hers, she's worried."

I whip my head back around the stands, and sure enough, she's standing from her seat. Her eyes are locked on me, and her teeth are torturing her bottom lip. "You okay?" she mouths.

I nod and smile, then give her a shrug. "You ready?" I ask, pulling my eyes from my best friend to look at Nixon.

"You know you're my best friend, right? I mean, aside from Tessa. I don't want you to take this the wrong way, but you're an idiot."

"What?" I ask in confusion. "What the fuck does that mean?"

"Reese."

My heart pounds just from the sound of her name. "What about Reese?"

"You're in love with her."

"Of course I love her. She's my best friend."

"That too, but that's not the kind of love I was talking about." He gives me a pointed look.

"Nix, we've been over this. I feel like it's a broken record at this point."

"One day, Reeves… one day you're going to wake up, and she's going to be gone. Not gone from your life but gone, and you're going to regret this 'she's just my best friend' bullshit you've been spewing all these years."

The announcer asks everyone to rise for the national anthem, which saves me from having to reply. I can't tell him that I think about us being together more each day. I can't tell him that I'm scared as hell because losing her as a part of my life is not something I'm okay with. I can't tell him that I already feel like I'm going to lose her, so it's a moot point. No, I can't tell him that. Instead, I line up with my team, place my hand over my heart, and stand tall for the anthem. I need to push Reese and what my future looks like without her out of my mind and play this game. I plan to leave it all out on the field. If this is my last game, it's going to be one for the record books.

We did it. Twenty-eight to fourteen. We brought home another CU championship. My eyes get just a little bit misty as I stand in the end zone. I just caught the final pass from the final play of the night. We have four touchdowns and all of them were mine. Sure, it was a team effort, but it was my legs and my hands carrying the ball that led us to victory. Hank's cannon of an arm, and the entire O-Line blocking, and the defense kicked ass. Hell, it was all of us combined, but the stats show those four passes landed in my hands, which resulted in numbers on the scoreboard. And Nixon with that fucking leg of his making all four field goals. We were on fire tonight, and the end result shows.

If this is my last game, what a way to go out.

My teammates attack me in the end zone, and we're a pile of black and red as we jump up and down and hug, and yes, there are some tears and a whole hell of a lot of yelling.

"We fucking did it!" Nixon screams as he barrels into me. We hug it out, and we're both wearing cheesy fucking grins. "Three years in a row, baby!" he cheers.

It's chaos, pure chaos on the field. Staff, players, media, families. Confetti, streamers, hats, and T-shirts are being passed out. It's absolute madness, so much so I can barely hear myself think.

"Cooper!" I faintly hear my name being called. I turn to look but don't see anyone. I hear it again, and that's when I see her. *Reese.* I should have known it was her. She's probably the only person other than my parents that I could hear in this loud-ass stadium. That doesn't even make sense when I think it, but it's the truth. She comes rushing toward me. I open my arms, and she jumps into them. Her legs lock behind my back, and her arms grip me around the neck. It's awkward with pads on, but it's perfect. In this moment, Reese and her hug are exactly what I need.

"Hey, Reese's Pieces," I whisper in her ear.

She pulls back, her green eyes are bright and filled with excitement. "I'm so damn proud of you. You killed it, Coop. You fucking killed it." She leans in close and gives me another squeeze before her legs release, and she slides down my body. Even with all the gear, my body still ignites from the contact. That's been happening more and more lately. It's been a struggle the past few months to not look at her and see the beautiful woman that she is. We're no longer kids, and my cock is all too eager to notice.

Once her feet are planted on the ground, I sling my arm over her shoulder and bend my lips to her ear. "Watch." I point to where Nixon and Tessa stand. They're huddled close together, both wearing matching smiles. One of the assistant coaches walks up to Nixon and shakes his hand. I see it, the exchange of the ring, but I would have missed it had I not been looking for it.

Reese looks up at me. "What's going on?"

"Just watch." I keep my arm around her and hold her close to my chest. She gasps, and her hands fly to her mouth as Nixon drops to one knee and stares up at Tessa. "Oh my God," Reese breathes.

The media catches on, as does everyone else in the stadium and out on the field. Suddenly, the jumbotron is displaying the proposal, and I'm sure that everyone watching at home is seeing this as well. You can't make this shit up. It's good TV, and I know we'll be seeing highlights not only from the game but from this moment for weeks to come, especially as Nixon and I enter the draft.

Tessa nods as tears stream down her face. Nixon slides the ring onto her finger before standing and kissing her. "She said yes!" he shouts, pulling out of the kiss.

"I'm so excited." Reese shimmies in my arms.

"I'm happy for them," I agree. Before I can say anything else, a female reporter steps in front of us.

"Cooper, good game out there. How does it feel to bring home your third championship for Central University?"

"Incredible. My teammates and coaches were on point again this year. It's a great feeling to go out on top."

"You and Nixon Barnes are good friends. Any plans to follow in his footsteps? Is there a proposal in your future?"

"We're just friends," Reese and I say at the same time. I smile down at her, and she playfully rolls her eyes.

The reporter asks a few more football-related questions and moves on to the next guy. That's how the next hour goes. Finally, when the dust has settled for the most part, I need a shower and out of these pads. "You and Tessa going to meet us outside the locker rooms?"

"Yeah. Our parents want to do dinner."

"I figured. Hotel lobby?"

"I'll tell them." She gives me another hug, and steps away. I watch her as she loops her arm through Tessa's, and they walk toward the tunnel. Spying Nixon ahead, I take off running to catch up with him. As soon as the locker room door opens, Levi is standing there, his smile a mile wide.

"Hell fucking yes! Three in a row." He's already got his arm around Hank's neck. "The three of you are unstoppable. If any team is lucky enough to get all three of you... that's a lethal combination."

"That's highly unlikely," Nixon speaks up.

Levi shrugs. "Yeah, but it would be badass. Where's the party?" he asks.

"Not until we get back home," Hank tells him. "We didn't want to plan it here and lose, and that would suck balls. So it's for when we get home. We figured it would be either a celebration or a goodbye to the season kind of party. We all agreed that no one would have felt like it tonight if we lost."

"That would have sucked." Levi chuckles. "I can't stay anyway. I'm heading out tonight. I have to catch the redeye. I have a game tomorrow."

Levi was drafted to the Dragons last year. He hasn't got a lot of playing time this year, but his time is coming. He's too good to just sit the bench. "Thanks for coming out, man."

"And miss this? Never. You guys take care. I'll catch up with you soon." He walks away with his phone at his ear.

"Where's he off to in such a hurry?" Hank asks as the three of us watch him leave.

"Reese says he's dating. Some model or something. My guess is that he's going home to her."

"Fuck, that's us in just a matter of months. I can't fucking wait." Hank slaps Nixon and me on the back and walks away.

"That gonna be you, Coop?" Nixon asks, raising his eyebrows.

I roll my eyes and groan. "Not this again. Come on. Leave it alone already."

"Your loss, my man. It's your loss." He heads toward the showers.

I want to scream after him that I know it's my loss. That I feel that weight of that impending loss as it sits heavy on my chest. I'm trying to hold out hope that maybe just maybe things might be different from how I imagine them to go.

Maybe.

REESE

We've been back at campus for almost a week, and the student body is still flying high and celebrating the win. The entire football team has pretty much reached full-on celebrity status. There have been news crews driving around looking to interview the players about what their next steps are, and even a few that have been snapping pictures of Nixon and Tessa, and her shiny new diamond ring.

My best friend is glowing. I've never seen her smile this much, and I couldn't be happier for her. Nixon is a great guy, and they deserve nothing but the best. I've been teasing her about putting my name on their wedding invitations as the responsible party for their nuptials.

"Hey, what about me?" Cooper asks. "I was there for this arrangement." He points his french fry at Tessa and Nixon before popping it in his mouth.

"When we get to that step, we will definitely discuss it," Tessa says to appease us.

"So, you ladies ready for this epic party tomorrow?" Hank asks, sliding into the seat next to me.

"Epic, huh? You sure you're at that level?" I tease him.

"Oh, sweetheart, it's going to be legendary. Students for years to come are going to hear about this one." He winks.

"I'm going to pick up the kegs when we're done here," Nixon tells him.

"Reese and I are going to stop and pick up some cups, chips, and maybe some dip or some brownies or something."

"You two"—Hank points at me then Tessa—"have been stingy on the brownies lately. What's up with that?"

"Well, you see, it's this little thing called college. We're trying to finish it. Not to mention, we've traveled to more of your away games this year," I defend.

"Because these two are pussy-whipped," he quips.

"Watch it," Cooper growls.

"Yep," Nixon says, not a care in the world. I love how much he loves Tessa. It gives me hope to find a love like that one day. To find a man who's not afraid to tell the world what you mean to him. As for Cooper, he's just being the protective best friend he's always been. If anything, he's consistent.

"Hey, Hank." Some tall, leggy blonde slides up to him.

"Hey, gorgeous." He winks at her before turning back to us. "I'll catch you guys later." Just like that, he's gone, the leggy blonde hanging on his arm as they walk out of the building.

"That's the third girl I've seen him with this week," Tessa comments.

"He's living his best life, that's for sure. I just hope he doesn't catch something or get one of them pregnant. That's all he needs is some cleat chaser getting her claws into him right before the draft," Cooper says, shoving the last of my fries into his mouth.

"Fuck, I'm glad I'm not there." Nixon leans in and kisses Tessa on the corner of her mouth.

Cooper grumbles something under his breath that I don't quite catch. "What was that?" I ask him.

"Nothing." He shakes his head. "You about ready?" he asks Nixon.

"Yep. Those kegs aren't going to pick themselves up." He stands and gathers their trash and ours before walking to the nearby trash can to throw it all away.

"How many kegs are we talking?" I ask Cooper.

"Three." He grins. "This is our last hoorah. Those of us who are declaring for the draft have the Combine coming up, so we have to stay focused—no booze and no parties. So we're doing it up big."

I look across the booth at Tessa. "This could get interesting." She throws her head back and laughs.

"You can count on that," she replies.

After a round of goodbyes, we part ways. "So, what are you thinking as far as snacks go?" Tessa asks.

"Let's see. There's going to be an abundance of drunk college kids. Chips and beer are all you need." I chuckle.

"You're probably right. I was thinking we make the guys go to an early dinner beforehand. Me drinking on an empty stomach is not a good plan."

"I'm going to take it easy. I don't think I've recovered yet from my junior year bender," I tell her.

"I'd hardly call that a bender. One night of letting loose and drinking is far from it."

"Well, I can still remember the vomiting." I shudder at the thought. "I hate to vomit, Tess. I really, truly hate it."

"Nobody likes to vomit," she says. "However, it's the last party with the guys. You have to let loose and enjoy yourself."

"We'll see how it goes. Come on. We have Solo cups and chips to stock up on."

"And brownies. Even if we hide them, we need to make Hank some brownies."

"Agreed."

We spend the next few hours shopping and getting everything we need to make six batches of brownies before heading over to the football house. We're going to cook, and the guys can clean up. We'll hold the brownies hostage until they do. It's a fair trade that they've never turned down in the past.

A few hours later, the brownies are done and packaged in a few containers. I take three and hide them in Cooper's room, and Tessa takes three and hides them in Nixon's room. We have the place to ourselves as the guys went to the gym. They decided not to replace Levi this year, since next year all five of them will be gone. This house will have a new set of students. We've made some good memories here. This year we've missed Levi, but he's off living his dream, just like Cooper, Hank, and Nixon will be soon. They're all declaring for the draft this year.

"I feel like we should clean the kitchen," I tell Tessa as we kick back on the couch. The furniture has all been pushed to one side of the room, so it's not exactly comfortable, but we're managing.

"Nope. They said they would be home by two. That gives them plenty of time to load the dishwasher and wipe down the counters. Because, let's be honest, we didn't exactly make a huge mess."

"True," I agree as the front door flies open.

"Ladies, I smell the goods. Where are they?" Hank jets off to the kitchen. "I can't find them!" he calls out, and we both laugh.

"What's so funny?" Cooper asks, sitting on my lap.

"Oompf. Get off me, you giant." He's not putting all of his weight on me, but still. He wiggles his ass, laughing his head off before he finally stands, pulls me up from the couch, takes my seat, and pulls me onto his lap.

"Better?" he asks, resting his hand on my thigh.

"Much."

"Hello? Brownies?" Hank asks.

"We made them," Tessa tells him.

"I can smell them. Where are they?" Hank points over his shoulder to Dustin and Trey. "We all three looked."

"We hid them," I say, barely containing my laughter at the look on his face.

"Why would you hide them?" Dustin asks as he literally scratches his head.

"You have kitchen duty."

"Come on. We just put in two hours at the gym," Trey moans.

"And we put in two hours of making your damn brownies," Tessa fires back.

"Hey, you." Nixon walks in the room, and pretty much mimics what happened between Cooper and me a few minutes earlier; however, he doesn't squish her before pulling her to stand and then sets her on his lap.

"Where were you?" she asks him, kissing his cheek.

"I moved my truck around back. The guys all moved theirs before we left this morning."

"Do we need to move?" I ask him.

"No. That's why we all moved. We want the two of you to be in the driveway. Everyone else can fend for themselves or park on the street," Cooper speaks up.

I turn my head to look at him. "Thanks, Coop." He pats my leg where it's resting on my thigh.

"Go on now." Tessa waves her hand toward the kitchen. "I can't eat all those brownies on my own. Nixon will want this shiny new ring back," she teases.

"No way." Nixon cuddles her close to his chest.

"What about the two of you?" Dustin whines.

"Our girls baked," Nixon says with a smirk.

"Thought she wasn't your girl?" Dustin counters. His gaze is locked on Cooper.

"Best friend is close enough," Cooper fires back.

"Come on," Hank grumbles. "The sooner we get this shit over with, the sooner we get the goods." The three of them amble off to the kitchen.

Tessa looks at me, and we both burst out laughing. "We better go get the goods," she says in her best Hank impression.

"Agreed." I turn to look at Cooper. "We hid them in your rooms. Be right back."

Tessa and I race upstairs and grab our three containers each. Our thought process was each guy could have their own, and then one left over for the party. The guys are already in the living room by the time we make it back downstairs.

"That took like three seconds," Trey says, holding his hand out.

"Your reward." I hand him a container.

Tessa gives one to Dustin, Hank, and Nixon. I put one on the table next to the chips on the far wall and hand the other to Cooper.

"Thanks, Reese's Pieces." He pulls me back onto his lap, and I go willingly. I'm just a friend, sitting on another friend's lap. No one has to know that I'm pretending it's more—that it's real, and his intentions are just like Nixon's. A girl can dream.

The party is in full swing, and I've lost count of how many times my cup has been filled, and emptied. I said I wasn't going to drink too much, but watching all the cleat chasers hang all over Cooper made the decision for me. I don't have the right to be upset or even irritated. He's not mine. However, I care about him. He's still my best friend, even if my heart sometimes forgets that's all he is. I don't want him to get trapped by some floozie and be stuck with her for the rest of his life. Everyone at CU knows that Cooper, Hank, and Nixon are going to the draft. They all know they're kickass football players. They also know that comes with fame and fortune.

"Hi, Reese, right?" a masculine voice asks.

Slowly, I turn my head to find a guy standing there who I've never met before. "Yeah."

"I'm Hunter. It's nice to meet you." He holds his hand out for me to shake. He offers me his left, and well, my beer is in my right, so I offer him my left as well. A giggle escapes me when I realize what I've done.

"Sorry about that," I say, barely managing to get the words out without slurring.

He smiles. "I've seen you around. This is the first time you've ever been without a group of guys around. That's pretty intimidating, considering it's usually the entire CU football team."

"Meh." I wave my hand in the air. "They're all harmless."

"So, which one is your boyfriend?" he asks, taking a drink from his own red cup.

"None of them. We're all just friends. Well, Cooper is my best friend. We grew up together, but nope, none of them is my boyfriend, you know, like sexually," I ramble. I have a feeling sober me is going to be embarrassed about this conversation in the morning. That is if I can even remember it.

"Good to know. It's hard to tell sometimes."

"Really?"

He nods. "It's kept me away from you all year," he confesses.

"I don't think I've ever seen you around."

"I transferred last year. We've had a few classes together, but like I said, you're always with a pretty big group of guys. I just assumed one of them was yours. It's not until now I decided to take a chance and say hello."

"I'm glad you did." I smile up at him. He's tall but not as tall as Cooper. Then again, I'm short, so everyone is tall to me.

"You want to dance?" he asks.

It might be the alcohol, but I swear I see a slight blush on his handsome face. "Yes." Tilting my cup to my lips, I drain it and toss it into one of the many trash cans we set around the house. No way am I drinking out of it again after leaving it unattended. Nope. I'm not that drunk.

Hunter takes my hand and leads me to the middle of the living room floor, and wraps his arms around me. We sway to the music, and I rest my head on his chest. He's not as muscular as Cooper, but he still feels sturdy and in good shape. Don't ask me what that means, because I'm not really sure either. What I do know is that this is nice. Dancing with a guy who's not one of my close friends. It's been way too long since I've let that happen.

When the music changes to a fast song, we begin to groove, rocking our hips. Our arms are swaying right along to the beat. I'm lost in the music, dancing my heart out when I feel a shove from behind me. I stumble into Hunter, at the same time that he's shoved as well. I feel my legs fall out from under me as I land on the floor. I curl into myself to keep from getting trampled. Looking around, I search for Hunter, for anyone that can help me up, because from the alcohol and the fall, I'm not sure I can do it on my own.

I scream when two large hands slide under my arms and lift me to my feet. His scent captures me before my eyes can focus on him.

Cooper.

"My hero," I slur, batting my eyelashes. At least that's what I meant to do. In reality, I probably looked like one of those creepy baby dolls that blinks every time you move it. I shudder at the thought.

"Thanks, man." Hunter approaches us. His eyes are wide, and his breathing is accelerated. "I was trying to get to her."

"You should have tried harder. No, you should have held onto her and made sure she was safe." Cooper growls the words.

"Coop." I reach up, placing my hand on his cheek. His eyes instantly drop to me. "I'm okay."

He gives me a stiff nod. "You're not to leave my side the rest of the night."

I should argue with him. I should tell him that he's not the boss of me. I should tell him that it kills me to see all those women hanging off him when in my heart, I know it should be me. I don't say any of those things. Instead, I nod, then turn my attention to Hunter. "Thank you for the dance," I say politely.

He gives me a stiff nod, and I'll never know if he was going to say anything because Cooper, with his arm tight around my waist, moves me through the crowd and over to the corner of the room where Tessa and Nixon are standing.

"Are you all right?" Tessa asks. She pulls away from Nixon to give me a hug.

"I'm fine. Just lost my footing when we got jostled in the crowd."

"Fucker should have been watching. I knew I should have busted that up," Cooper grumbles.

"What?" I ask him.

"I saw him lead you out there." He motions to the middle of the floor. "I don't know him; therefore, I don't trust him. I wanted to pull you away from him, but these two," he points to Tessa and Nixon, "talked me out of it."

"He's a nice guy."

"Oh, yeah? When did you meet him?"

"Tonight."

"Exactly." He runs his fingers through his hair. "Reese, you have to be careful. You've been drinking, and you don't know him. What if he slipped something into your drink? What if he got you so drunk you didn't even know your own name and took advantage of you?"

"Being taken advantage of doesn't sound so bad," I tease. "It's been too long."

"What the fuck!" Cooper raises his voice. "Do you hear yourself right now? He could have raped you, Reese."

"T-That's not what I meant." My foggy alcohol brain is trying to keep up. Surely, he knows that's not what I meant. "I meant that it's been a long time and random sex, it's not so bad. I mean, I'm weeks away from graduating from college, and I've never had just random sex. It's a pastime, right?"

"No, Reese." His voice is low, his words tight. "It's not a fucking pastime. You could have been hurt."

"How? How could I have been hurt when you were watching me. You're always fucking watching me. He's the first guy who isn't a close friend that's noticed me in a long time. What's bad about that, Cooper? Huh? You have girls hanging off you every fucking day, and I say nothing. I let you make your choices. As your best friend, I support you. Why can't you do that for me?" I stomp off into the kitchen. I need more alcohol. I can't have this conversation with him right now. I just can't. I might say something that I regret, or that I can't take back. What's worse is, my lips are loose, and my heart is wide open. For him. I can't tell him that I wish we were more; that would ruin what we have. I need to clear my head, and a shot sounds like a great way to do it.

Walking away is the best choice for me.

Chapter 15

COOPER

My hands are fisted at my sides, my chest rising and falling as I try to catch my breath, and my eyes, they're locked on Reese as she disappears into the kitchen. "She fucking walked away," I grumble. I don't really care if Nixon and Tessa are listening. The words needed to be said. We've never argued like this. Never. Not even when we were kids. We just… don't fight.

"Do you blame her?" Nixon asks. "You're acting like a jealous boyfriend."

"What?" I whip my head away from staring at the door Reese disappeared behind to look at him. "That's insane."

"Is it? You saw that she was drinking too much, so you stopped." He points at the water bottle in my hand.

"How is that a jealous boyfriend? I'm being a good friend looking out for her. Reese never drinks like this. In fact, this is maybe the third time it's ever happened."

He nods. "I get that. But what about the way your eyes watched her no matter where she was in the room? What about when that guy offered her his hand and led her out there to dance, you pushed off the wall and was ready to fight? How do you explain that, Cooper?"

"He's a stranger."

"Cooper." Tessa's soft voice breaks into our heated exchange. "You're her best friend. We get that. But you have to remember that you're leaving. You're not going to be there to scare off some guy who you don't know that talks to her. She has to live her own life, Cooper. She's lived in your shadow for years. For the last four years, I've watched you protect her, scare guys off before they even have a chance to utter a single syllable to her. You're leaving, Cooper. You're leaving, and she's not. You have to let her live her life." Her words are soft, gentle, as if she's trying to calm an angry bear and, in a way, I guess she is.

"Fuck." I run my fingers through my hair, letting her words sink it.

"She's been trying not to think about it," Tessa adds.

"That's all I've been able to think about. I've considered asking her to come with me a million times."

"Think about that, Reeves. Don't you want her to be happy? Fuck, man, it's not all about you."

"I know that," I grind out. "I know it's not all about me, but I also know Reese and my leaving is going to be hard on her. Hell, it's going to be hard on me. I didn't say I was going to ask her to come with me, just that I thought about it."

"I think the two of you need to talk, Cooper." Tessa gives me a soft smile.

"You should tell her," Nixon says pointedly.

"I know. I'm going to apologize."

"That's not what I meant, and you know it." Nixon stares me down.

"Fuck, not this shit again." I know exactly what he's thinking, and he's wrong. I don't know what I have to do to prove that to him.

"What did I miss?" Tessa asks Nixon.

"He's in love with her." He says the words casually, as if we're discussing the damn weather. As if it's a foregone conclusion.

"Oh." Tessa's eyes grow wide. "Is that true?"

"Yes. I love her." Tessa opens her mouth to speak, but I beat her to it. "She's my best fucking friend. Yes, she has a pussy, but I've never been privileged to see it, and I don't plan to. That's because she's my best fucking friend," I say again. I don't tell them that I've fantasized about seeing her pussy, feeling it, tasting it, but I'm a guy. I'm young, and it's been... a while since my cock has seen any action. A long fucking while. Reese is beautiful and sexy, and even though she's my best friend, I'd be blind not to notice. Who am I kidding. I've always noticed when it comes to her. I just learned to keep that shit in check.

"Cooper," Tessa starts again, but I hold my hand up.

"I have to go find her. I need to make sure she's okay." Without another word, I take long strides as I make my way to the kitchen. I find Reese sitting on the floor in front of the dishwasher with a bottle of vodka in her hands. She's drinking right out of the bottle.

"Hey." I crouch down to face her.

"Hey."

I point to the bottle. "How much of that have you had?"

"Just... a couple of drinks." She hugs the bottle to her chest like she knows that I'm going to take it away from her. She would be right.

"Why don't you let me take that?" I reach for the bottle, and she hugs it tighter.

"No. I'm not done with it."

"Reese." I move a wisp of hair from her eye, tucking it behind her ear. "Remember the last time you were miserable."

"I know, but I'm miserable now too."

My heart lurches in my chest. "Why?" I ask softly.

"You're mad at me. You're never mad at me. And... I'm mad at you too, and I'm never mad at you."

I exhale. I can work with this. "Why don't we leave the bottle down here, and we can go upstairs and lie down?"

"This is your party."

"Nothing is more important than you, Reese. Surely, you know that by now?" Her green eyes shimmer with tears, and she nods. "Come on, you." I take the bottle, which she lets me do, and set it on the counter. I then offer her my hand and help her stand. She wobbles on her feet, and instead of risking her falling, I lift her into my arms, bridal style, and carry her out of the kitchen. I don't make eye contact with Nixon or

Tessa when we walk past them. I don't need to hear anymore. They've said their piece, and I heard them loud and clear. Right now, all I want to do is get her upstairs and away from all these drunk assholes. And maybe when she sobers up, we'll talk. Talk about all the things we've been avoiding. Namely, me leaving. Maybe I'll get the courage to broach the subject with her.

Maybe.

"Do you need to use the bathroom?" I ask once we reach the top of the stairs.

"No."

I walk on past and down the hall to my room. Once inside, I carefully lower her to the bed, then go back and shut the door and lock it. Kicking off my shoes, I walk to the bed and sit next to her. She rests her head on my shoulder, and I feel as though I take the first deep breath I've taken since the party started.

"I don't like it when you're mad at me." Her voice is soft.

"I'm not mad at you. I was worried about you. There's a difference."

"Yeah." She sits up and kicks off her shoes before lying back on the bed. "Lie with me?"

Never able to deny her anything, I move to lie next to her. We're both on our sides, staring into each other's eyes. It's intimate, but it doesn't feel wrong. The party is loud below us, but here, in the confines of my room, we're both calm. Our silence isn't uncomfortable; in fact, it's comforting to me. She's here with me; she's safe. That's all that matters to me. Reaching over, I move her hair that has once again fallen into her eyes.

"I was watching you," I confess, breaking our long stint of silence. "Like I always do. You looked like you were having fun. Then you went down. I waited three heartbeats before I was pushing through the crowd to get to you. He was just standing there. Sure, he was being backed away from the crowd, but I got through." She nods. "You deserve someone who will always get through, Reese. Someone who won't stop until they get to you."

"You deserve someone who will love you for who you are. They'll love that football is your life, they'll respect that. I'm so afraid that you're going to end up with someone who wants to use you for your name or your contract," she responds.

"What contract?" I tease to lighten the mood. "I need to get one first."

"Come on, Coop. We both know that it's going to happen."

Her smile, the same one she's been giving me for years, it does something to me. Turns me inside out. My eyes fall to her lips, and I ache to kiss her. Just once, I'd like to know if her lips are as soft as they appear.

"When you look at me like that," she swallows hard, "it makes me think you want to kiss me," she whispers.

"You ever thought about that, Reese? Kissing me?" I toss the question out there. I know that I have more times than I care to admit.

She nods. "Have you?"

"Yes." I'll never lie to her. Never.

"All these years, and we've never crossed that line."

"Nope."

"Maybe we should. You know, just for curiosity's sake?"

"You want to kiss me?" I smirk. I need to lighten up this mood before we fall into something that we can never take back.

"Yes." She's deathly serious. No shadow of laughter in her expression.

"Reese." My tone is a warning.

"Cooper," she challenges.

It's wrong. She's my best friend, but best friends do this kind of thing, right? They experiment? I mean, college girls who are just friends do it. I'm sure the guys do too. Why can't Reese and I try it? Just once. Just a small little sample to experience what it's like. After the thousands of times over the last couple of years that I've thought about it, I could put the question to rest.

Her tongue peeks out and wets her lips, and just like that, my decision is made. Moving my hand to rest against her cheek, I move in slow. My eyes hold hers, looking for a sign that she doesn't really want this. Looking for anything from her that tells me I should stop.

"Kiss me, Cooper."

All right then. I close the distance and press my mouth to hers. Her lips are soft and sweet, just like I imagined they would be, minus the hint of alcohol on her breath. I need to pull away, but I can't do it. When her mouth opens, and her tongue swipes at my lips, any thoughts of pulling away from her are lost. Together we move closer. We're now a tangle of arms and limbs, but our lips are busy kissing. It's a kiss that I feel deep in my gut and has my cock pressing painfully against my zipper.

We lose all track of time, getting lost in the kiss. My hand slips under her shirt, and she moans. It's a deep throaty sound from somewhere deep inside, and it gives me purpose. She wants this as much as I do.

"Tell me to stop." My words are a breath against her lips.

"No," she says before sliding her tongue past my lips once more.

Bliss.

That's what this feels like. Pure, utter, complete bliss to have her in my arms. My hands having free reign to explore her soft skin. My finger brushes across her nipple, and she moans. My cock twitches, wanting in on the action, but I ignore it.

Reese pulls away, and I think she's finally come to her senses. She finally realizes that we're kissing and touching, and… it's not what best friends should be doing, but she surprises me when she sits up and pulls her shirt over her head. What's even more surprising is when she reaches behind her and wiggles and grunts until her tits spring free from her bra. What's not surprising is the way my mouth waters when I take in the beautiful woman before me.

Unable to resist, I reach out and test their weight in the palm of my hands. My thumb glides over her nipple, and she shudders, tilting her head back.

"Come here." My voice is gruff and full of need.

Once she's lying back on the bed, I capture a nipple in my mouth. Her back arches off the bed and her hands find their way to my hair. I nip and suck like it's my fucking job, and with each pass of my tongue, with each taste, I fall even further under her spell.

Somewhere in the back of my mind, I know that what we're doing is a bad idea. How do you come back from this? However, with Reese in my arms, I can't seem to find it in me to care. My hand slides to her waist and easily slips under the band of her leggings. I can't seem to rip my mouth away from her tits, but when my hand reaches her pussy— when I feel how wet she is for me—I pull back to find her watching me.

"Fuck, Reese."

"Don't stop." Her cheeks are flushed, but her voice is clear.

Sliding my fingers through her folds, I push one long digit inside her. "Oh, God," she moans.

My cock is hard, painfully so, but I push forward. Giving her what she asks for. Slowly, I pump in and out of her, until my hand is coated. I add another digit, and her hands that are buried in my hair, tighten their grip.

"God, Coop, what's happening to me?" she asks, breathless.

That gives me pause. I stall my movements and look up at her. "Have you ever had an orgasm, Reese?" Fuck, I hate thinking about her with anyone but me.

She nods. "But only ones I've given myself."

I don't ask who she's been fucking, because I'll kill him, so instead, I push the thought of someone else seeing her like this and begin to pump my fingers inside her. My mouth clamps down on her breast, and my thumb swipes across her clit. I have one goal. I want to make her come. I want to be the first man to ever give that to her.

I wish I could be the last.

That sobers me up. What the fuck are we doing? Reese is my best friend, not some random girl. She's more than a drunken hookup. I worry that we've gone too far, but I can't stop. I won't stop until I give her what she needs. Turns out, that doesn't take long. I suck hard on her nipple, as my thumb presses harder on her clit. I feel her walls squeeze my fingers. Her hands about rip my hair out of my head, and she cries out my name.

I don't worry about anyone hearing her, not with the party going strong downstairs. What I do worry about is if I just fucked up? Did I just lose the best thing that ever happened to me, for a quick taste? For a quick feel? I don't remove my fingers until she settles into the mattress, and her hands fall from my hair.

"Cooper." I move up her body and stare down at her. Her green eyes are bright, and she has a dopey satisfied look on her face. My chest swells, knowing I'm the one responsible for it. She gives me a lazy grin, lifting her head and pressing her lips to mine.

The alcohol on her breath is just another reminder that this is wrong.

"What's wrong?" she asks, pulling away.

"Nothing." I smile, trying to hide my panic, but Reese sees right through me.

"You regret it." It's not a question but a statement.

"No. I could never regret any amount of time spent with you." That's the truth. I don't regret it, but I'm scared as hell that I'm going to lose her. I don't ever want to know what a life without Reese is like.

"You don't want me?"

Grabbing her hand, I place it over the bulge in my jeans. "Does this feel like I don't want you?" *I want you. I want all of you.*

"Then what's wrong?"

I'm scared. "I don't want to lose you. Reese, I'm leaving in a few months. I have no idea where I'm going to be living." I pause, taking a deep breath. "You mean the world to me, Reese. I don't want to ruin our friendship for a quick fuck."

"I-Is that what this is to you? A quick fuck?"

"No. Not even in the slightest, but if we take this any further, I don't know if we can come back from it." *I know that I can't come back from it.*

My words seem to pull a mask over her face. Her happy, sated smile is gone. It's replaced with a smile that I can only describe as fake. "Of course, you're right. We got carried away. This doesn't have to change anything. It was one night of a little too much to drink, and we stopped before… well, we stopped, and we can move on past this." She takes a deep breath and slowly exhales. "I'll never forget it, but it never happened. Does that make sense?" she asks.

I nod. I can't speak. I can't seem to form words. I don't know if it's from the fear of losing her or the fear of never having her like this again.

This changes everything.

"Reese." I force her name past my lips.

"Cooper." She gives me a bright smile as she pulls the blanket up over her bare breasts. "It's fine. *We're* fine. You're the most important person in my life." Her voice cracks, or maybe that's my heart at the thought of losing her. "Nothing is going to change that or take that away from us."

"Promise?"

"I promise." She looks down at the blanket clutched to her chest. "Can you grab me a shirt?"

Scrambling from the bed, I reach into my dresser and grab a T-shirt and hand it to her. "I'm going to go grab a quick shower. You need anything?"

"No. I'm just going to change and go to sleep."

I take a step forward to what? Kiss her? I fucked that up. No more kissing from those lips. "Okay. I'll grab us a couple of waters on my way back."

"Thanks, Coop." Her voice is small. Sad. And I'm kicking my own ass for making her feel that way. I want the happy, satisfied Reese back.

Grabbing some clothes and the key, I keep my back to her as I slip out of the room. It's cowardly. I tell myself I'm giving her privacy, I'm still fully clothed, and well, she is not. Tossing my clothes in the bathroom, I rush downstairs and grab two bottles of water, and race back up unnoticed. At least, I hope I was unnoticed.

Locking the bathroom door, I set the bottles on the counter and rest my head back against the door. What the fuck did I do? "Please, God," I whisper. "Don't let me lose her over this. I can't lose her." Rubbing my hands over my face, I freeze.

I smell her.

Reese.

Fuck me.

I tear at my clothes, not stopping until I'm naked, and then I step into the shower. I turn on the water, and the shock of the cold jolts my system but does nothing about the ache between my legs. My cock is hard and angry. Angry that I walked away. It's for the best. I know deep down that not letting things go any further was what was best for us. That doesn't mean I don't feel shitty about it. That doesn't mean that my heart isn't aching at the thought of losing her. I fucked up. I was sober as I only had a few beers. She's been drinking. I should have stopped us. I never should have given in to temptation.

Resting both hands on the wall of the shower, I tilt my head forward and get lost in my thoughts. Every second of what just happened replays in my mind. She's fucking incredible. Turning my back to the wall, I grip my cock in my fist. I squeeze and tug root to tip. Closing my eyes, I see firm, round tits, pert, hard nipples, and gorgeous green eyes full of need.

I see Reese.

My hand pumps faster as I remember the taste of her skin, the softness, and the way she fell apart at my hands. My balls tighten. My back grows stiff, and with one last stroke, I'm exploding. "Reese," I moan.

My legs are trembling as I try to stand. It takes me longer than usual to get my bearings and finish my shower. Even just the memory of her has rocked me to my core. Once I manage to wash off, I turn off the water and step out of the shower. I take my time drying off and getting dressed. I'm stalling, being a pussy, and she deserves better. Grabbing the two bottles of water and my room key, I open the door and head back down the hall.

The room is dark. I find my way to the bed, setting the waters on the nightstand and crawling in beside her. I'm lying on my back, hands behind my head, staring up at the shadows on the ceiling. I want to hold her. I've done it a million times in the past, but this time, it's different. It's not just the companionship of my best friend. No, it's the gorgeous, sexy woman that she is. She's so much more. I'm battling with myself when she makes the decision for me. She rolls over and moves until her head is resting on my chest. My arms wrap around her and hold her tight.

"Night, Coop."

"Night, Reese."

We lie here unmoving, and eventually, her breathing evens out. I place a kiss on the top of her head and close my eyes. It doesn't take long for me to start to drift off to sleep. Tomorrow is a new day, one I hope greets both of us with no regrets.

Chapter 16

REESE

I've been lying awake, for I don't know how long, listening to Cooper breathe. The sun has just started to rise as the low dim light filters in through the window. We crossed a line last night, and it was blissful, and... everything. Then it wasn't. For the last few years, hell, even longer if I'm honest with myself, I've harbored feelings that are more than just friendly for my best friend. Last night, I thought he felt the same way. Sure, he was hard—he's a man, I was naked, that's going to happen. But he pushed me away.

He couldn't hear it, but my heart shattered.

Tiny shards of hope blasted into a million pieces. I don't blame him. I'm not even mad at him. Cooper is and will always be special to me. However, it's time I realize that we will never be anything but friends. That's our story. That's how it ends. I have to find a way to get past that. I can't let it affect our friendship. I refuse to let it. Not having him in my life is not an option. I need to tramp down the pain and cover the scars from last night. That's exactly what I plan to do, but I need a minute. Maybe a few hours to decompress. To get my head on straight.

Cooper has a lot of changes coming up. Changes that will not only impact his life but mine. The Combine is in a couple of months, the draft, finals, graduation, and then he's leaving. I know it's what's best for him. I know he's going to be fucking fantastic, and I couldn't be happier for him that he gets to live his dream.

I just... need a minute.

Carefully, I climb out of bed, trying not to wake him. With my back to the bed, I slip off his T-shirt and slide back into my bra and sweater. With my boots in hand, I grab my bag, which holds my car keys from the floor. Slowly I turn the knob and let myself out of his room. I feel like I'm doing my first ever walk of shame, and in a way, I am. Although, I'm not ashamed of what we did. I am, however, embarrassed that I offered him more, and he shut me down. That's my scar to bear, and one I need to learn to mask quickly.

This is the coward's way out, and I'm fully aware of that. I just need to go home, get a few more hours of sleep, shower, and then I'll be fine. Things will go back to how they used to be, and I have to be okay with that. The alternative is losing Cooper in my life, and that just won't do.

Thankfully, my car isn't blocked. Tossing my bag into the back seat, I hustle to slide behind the wheel and back out of the drive. I keep my eyes on the road, refusing to glance back at the house. No, I can't do that. I can't keep hoping and wishing for something that will never be. When I make it to the Stop sign at the end of the street, a single tear rolls across my cheek. Quickly, I swipe it away and roll through the Stop sign. I just need to get home. I need to hold it together until I'm in the confines of my room.

Fifteen minutes later, I'm unlocking our apartment door. Sliding the lock back into place, I go straight to my room and plop down on the bed. My eyes land on a picture of Cooper and me at our high school graduation. One tear falls, then another, and another. I don't bother to try and stop them. I know there's no use. This is my issue, one I need to get past. I changed the game. I'm the one who wants more. I'm the one who went and fell in love with my best friend.

After years of hoping, it's time to lay that to rest. I need to move on. There is never going to be more than friendship between us. I just need to mourn the loss of what my heart wished it could have been. Then somehow, I need to pick up the pieces and move on. One thing is for certain, I will always love Cooper Reeves.

The sound of my phone vibrating pulls me from my slumber. Glancing at the clock, I see it's two in the afternoon. Tossing the covers off, I scramble to my bag that I dropped on the floor and fish out my phone.

Cooper.

"Hello," I answer, my voice gravelly from sleep.

"Reese. Where are you?" I can hear the worry in his voice.

"At home. I was sleeping. What's wrong?"

"You left."

Shit. I'm not ready to have this conversation. "You were snoring," I lie. "I came home to sleep."

"Oh." He pauses. "Are you coming back over? We were going to grab something to eat."

"Sure. I just need to shower." Looks like my alone time is busted. If I refuse to go, he's going to know that him pushing me away killed me. I can't let him know that, because it's not his fault that I fell in love with him.

"Okay. We'll wait for you."

"I can just meet you there. Where are you going?"

"We'll wait, Reese. See you soon." With that, he ends the call. He's moody today, but I should have known he would be. Cooper worries, and when he woke up alone, I'm sure he thought something had happened. I know he's worried about last night as well. He thinks things are going to be different. He's right. He just has no idea that it's my broken heart that pulled me from his bed during the early morning hours. Our friendship will remain the same. I'll give it my all to ensure that it does, but my heart, well, my heart needs to move on.

I can do this. *I have to.*

Grabbing my clothes, I head to the shower. The entire time, I'm psyching myself up to act as if things haven't changed between us. I'm not an actress, but I need to be ready to put on a show. I can do this. I don't want him to see the pain, or the hurt. I need to be just Reese. His best friend. I'll pick up the pieces without him knowing. What choice do I have?

Thirty minutes later, I'm pulling into the driveway of his house.

Taking my keys from the ignition, I grab my purse and put on my "everything is fine" face. I walk into the house without knocking, just like I always do.

"Hey, there she is." Tessa smiles at me from her seat on the couch.

"Finally. We're starving," Hank grumbles.

"You look like you just rolled out of bed." I raise my eyebrows, and he chuckles.

"Busted, but I'm still starving."

"Come on, you big baby." I walk around the couch and hold my hand out to him, pulling him to his feet.

"Thanks, Reese." He hauls me in for a hug, and just like every time before this one, I hug him back.

"I need my shoes." Tessa stands and moves to find them.

"I'm going to run upstairs to get my wallet," Nixon says, and dashes up the steps.

"Where are Trey and Dustin?" I ask Cooper. It's my lame attempt at conversation pretending that everything is normal. Pretending that my heart doesn't ache.

"Still sleeping. We tried everything to get them up." His eyes are locked on mine.

"I know the feeling. I was exhausted," I say, averting my gaze to look around the room. "It's not too bad this time."

"Yeah, I cleaned up some when I woke up and found you gone. Gave me something to do since you weren't answering your phone."

"Sorry about that. I was out. But, hey, at least you got a head start on clean up." I turn back to face him and smile.

"Reese." He steps close and grabs my hand. "Are we okay?"

"Of course, we are. Why would you ask that?" I know why. Like I said, an actress I am not.

"Reese." His eyes are soft, his voice pleading.

With more courage than I ever thought I had, I tell him what he needs to hear. "It's fine, Coop. We were both drinking, and one thing led to another. We stopped before the point of no return. It's all good. I promise." I give him a forced smile, one I hope he can't tell isn't real.

"Now, you dragged me out of bed for food. Are you planning on feeding me anytime soon?"

"Come here." He tugs me into a hug. I close my eyes and fight off tears. I can't let him see me cry.

"Come on, you two, time's a-wasting!" Tessa calls out, dragging Nixon behind her as they pass through the front door.

"The others are meeting us there," Nixon announces. I guess he was able to get them up and moving.

"I'm starving. I might wither away," I say, putting some distance between us. I grab his hand, just as Tessa had with Nixon and pull him outside. This is us. This is what we do. My heart will just have to get over it. I'll take Cooper Reeves any way that I can have him. Best friends, that's what we are, and how we shall remain. As for the pieces of my heart, with time, I'm sure I can mend them back together.

We end up at a small diner in town. The food is cheap and better than most five-star restaurants. Trey, Dustin, and Hank are on one side of the table. Nixon, Tessa, and Cooper are on the other. I'm sitting on the end between Cooper and Hank. Which is why Hank has free access when he reaches over and steals a fry from my plate.

"Hey." I swat playfully at his hand.

"What? I'm a growing man, Reese." He snatches another one. Not that I care. They give you huge portions, and I'm never able to finish all of mine. Normally, I could offer them to Cooper.

"Fine," I say, pretending to be put out, but I slide my plate with a pile of leftover fries his way.

"Those are mine." Cooper reaches over to grab a fry, but Hank is faster, anticipating his move, and slides the plate out of his reach. "Ah ah ah." Hank holds up his pointer finger and wiggles it back and forth. "Reese's Cup gave these to me."

Cooper glares at him. "I feel like I'm babysitting." I laugh. I grab a handful of my leftover fries and drop them on Cooper's plate. His eyes find mine, and the look he gives me tells me that this is about more than just french fries. I thought I was doing okay pretending things are normal between us. I guess maybe I'm not. Damn it, I should have made sure Cooper had all the fucking french fries.

"Those were mine." Hank pretends to pout before grinning and popping a fry in his mouth.

"You have to share," I tell him in my best mothering voice, and our table of friends break out in laughter.

"We all know that Hank likes to share," Trey quips.

Hank opens his mouth, but I hold up my hand to stop him. "Nope. We're not going there. What you do behind closed doors, needs to stay behind the door."

"But what if it's not behind closed doors?" He gives me a wicked smile and shrugs his shoulders.

I look over at Cooper and point to Hank. "He's your friend," I say, teasing.

He studies me for several long seconds that seem like hours. When he finally opens his mouth to reply, a leggy brunette walks up to the table and interrupts him.

"Hi, Cooper." Her voice is sugary sweet. "I'm still waiting on that date."

The food I just consumed sours in my stomach. I turn to look at Hank to find his eyes already watching me. "You better eat up before I steal them back," I tell him when I want to do anything but. I already feel like I'm going to lose what I just ate, adding more food to that would be a huge mistake, but I couldn't think of anything else to say.

"Reese, we're long overdue for a girls' night," Tessa announces.

I offer her a grateful look, and her subtle nod tells me she knew she was saving me. "Yes. It's been too long."

"Aw, babe, why's it have to be girls' night?" Nixon whines.

"Because sometimes we just need the girls. You get me all the time," she tells him.

"That's how I like it."

"You'll be fine." She pats his shoulder as he leans in and kisses her before she turns back to me. "Tonight?"

"It's Sunday."

"So? You don't have class tomorrow until ten, right?"

As my best friend, she knows my schedule just as well as I do. She also knows me well enough to know that I need this even though I haven't said anything to her about last night. "Yes."

"Then, why not tonight? My first class is at ten thirty, so we can go out and have a few drinks, do some dancing, and be home in time to sleep it off and drag our asses to class tomorrow."

"I'm in."

"Reese." Cooper's deep voice pulls me in. I turn to look at him. The look he gives me is pleading.

"Oh, come on, Cooper. You know we're not reckless," Tessa says, saving me once again. "You boys will just have to do without us for one night."

"Cooper." The brunette, who is still standing between us, places her hand on his shoulder. "Maybe you and I can get together tonight."

"Not interested," he says through gritted teeth.

Looks like it's not just me who's not doing it for him.

"Let's go back to the house and get our cars, and we can go home and get ready," Tessa says, taking the final drink of her sweet tea.

"Wait. Where are you going?" Nixon asks.

"I'll text you and let you know we're safe. I promise to call if we need a ride." Tessa kisses his cheek.

"Damnit, Tess. I'm your fiancé. I should know where you're going to be," Nixon says, his voice firm.

"I'm going to be out with my best friend. Are you saying that you don't trust me?" she challenges.

"No. Damnit, I worry about you." Nixon runs his fingers through his hair.

Grabbing the check, I stand. "Nix, you're welcome to come with us," I offer. I don't want them to be at odds because she's trying to make me feel better.

"No. He's not," Tessa says adamantly. "Nixon, you know I love you. I'm not sure where this is coming from, but I'm going out with my best friend. We're going to have a few drinks and then come home. I'll check in so you know we're safe."

"I don't understand why you can't just tell me where you're going?"

"For one, I don't know yet, and two, you and your posse of hulking football player friends will show up, and it's girls' night."

"It's fine, Tessa."

"No, it's not fine. You're single, and with these goofs hulking out their muscles, you're never going to find you a good man."

Cooper makes a strangled sound from deep in his throat. A quick glance at him and his fists are clenched, and his eyes are closed.

"They're not going to stop me," I tell her, with less bravado than I was feeling a few seconds earlier after seeing Cooper. I don't know what's going on. He can't have his cake and eat it too. He doesn't want me. We've established that. I need to move on. He doesn't know he broke my heart—I have to remind myself of that—but I know that going out and meeting new people is what I need to do. Cooper and his friends, who have become mine, are leaving, that includes Tessa. She's following Nixon wherever he gets drafted. I'm about to be flying solo. I need to put myself out there.

"You and I both know that no guy is going to come near you if he's there." Tessa points across the table at Cooper. Then she turns her attention to Nixon. "I'll text you where we're going, and I'll check-in. However, you are not to show up unless I tell you that I need you to. Do we have a deal?" She holds her hand out for him to shake it.

He nods, and bypasses her hand, opting to lean in and kiss her. "Love you," he whispers.

My eyes water. I want what they have. I want someone to call my own. Someone that will be there for me in good times and in bad. Someone I can share that intimacy with. I bite down on my bottom lip to keep the tears at bay when I think about that person not being Cooper.

It's time for me to gather the broken pieces and glue them back together. It's time to move on.

A few hours later, Tessa and I are walking into Bob's. It's a local bar that has a designated dance floor. There's a jukebox in the corner, and on Friday and Saturday nights, they have live bands. We come here a lot, mostly with the guys in tow, but tonight, it's girls' night.

"Thank you for this," I say once we're seated at the bar.

"You ready to tell me what happened?" she asks.

"Not really, but I know you're going to keep giving me that look, the one that says that you and I both know I'll tell you eventually." Tessa is the only person I've ever told my true feelings about Cooper. "We kissed. There was some… touching, and then he reminded me we're just friends and that he didn't want to go too far and not be able to come back to that." Sure, I'm leaving out some details, but that's the gist of the story. Besides, it's still too raw, too painful to relive the entire night all over again. I'm just not there yet.

"This is the PG-condensed version, but I can work with this. How are you feeling?" she asks me.

"Broken," I say as I blink back tears. "He has no idea, so I need to hide it. He would feel guilty, and I don't want him with me out of guilt. I'm a big girl. I can handle this. I just need to pick up the pieces and move forward."

"I'm so sorry, Reese. I could have sworn that he was in love with you."

"He loves me." I nod. "He's protective like a big brother. As close as we are, and since we're not really related, I could see how it would appear that way." I had hoped that his love for me was more too.

"Well, you know what they say." She grins. "The best way to get over a man is to get under another one."

I can't help but laugh at her. "I'm pretty sure I'm not ready for that. Casual has never been my thing."

"Of course it's not. You've been in a one-sided relationship for years. Your heart doesn't know anything else."

Her words sting, but they're true. "One step at a time. I know I need to put myself out there. You're all leaving. All of you are moving on to bigger and better things. I'll just be me, sitting on the couch on Sundays, hoping to catch a glimpse of my best friends."

"Your ass is going to visit, and I promise I'll come visit too. Have you decided if you're moving back home or staying here?"

"Not yet. I guess it all depends on if I get that job with the county that I applied for."

"How does your mom and dad feel about that?"

I shrug. "I'm sure they wished I moved closer to home, but this is a really good opportunity, and would afford me the luxury of taking over our apartment. I wouldn't have to move, which is a plus."

"Well, regardless, you better tell them that you are best friends with several pro-football players and their wives and that you're going to be taking lots of long weekends."

"I don't think that's how it works. And wives?" I raise my eyebrows in question.

"Sure, eventually those knuckleheads are going to get married. Levi is getting pretty serious with his girl."

"I guess you're right." The thought of Cooper moving on and getting married has my stomach twisting. My heart is so entangled with his, I don't know how I'll ever make it through that. I'm sure with time I'll be okay. I just need to get past the hurt of his initial rejection of... more.

"What can I get you ladies to drink?" the bartender asks.

"Two vodka cranberries," Tessa orders for us.

"Reese?" a male voice asks. I feel a warm hand settle on the small of my back. Turning, I see Hunter smiling at me. "Hey. It's good to see you. Hi, Tessa," he greets. His eyes dart around. "Where are the guys?" he asks.

"Girls' night," Tessa speaks before I can.

"Nice." He bobs his head and grins. "What are you drinking?"

"Oh, we just ordered." Again, Tessa answers.

He slides into the seat next to me, and the three of us begin to chat about what comes next. Hunter is an accounting major and has a job here in town at a local firm.

"Where's home?" Tessa asks, keeping the conversation going.

"Florida. My parents aren't too happy that I'm not moving back, but this town has grown on me, and the position is a good one. The pay too." He grins. "What about you?" he asks Tessa.

"I'm going with Nix, wherever that leads us."

"You?" he asks me.

"I'm not sure yet. I've applied and had the first round of interviews for the county as a social worker. It just depends on that."

"Maybe we can catch up, have dinner sometime." He throws the offer out there.

"Yeah." I smile. Hunter is an attractive guy. He's got light brown hair and big blue eyes. He's slender, yet you can tell he takes care of his body. He's at least a couple of inches shorter than Cooper, but still taller than me. He seems like a really sweet guy. "That would be nice," I add when I realize I've just been staring at him.

Daughtry's "Start to Something Good" filters through the speakers. "Want to dance?" Hunter motions his head toward the dance floor.

I open my mouth to decline, but remember this is what I need to do. I need to branch out, spend time with people other than my core group of friends that are all moving on. I need to let a man other than Cooper have some of my time. "Sure." I finish the last of my drink and slide off my stool.

"You know what, I'm not feeling so well. I think I'm going to head home," Tessa says. She looks at Hunter. "Can you please make sure she gets home safe?"

"I'll come with you," I tell her, flashing Hunter an apologetic look.

"No," she says quickly. "I'll be fine. I'll order an Uber and see you at home." She leans in for a hug and whispers, "He might not be your forever, but you need this. Enjoy tonight, Reese." With that, she's gone.

My eyes follow her until she disappears. Then flash back to Hunter. "Shall we?" I ask, offering him my hand.

He takes it and leads me out on the dance floor. His hands settle on my waist as I slide mine behind his neck. We're quiet as we sway back and forth and listen to the song. It gives me faith that there is someone out there for me. I just hope that I have room in my heart for someone else. Only time will tell.

Chapter 17

COOPER

When Nixon told me that he was going to the girls' apartment to wait on them to get home, I was all in to tag along. It's something that I wouldn't have thought twice about before last night. However, here I am sitting on their couch, staring blindly at the TV, wondering if she's going to be mad that I'm here. Normally, we'd hang out and then go to bed. Her bed. I would sleep next to her, and all would be good. Nothing sexual, just friends. We've shared a bed countless times, but tonight, I feel as though she might not want me here.

It's not just that. How am I supposed to lie next to her and not touch her? Not kiss her? I don't know that I can, and that scares me.

"My girl," Nixon says, smiling at his phone.

"What?" I ask.

He looks up as if he just remembered I've been sitting here with him. "Tess is on her way home."

I nod. Glad they're not going to be out late. Two women on their own is dangerous late at night. Then his words register with me. "Just Tess?"

He cringes. "Yeah, I guess she didn't want to be the third wheel."

"Third wheel?" I'm aware I'm repeating everything he says, but I can't seem to form words otherwise.

"That's all I know, man." He gives me a sympathetic look.

Fuck. I run my fingers through my hair. Tessa wouldn't feel like a third wheel if it were another female in their group. Leaning forward, I rest my elbows on my knees, my head bowed as I calm the fuck down. I can't have her; she's my best friend. I need to be happy for her.

"Coop?"

I look up to find Nixon watching me. "You good?"

"No." My voice is gritty.

He nods. "Just tell her that you love her, man. Why put yourself through all this?"

"She's my best friend."

"You're a fucking idiot, Reeves."

I don't reply because he's right. My fear of losing her is causing me to be miserable with the possibility that another man gets to kiss her, hold her close at night, and be the most important person in her life. "We fooled around last night," I blurt. "Just kissing and… touching, but she wanted more, fuck me, I wanted more, but I stopped us."

"What?" The disbelief is evident in his voice.

"I can't lose her, Nix. She's been by my side for every major moment in my life. Sex complicates things, and if it didn't work out, and I lost her…" I shake my head. "I couldn't deal with that."

"So you let the girl you've been in love with for years just walk into the arms of another man?"

Pain slices through my heart. "You don't understand."

"You're right. I don't understand." He pauses before speaking again. His voice is calm, but his words pack a punch. "What I do understand is that you're letting the fear of losing her control you. What you don't understand is that things are going to change, Cooper. You're moving to who knows where, and she's going to be here. You can't expect her not to have a life. She's going to move on, and things are going to change with the two of you. Regardless of whether or not you confess how you feel about her or not."

"No. Distance won't change the connection we have." I say the words and will them to be the truth. Our truth.

"I know you have good intentions, but long-distance is hard. Even if it's just friendships."

"I don't have any other choice. I can't ask her to come with me. That's not fair to her."

"Not as your best friend, but as the woman in your life, the love of your life, there's nothing wrong with that. Tessa is coming with me."

"You're engaged."

"You could be too. There are these things called jewelry stores."

"Fuck you."

He throws his head back and laughs. "Look at you, man. You're a fucking mess."

He's right, and I don't want Reese or hell, even Tessa to see me like this. "I need to go."

"What? Why?"

"I can't be here. What if she brings him home? I can't…. I've gotta go. If Tessa can't bring you home tomorrow, call me." I stand and stalk toward the door.

"Running away isn't going to solve the problem, Coop."

"No, but that's the best I've got right now." With a wave, I disappear out the front door. In my Jeep, my chest heaves as if I've just run a marathon. I don't like that she's with a man I don't know. What if he hurts her? "Fuck!" I scream, slamming my hands down on the steering wheel. "You fucked up, Reeves. That's what you get for touching your best friend," I say to myself. Grabbing my phone, I send her a text.

Me: Hey, you. If you need me, or a ride home, you know how to reach me.

I stare at the screen, waiting for the screen to show me that my message has been read. My eyes stay glued to the screen, and I have to keep tapping it to keep it from going into sleep mode. I can't move from this spot until I know she's safe, and that if she needs me, I'm there.

I'll always be there.

I don't know how long I sit in my Jeep, staring at my phone like it holds the answer to world peace. Finally, my message shows as read, and those three little bubbles bounce.

Reese: Thanks, Coop. Hunter is taking me home.

Hunter. Fuck. That's the guy who was dancing with her at the party. The night we kissed. He's had his sights set on her, and now he's with her. He seems like an okay guy, but Reese deserves more than just okay. She deserves everything.

Me: Be safe, Reese.

Reese: Always.

That's it. She doesn't need me. I don't know how I feel about that. I gave into temptation, and now she's leaning on someone else. She doesn't need me to pick her up because he's with her. Someone who's not me. Putting my Jeep in Drive, I pull out of the parking lot and point the it toward home. I'm in a daze most of the drive, imagining Reese and Hunter together.

When I pull into the driveway, the house is dark, which fits my mood perfectly. I don't want to talk to anyone. I just want to be alone. I don't bother with the lights and head straight for the stairs. In my room, I shut and lock the door and blindly make my way to my bed, falling face-first onto the mattress.

My bed smells like her.

Emotion wells in my throat at the thought of losing Reese in my life. I can already feel her slipping away. I knew better. I knew I shouldn't have kissed her or touched her, but the temptation was too strong. Now, my careless actions may have lost me my best friend. I don't know how to deal with that.

Sliding my phone out of my pocket, I scroll through my pictures. Ninety percent of them have her in them. Just like my memories. There are few that don't have Reese in them with me. I knew leaving her would be hard, but it's worse with this… divide I suddenly feel. Is it all in my head? Is it my regret that's making me feel this way? Is it our new reality? Whatever it is, I don't like this feeling.

My phone vibrates with a message from Reese. I fumble to click the icon and read her message.

Reese: Just got back to the apartment. I didn't want you to worry. Night, Coop.

The agony roaring through my gut calms. I read her message three times before I reply.

Me: Thank you. Goodnight.

I want to say more, but I'm at a loss for words. I've never not had something to say when it comes to her. We talk about anything and everything, but it all suddenly feels different. *We* feel different. I told her that we had to stop before we couldn't go back. What I didn't realize was that we had already crossed that line.

It's just after four, and I know her last class of the day just ended. I also know that she doesn't have to work tonight. Normally, that would mean that I end up at her place, or she ends up at mine. Today I don't know what to expect. I tossed and turned all night last night, and no matter how hard I tried, I couldn't fall asleep. It was the early morning hours before I finally lost the battle to exhaustion.

My ass was dragging at the gym this morning, and it's still dragging as I plop down on the couch next to Nixon. "You talked to Tessa?" I ask him.

"What kind of question is that? She's my fiancée."

"You know what I mean."

"Yes. I've talked to the love of my life. Have you talked to yours?"

I give him a hard look, causing him to laugh. "What's so funny?" Dustin asks with a bag of Doritos in his hands. He takes a seat on the loveseat across from us.

"Nothing." Nixon sobers.

"What are we doing for food? Are the ladies coming over?"

"Tessa should be here around five," Nixon says.

Dustin looks at me, and I shrug. I'm not sure if Reese is coming over or not, and I hate that just as much as I hate this distance I feel between us. My phone is already in my hand, so I hit her name and place it next to my ear.

"Hey." She sounds happy and not at all upset about this weekend.

"Hi. Are you coming over with Tessa?" I get straight to the point.

"I was planning on it. Is that okay?"

"Yes," I say quickly and way too loud. Dustin gives me a strange look, and Nixon smirks, keeping his eyes downcast at his phone. "I just wasn't sure. I hadn't talked to you today."

"Yeah, we're stopping at the store to get stuff to make spaghetti. Didn't Nixon tell you?"

"No." I turn to look at my ex-best friend. "Nixon didn't tell me." He shrugs and blows me a kiss. *Bastard.*

"We should be there around five. You need anything while we're out?" she asks. That's Reese always thinking of others.

Just to see you. "No, I'm good. I'll see you soon."

"Sounds good. Bye," she says, and ends the call.

"What the hell, Nix? You knew she was coming and didn't tell me."

"Nope. It's not my job to be the go-between with the two of you."

"What did I miss?" Dustin asks.

"Nothing, just that the girls are making dinner. Spaghetti."

"Yeah. Tessa asked me what sounded good. I told her if she stopped and picked everything up, I'd pay her, so cough up some cash." He holds his hand out. I dig into my pocket, and so does Dustin to give him some cash.

"Trey and Hank are out for the night. I guess they met a couple of girls at the party, and they're all getting together tonight," Dustin tells us.

"He needs to be careful. You don't know who you can trust, and some of the cleat chasers are like vultures wanting to sink their teeth into a pro career."

"True dat," Dustin says, shoving another Dorito into his mouth.

"So, you ready for the Combine?" Dustin asks us. He's not declaring for the draft. He doesn't love the game like we do. He likes it, and he's a damn good player, but it's not in his blood like Nixon's, Hank's, and mine.

We spend the next hour while we wait for Tessa and Reese to get here talking about the Combine and the upcoming draft. I'm nervous as hell but excited at the same time. This has always been my dream, and it's so close that I can taste it.

When the front door opens, I stand to help, as do Nixon and Dustin. We take the bags from their hands. "Are there more?" I ask Reese.

She smiles up at me. Her green eyes are bright and don't hold a single worry or regret. "Nope, this is it. However, you can help us with salad prep." She hip checks me and laughs all the way to the kitchen.

"You got a little something…" Nixon taps at his chin. "That's your best friend, you know?" he snarks.

"Damn right," I say as I follow the path Reese just took to the kitchen. I do as I'm told and start dicing a tomato for the salad. The five of us talk and laugh, as we always have. Nothing seems off between us. Reese laughs and smiles. She sits next to me at dinner and swats at my hand when I try to steal her breadstick.

"Hands off, Reeves," she says, swatting at me with her fork.

With each passing minute, my anxiety begins to fade, and we're just us. Just Cooper and Reese, two best friends hanging out with a group of mutual friends. It's exactly what I needed, and nothing like I was expecting. It gives me hope that nothing will ever change between the two of us. Not time, not distance, and not other people.

We will always be Cooper and Reese.

Chapter 18

REESE

"**D**o you have to go?" Hunter asks. We're sitting in the theatre waiting for our movie to start. We've been casually seeing each other since girls' night a few weeks ago. If you can call it girls' night since Tessa bailed on me. We have dinner at least once a week, and this is the second time he's brought me to the movies.

It's been nice to have someone other than Cooper's friends—well, I guess they are my friends too, but Hunter, I met him all on my own. Sure, it was at a party at the house, but still, he introduced himself, and then that night at the bar, he drove me home and asked for my number. Four days later, he called, asking me to dinner that weekend. I accepted. Cooper wasn't impressed. He didn't say a word, but his actions told me his true feelings. He's never going to stop worrying and protecting me. That's what best friends who think of you as a little sister do.

"Yes, I have to go. Cooper's family. He's been working toward this his entire life. My parents and his are going to be there too."

"Does that interest you? Watching the Combine?"

"Yes." I shrug. "I've always loved football."

"I wasn't sure if it was because Cooper played or if you shared the love for the sport." He smiles, and it's warm and inviting. He's not jealous of Cooper; he really is just trying to understand me and my likes.

"I love it. I watched it with my dad growing up, even before we moved next door to Cooper and his parents. It was kind of our thing. When Cooper came into my life and I found out he played, I was excited. My dad taught me about the game, so it was something we had in common."

"Did you ever play?" he asks.

"No. No way. I'm not that brave. Have you seen the size of those guys? Nope. I want no part of that. I was never a cheerleader either. Well, at least not on the sidelines. I prefer to watch and cheer from the stands."

"You know, I'd never been to a football game until college."

"Really? Did your high school not have football?"

"Nope. We were a big basketball school."

"Did you play?"

"Nah, I did go to the games, though." He pops a few pieces of popcorn into his mouth as the lights go down, and the movie starts.

For the next two hours, we sit side by side, sharing a tub of popcorn with our eyes riveted to the big screen. It's not uncomfortable. There are no awkward moments when we both reach for a handful of buttery goodness at the same time. But there's also no spark, and I blame myself for that. Hunter is a great guy, but I'm still healing. The broken pieces of my heart are going to take some time to mend back together.

"Well, what did you think?" Hunter asks once we're outside the theatre.

"It was really good. I thought for sure it was her dad who was the killer."

"Really? I was thinking the brother," he volleys back.

"We were both wrong." I laugh.

He holds his arm out for me, and I slide mine into his as we walk to his car. It's late February, and the weather is still cold out. Hunter walks me to the passenger door and opens it for me. Like the gentleman that he is, he waits for me to put on my seat belt before closing the door and rushing to the driver's side.

"I'm ready for warm weather," he says, rubbing his hands together once he's in the car.

"I don't know… I'll miss my sweaters and boots."

"There's that." He laughs.

Hunter is different from the group of guys I'm used to hanging out with. No doubt, any one of my friends would have made a comment about my ass in my jeans or leggings that I pair with my boots and sweaters. Not Hunter. No, instead, he gives me a kind smile.

"Where to next?"

"I should really get home. I have to pack as we leave early in the morning." Cooper's parents rented us an Expedition to drive to the Combine. It's about a three-hour drive from where we are in Ohio to Indianapolis. Hank, Nixon, Cooper, Trey, Tessa, and I are driving down. Dustin has to work and made us promise that we would keep him updated. He's currently working at a local physical therapy office doing an internship and is hoping to get hired full-time once we graduate.

"Let's get you home then." He backs out of the parking space, and we're on the road. It doesn't take long to reach my apartment, and the conversation is easy as we chat about graduation.

"Thanks for tonight. I had a good time." We had pizza before the movie. It was simple and perfect. I'm not one for all the frills.

He reaches over and laces his fingers through mine. This is a first for us. He's led me into rooms with his hand on the small of my back, we've hugged a few times after dates, and of course, we've danced, but hand-holding, that's new. "You're welcome, Reese." He traces his thumb softly over mine. I can't help but think of the contrast of his soft hands to Cooper's rough and calloused ones. "Am I allowed to say that I'm going to miss you?" he asks.

"It's only a week. Well, nine days. I'll be back before you know it."

"Nine days is a long time."

I laugh. It's part nerves and part disbelief because this is all new to me. "I'll text you while I'm gone. I promise."

"What about all of your classes? Work?" he asks.

"Classes… all my professors know we're going to be gone, and I've turned in most of my work early. Work knows too. It's no different than a vacation. I mean, my family is going to be there." My parents wouldn't miss this for anything. They're riding to Indy with Cooper's parents.

"Drive safe."

"Oh, I'm not driving. The guys are doing all of that. It's just a three-hour trip, so Tessa and I have already declared that we're just the passengers."

My phone buzzes. "Sorry, that might be my parents." Glancing at the screen, I see Cooper's name. I know if I don't answer, he'll worry. "Hey, Coop." I mouth "Sorry" to Hunter.

"Hey, you still coming over tonight so we can leave here in the morning?"

"Yes. Hunter is dropping me off now. I just have to pack, and then I'll be there. Is Tessa already there?"

"Yeah, she got here a few minutes ago. You want me to come and pick you up?"

"Nah, as long as my car won't be in the way there."

"No, it's all good. Drive safe."

"See you soon." I end the call and slide my phone back in my purse. "Sorry, that was Cooper. He was asking if I was still staying there tonight, since we're all heading out in the early morning hours."

"You're spending the night there?" he asks.

"Yeah, I do it all the time. It makes sense since everyone who's going is already there. Tessa is staying over with Nixon. This way, they don't have to wait on me or pick me up."

He's quiet, and I'm worried he's pissed off. "You need me to drive you over there?"

"No, that's okay."

"Reese." He waits for me to look at him. "I don't mind. That will give me more time with you anyway."

His words are sweet, just like the man. "Okay. Just let me run upstairs and pack. Do you want to come up?" I offer. He's never been in my place. He's walked me to the door, but he's never actually been inside.

"Definitely. I can carry your bags for you." He reaches for his door handle and follows me down the walkway into the building and into my apartment.

"This is home," I say, waving my hands around the room. "Have a seat." I point to the couch. "Do you want something to drink?"

"No. I'm good."

"Okay. Just give me a few to pack." I rush to my room, toss my suitcase on the bed, and begin grabbing everything I'll need for a week. Sweaters, leggings, jeans, hoodie, long-sleeve T-shirts. I make sure I bring everything I have that has *Reeves* on the back with the CU colors. I'm there to support my best friend, and that's what I intend to do. I see Cooper's CU hoodie, one that I didn't steal this time, resting on the back of my desk chair. I toss it in as well in case he wants it. Socks, bras, and underwear get tossed in. I grab some sweats just in case, and some pajamas. I packed my toiletries this morning, so I grab that bag and go through it one more time, making sure that I haven't missed anything.

As I'm wheeling my suitcase into the living room, my phone rings. Cooper. "Hey, you. I just finished packing."

"Is my CU hoodie at your place? My new one?"

"Yes. I already packed it. It was on my desk."

"Thanks, Reese. So, you're on your way?"

"Yeah. Hunter is going to drive me over, so after I do one more mental check to make sure I have everything, I'll be there."

"Oh, okay. Have you eaten? I saved you some pizza. We ordered out. Didn't want to have to clean or leave a mess for Dustin."

"We ate earlier, but maybe a slice," I tell him.

"Okay. I'll see you soon, Reese."

"Bye." I slide the phone in my back pocket.

"Cooper?" Hunter asks.

"Yeah. He wanted to know if he left his hoodie here. It was in my room."

"The two of you never dated?" I can hear the disbelief in his voice.

"Nope." It's not a lie. Kissing him, and well… everything else we did wasn't a date. It was a moment in time that I need to forget, but my heart won't let me. "Just best friends since we were kids. He's like a brother to me." I add that on to calm his fears. He has nothing to worry about. Cooper doesn't see me like that. Sure, he's a man, and he gets aroused, but to go through with something more… he's just not interested.

I've done well the last few weeks. I've been able to be around him and not let my broken pieces fall to the floor. I'm slowly gathering them, holding them close so that one day, maybe my heart can be put back together.

Hunter nods. "You got what you need?" He asking and coming to stand next to me, taking the handle for my suitcase.

"Yes." I pause, going through my mental checklist. "Oh, hold on. I almost forgot." I rush back to my room and grab the giant sharable bag of Reese's Pieces. Cooper gives them to me, but they're his favorite. He used to say it was because I was his favorite, but deep down, he loves the peanut butter pieces. To be honest, so do I. They're addicting. "Ready," I say, holding up the bag.

"Sweet tooth?" Hunter smiles.

"No, well, yes. These are for Cooper. They're his favorite, and mine too actually, despite the name." I grin up at him. "It's more of a good luck kind of thing. He used to give them to me all the time when we were kids, and he still does. It's usually when something good is going on, when I'm sad, for any reason really. The Combine is a big deal to him, so…." I hold up the bag again and shrug.

"You're one of the good ones, Reese Latham."

"Ready?" I ask, ignoring his statement. I know he's being nice, but I'm not ready to go there. To talk about being a good one and what that means to him. We're not there yet. I don't know that we will ever be. I know that he's nice, and I enjoy my time with him. For now, that's the best that I can do.

When we pull up to the house, Cooper steps outside onto the front porch. I wave through the window, and he waves back, wearing a grin. I know he's both excited and nervous about tomorrow. I turn to Hunter. "Thank you for the ride. I'll text you when we get there."

He reaches over and cradles my cheek in the palm of his hand. "I'm going to miss you, Reese."

I want to say I'll miss him too, but to be honest, I'm just not so sure that I will. That makes me sound like a horrible person, but I refuse to lie to him. This thing between us, whatever it is, is still new. I don't know that I'm at the "I'm going to miss you" stage. Luckily, Trey pulls in behind us and taps on the window. I lower it to talk to him. "Hi."

"Hey, you got bags? I'll carry them in." He bends down to peer into the car and waves at Hunter. "What's up, man?" he says in greeting.

"Yes. Thanks. Trey." I reach the handle and push open the door. Looking over my shoulder, I say, "Thanks again, Hunter, for tonight and the ride. I'll text you," before climbing out of his car and grabbing my purse and small tote, while Trey removes my suitcase from the trunk. I wave at Hunter and follow Trey up onto the porch.

As soon as I'm within reaching distance, Cooper lifts me from my feet and spins me in the air, causing me to laugh. "Woo!" he cheers. "Combine, baby." He puts me back on my feet, and his brown eyes are filled with excitement when he looks at me. "I can't believe it's here, Reese. This is… everything I've been working for. I can't believe it's finally here."

I wrap my arms around him and hug him tight. "You deserve this, Coop. You're going to be great."

The sound of a horn beeping pulls our attention to the driveway. Hunter sticks his hand out the window and waves as he slowly drives away.

"Let's get you inside. It's too damn cold out here." With his hand wrapped around mine, Cooper pulls me into the house. My suitcase joins the bevy of others in the living room. Everyone is packed and ready to go on this adventure. I'm so excited for all three of them and what the future might hold.

Cooper pulls me behind him into the kitchen and lifts me onto the counter. Grabbing a paper plate, he adds a slice of pizza and pulls a bottle of water from the fridge before handing it to me.

"Thanks." He nods. "How are the nerves?"

"Okay. I think. I'm sure once we get there, it will be way worse. Then again, maybe not. I'm just going to go out there and do what I do. I'm in shape, and these hands—" He holds them up to show me. "—are on fire."

"Modest as always," I tease.

He flashes me a grin. "Thanks for coming. I wasn't sure you were going to."

"Of course I was going to come. No way am I missing this. I feel like it's been me on this journey with you. All the way."

"You and me," he says as Tessa comes into the room.

"Road trip," Tessa sings, hopping up on the counter next to me. "How was your date?"

"Fine. We had pizza and went to see a movie."

"Fine," she mocks.

"What? It was fine. Hunter's a nice guy."

"The train's rolling out at seven in the morning," Nixon says, joining us. He walks over to stand in front of Tessa, giving her his back. She doesn't hesitate to wrap her arms and legs around him, climbing onto his back.

"We better get to bed. You guys especially."

"Nah, that's why we're going down a day early. That way, we can get there, chill, and get a good night's sleep."

"Night!" Tessa calls as Nixon carries her out of the room.

"I guess we better get to bed," I say, jumping off the counter and tossing my plate. I keep my water to take with me to bed.

"You coming to my room?" Cooper asks.

This will be the first time I've stayed over since that night. "The couch is fine."

"Reese." He reaches for my hand. "Please." His voice is soft yet pleading. "I promise I'll keep my hands to myself. This is big, and every time I've ever thought of this moment, you were there every step of the way."

I love him.

I'm in love with him and can't find it in myself to deny him this. "Okay." I nod, and his shoulders relax. With my hand in his, he guides me through the house as we shut off the lights and lock the door. Then he leads us upstairs to his room. I send up a silent prayer that I can make it through this night, and this weekend, unscathed.

COOPER

"I'll get you something to sleep in," I tell Reese as I guide her into my room. I wasn't sure she would stay with me. I know it's wrong to ask that of her, but I need her. I need my best friend. No way could I sleep knowing she was downstairs on the couch. I need to feel that connection with her. The Combine is a huge deal, and Reese has always known how to calm me down. Hell, just her presence alone has a calming effect on me.

Reaching into my dresser drawer, I grab a pair of sweats and a T-shirt and toss them on the bed. "I'll... uh, just step out. Give you time to change."

"Just turn around, Coop. It's fine," she says, reaching for the clothes.

"Okay." I nod and turn my back to her. I hear her rustling around, and I close my eyes just to be safe, giving her the privacy she deserves. However, in my mind, I'm undressing her. I'm staring at her perfect tits and am raking my eyes over every curve. Every single fucking curve that I will never in my life be able to forget.

"Done," she says softly.

I don't want to open my eyes. I don't want the vision in my mind to be swept back into my memory bank. I'm not ready to let it go. I stand here, my eyes tightly closed, fighting my internal battle.

"Coop." Her soft hand lands on my arm. My eyes fly open and land on hers. "I'm changed."

"Okay." I clear my throat. "Good. I'm just going to grab some clothes and change."

"My turn to focus on the door." She grins and steps in front of me. Her body is so close I can feel her warmth seep into my skin. Fuck me, this is a hell of a lot harder than I thought it would be.

Forcing myself to step back, I grab what I need and quickly change. "You're good," I say, tossing my jeans into a pile in the corner of my room. Reese turns and walks to what I like to refer to as her side of the bed. It's the side she always sleeps on when she's here. The side that smells more like her. The side that I admittedly like to sleep on when she's not here.

I wait for her to climb into bed before turning off the light and climbing in next to her. I'm lying flat on my back, covers pulled up to my chin as I stare up at the ceiling. The shadows are dancing from the moonlight shining in through the blinds.

"Coop." Her voice is soft, barely a whisper, but I hear her.

"Yeah?"

"C-Can I—Can I lie next to you?" Her voice cracks, and it kills me that she's worried about us, about being close to me. She's laid in this bed next to me hundreds of times, and she's never had to ask.

"Always, Reese. Always." I hold up my arm, and she moves closer, resting her head on my chest. "You never have to ask me, Reese," I say into the quiet of my room. We lie in silence for several long minutes that feel more like hours. I run my hands through her hair, relishing the fact that she's here with me. "I missed you," I murmur.

"Me too," she says, and if I didn't already hear the crack in her voice, the wetness that coats my skin through my shirt would have been all I needed to know she is upset.

"I'm sorry, Reese. I never want anything to come between us. I never want to lose this." I hold her tighter, and just a little closer, needing to feel connected to her.

"Things can't always stay the same, Coop."

I know she's right, but damn it, I want them to. I wonder if she can feel my heart as it beats heavy in my chest. "We won't let it change." It's more than just words; it's a vow. I'll do everything in my power to see it through.

She nods but is otherwise silent. There are no more words spoken as we lie in the quiet of my room, lost in our heads. Her breathing eventually evens out, and I know she's asleep. Lifting my head from the pillow, I press my lips to the top of her head. "Goodnight, Reese," I whisper into the night.

When my alarm goes off at six, I groan. What I don't do is move from the warmth of the cocoon I'm wrapped in. The covers are pulled up over us, and Reese is in my arms, her back to my front. My cock is hard and pressing into her ass, and her body is warm bundled up in mine.

"Coop," she grunts. "Alarm."

Pulling away from her, I roll over and smack at the nightstand until the offending beeping stops. I roll back over and wrap my arms back around her. It's wrong, but I can't help it. I've missed her.

"I don't want to get up," she says over a yawn.

"We can lie here a little longer." As soon as the words are out of my mouth, there's a pounding on my bedroom door.

"Get your asses out of bed!" Trey says. "We got some ass to kick and some names to take!" he yells loudly, before tromping down the stairs.

"So much for a little longer." Reese chuckles and throws the covers off her before climbing out of bed.

Just like that, my moment with her is over, and I don't know if I'll ever have one like it again. I hate that I feel so off-balance when it comes to her. When it comes to us, it was always easy. I never questioned anything, and now that seems to be all that I do. I need to get my head screwed on straight before people start to notice.

"Time to get up, lazybones." She grins. "I need to run downstairs and grab my bag. I forgot that I didn't have anymore clothes here."

"You do. They're in the bottom drawer," I tell her.

"Oh."

I watch her as she bends over and pulls open the bottom drawer. She pulls out a pair of leggings and a long-sleeve CU T-shirt. Then her bra and panties. She always leaves a full outfit here just in case. There are even pajamas in there, but I pretended to forget that from last night. I'd rather see her in my clothes.

"Looks like I have what I need." She turns to face me with her clothes in her hand.

"Your bag with all your bathroom stuff is in the bottom of my closet."

"Perfect. Thanks, Coop." She grabs the bag and leaves the room.

I took my shower last night before she got here, so I climb my ass out of bed and get dressed. By the time I'm done, Reese is back with a towel on her head. "I didn't want to hog the bathroom, so I'll just get ready in here."

That's not an issue. She's done her hair in her before. What the issue is is that my room will smell even more like her. I'm struggling as it is. The only saving grace is that we're going to be gone a week.

"I need to piss and brush my teeth," I say, giving her shoulder a soft squeeze as I pass her to leave my room. I shut the door behind me and force my legs to move away from her. I don't know what's going on with me. Reese seems fine. Sure, last night she was sad, but today she's just my Reese. I need to get past this.

Thirty minutes later, the Expedition my parents rented is loaded, and we all pile in. Reese and I are in the front as I'm driving the first leg of the trip. Hell, it's only three hours, I might just drive the entire way. Lord knows my long-ass legs would be more comfortable up front than squished in the back.

"Combine here we come!" Trey calls out, and we all cheer.

I've waited for this moment as long as I can remember. I can't believe it's finally here. Glancing over at Reese in the passenger seat, she's singing softly to the radio, taking in the scenery. Without a doubt, there is no one else in this world I'd rather have on this journey with me.

It's been a long, grueling week. The Combine was an experience I will never forget. Meeting the professional players, getting their advice and wisdom. Competing with the best of the best. If I never get drafted, I'll still be glad I came. It was definitely a good experience. It helped to know that Reese and our parents were here to cheer me on. You don't realize what the support of loved ones means until you are in this kind of situation. I know that they are here for me and no other reason.

"How do you feel about it?" Reese asks from her spot in the passenger seat.

Glancing in the rearview mirror, I see that everyone else is already asleep. They're all exhausted, and I am too, but I'm too amped to sleep. Maybe it was getting so much time with Reese and our parents? "Good. I'm feeling confident."

"As you should." She swats at my arm. "My best friend, a professional football player. I know this has been your dream. We've talked about it countless times, but to witness this past week... the hard work paying off... it's a sight to see. I'm really proud of you, Coop."

"Thanks. I'm glad you were there. It felt right, you know?" I have the urge to reach over and hold her hand, but I know that's crossing a line that I'm not allowed to cross.

There have been a lot of those moments this past week. She's the first person I wanted to see at the end of each day. That's nothing new, not really. We've always shared everything with each other. However, it does feel... different. I can't explain it. I guess it's just because of how weird things have felt between us lately.

"I'm glad I was there too. Just think, pretty soon, I can say I knew you when." She laughs. "Hey, I should get you to sign something. Get your autograph now. I could be rich one day."

"Turning into a cleat chaser, are you?" I tease.

"Hey, a girl's gotta eat. I bet you once you're drafted and make a name for yourself in the league, I could make more on one of your signatures than I could in a year as a social worker."

"Social work is more fulfilling."

"This is true. At least I hope it is. From all of my externships and job shadowing, I'm pretty confident. Sure, there are going to be bad days, but you have that with every job, right? I mean, look at you. You get taken down by tanks of men on the daily. I know that's not fun."

"It's fun when we win."

"It's a rush for me, and I'm just a spectator. I can't imagine the thrill or the high that it gives you. Especially with all those touchdowns you run in."

"Go on." I wave my hand at her. "Keep those compliments coming."

"Stop." She chuckles. "Truly, I'm so proud of you. You're going to do great things, Cooper Reeves."

The conversation lulls as she closes her eyes, resting her head against the seat. Now, I regret driving. I wish I could just watch her and take her in. It hit me this week that I'm leaving soon. After the draft, then graduation, I'll have very little time before reporting to training camp, wherever that might be. I'll have to find a place to live and get settled. My time with Reese is limited. I'll go from seeing her every day to daily text messages and calls. More than anything, I wish that I could ask her to come with me. However, I know that's not fair. I can't ask her to drop the plans she has for her life, the job she has lined up, her apartment, just to follow me. Besides, I'll be gone a lot. Between practice and games, and other team activities, I don't know how much time I would have to devote to her. To our friendship.

So, yeah, I wish I wasn't driving so I could soak up this time. I need to get it in while I can. I don't know what the future holds. As far as my career goes, I hope to be drafted. I'll be disappointed, but I have an education to fall back on. My degree as an athletic trainer will help keep me in the game that I love. As for Reese, that future scares me more than anything. I can't imagine my life without her. I hope I never have to find out what that feels like.

About thirty minutes from the house, her cell phone rings. "Hello." She pauses. "Hey, Hunter." Another pause. "Yeah, we're almost home." She listens to whatever it is he's saying. "Not tonight. I'm drained. Can I call you tomorrow?" Again, she listens.

I hate that I can't hear what he's saying.

"No. Coop can take me home." She glances over at me, and I nod. "Okay. I'll call you. Bye, Hunter."

"Thanks for taking me home," she says, sliding the phone back into her purse.

"You don't have to thank me, Reese."

"I know you've been driving all day."

"Wouldn't matter. You know that, right? That no matter what happens, if you need me, I'm there?"

"Are we there yet?" Hank asks, stretching his arms as far as they can go in the cramped space. He's a tall guy, hence the reason I'm driving. I didn't want to be cramped up in the back seat.

"Just about." Reese turns to look at him.

"Reese?"

I pull up to the Stop sign and look at her. "Tell me you know that."

"I know, Coop." She nods, and that's the end of it.

I wish it was just the two of us in this car so I could make her tell me like she believes it. I don't need to air our dirty laundry in front of our friends. I need to make sure that before I leave to… wherever I'm headed, that she knows that no matter what, I'll be there.

Chapter 20

REESE

"I wasn't sure you were going to make it," Cooper says when I walk into the house, dragging my suitcase behind me.

"You mean the fifteen million text messages that you sent me, and that I replied to, saying I would be here didn't convince you?" We're flying to Vegas today for the professional football league draft. Cooper, Trey, and Nixon are all going. All hopeful to be drafted and reach their dreams of becoming professional football players. Cooper has waited his entire life for this. Hell, I've waited for it as well. I've been there with him on every step of this journey, I'm not backing out now.

"I haven't seen much of you lately." He takes my bag and rolls it over next to his.

It's his dig at Hunter. I get it. I've altered our pattern, but I had to. I couldn't keep giving him all of me. It was too painful. Hunter is a nice guy and treats me right. We've been dating for a couple of months now. Nothing serious. Sure, neither one of us is dating anyone else, but we a far cry from professing our love to one another. He's easy to be around, and we enjoy our time together. For now, that's all I have.

"You've been busy with the draft and graduation, as have I. Between school, my job, and the externship, it's been hectic." That's all true. It's also true that I might be studying more and making myself busier than usual. He's leaving soon, and the distance is going to kill me. I needed to start the process of getting used to him not being there every day.

"And your boyfriend." He says it as if the word leaves a sour taste in his mouth.

"He's not my boyfriend."

"No? You sure do seem to be spending a lot of time together." His tone isn't accusing. If anything, I can hear the undertone of hurt. I hate that. I never want to hurt Cooper. However, he hurt me, and this is the only way I know how to deal. I'm slowly picking up the shattered pieces of my heart and laying them out on the table. One by one, I'm gluing them back together.

"We're dating, Coop."

"What does that mean exactly?" he asks, crossing his arms over his chest.

"It means that we enjoy each other's company. We're taking things slow. One day at a time."

"Is he pissed that you're here?"

"What? No. Of course not. And if he was, I wouldn't care. He's not my boyfriend. He's a guy I've been dating. Nothing more. You're my best friend." *The man I love.* "I wouldn't miss this. I've been on this ride with you since we were eight. No way am I missing the grand finale."

"The grand finale, huh?" He grins.

"Yep. It's all downhill from here. You've made it, Cooper. Tomorrow you find out where your future leads you."

"Tomorrow? You got me pegged for the first round, Reese's Pieces?" His grin is wide and contagious.

"Don't do that. Don't be modest with me. We both know how hard you've worked, and you know as well as I do that you're going to know your fate tomorrow. And if you don't believe me, I know your agent has been telling you what's up."

"Oh, you do, do you?" He chuckles.

"Stop." I push on his arm. "Where is everyone?"

"They're taking a later flight."

"So, it's just us?"

"Yep. Our parents are going to be there too. Did your mom and dad tell you they were going?"

"Yeah, Mom called me last night. I know they were on the fence, not sure if she could arrange the coverage at work."

"Yep. They fly out tonight with Mom and Dad."

"I'm so excited for you, Coop. I'm thrilled that we all get to be there with you to see your dreams come true."

He steps closer and engulfs me in a hug. "I'm so fucking glad you're here, Reese."

My arms wrap around him, and I hug him tightly. I've missed him something fierce. I've missed his hugs. I've missed our talks. Just missed Cooper. I missed all of him.

I thought that keeping myself away from him was the right thing to do. I need my heart to heal, but in this moment, I realize I was wrong. I need as much time with him as I can get. These hugs are just down the road, and soon could potentially be across the country. I know his agent has a good idea of where he's going. I know they've talked about it, but I've never asked. I don't want to know. Not until I have to. I'll deal with it then.

When he finally pulls away, his eyes catch mine. He stares down at me, and I swear if I didn't know better, it's yearning I see in his eyes.

"You all set?" I ask, breaking the moment between us. I can't handle anymore moments. My heart won't make it.

"Yeah. I'll get our bags." With a bag in each hand, he wheels them to the door. We're only going to be gone for four days, so carry-on is all that we really need.

"Let's take my car. It's easier to maneuver in the parking garage at the airport."

"Good idea."

He places our bags in the back seat and slides behind the wheel. I get into the passenger side and hand him the keys. He's driven my car countless times. In fact, he usually drives when we go somewhere, even if we take my car. This time though, it feels different. It's a glimpse of what domestic life would be like between us, yet, at the same time, it feels like a cruel joke. This will never be us. We're not going to be more than best friends. We'll never be loading up our kids to go on vacation or visit our parents. I guess this time the reason is different because I know that the hope I once held is gone. Like a puff of dust into the early morning sky. Somehow, I need to learn to stop loving my best friend.

We're three-wide, two-rows deep as we walk to the hotel where the draft is taking place. Cooper and his parents lead the pack while I walk with mine. Dad is in the middle, and Mom and I both have our arms linked through his. I'm glad because my knees feel weak. I'm so nervous for Cooper. I was reading last night that sometimes even if it's an assumption that you will go in the first round, that's not always the case. I know it's a privilege he was invited. Only those slated to go in the first round get picked. Cooper, Trey, and Nixon all got the invite. They're hell on wheels on the field together. I know the chances of them all going to the same team are slim, but those coaches, they'd be crazy to not attempt to be able to recreate the magic of the three of them on the field together.

We filter into the hotel and are directed where to go. Apparently, all players and their families and agents wait in an area they refer to as the green room. There are tables set up with players' names on them. We're led to Cooper's table, and everyone begins to take their seats.

"Reese." Cooper says my name to get my attention. He pats the chair next to his on the opposite side of the table.

I nod and join him. "How you feeling?" I ask him.

"Like I'm dreaming. Can you believe we're here?"

"*You're* here, Cooper. This is from all of your hard work, dedication, and love of the game. That's why we're sitting at this table. You did it." I reach over and give his hand a gentle squeeze.

"It's fucking crazy, Reese. It's all happening so fast. Soon I'm going to be packing and moving. I'll be heading to training camp."

"Yeah, you are," I say with a smile. I hide the pain of losing him. This is his day, his moment. I won't ruin that. My phone vibrates from its spot on the table, glancing at the screen I see Hunter's name.

"Checking up on you?" Cooper asks. His voice is tight.

"I doubt it. I haven't talked to him all day." Grabbing my phone, I swipe the screen and pull up the message. I know Cooper is reading over my shoulder, but I don't care. There's nothing in this message that he can't read.

Hunter: Hey, you. Just wanted to tell you I'm thinking about you.

Hunter: Tell Cooper good luck tonight.

Me: Thanks.

I send him a picture of the wall that has the professional football league's logo.

Hunter: Surreal!

"He makes it hard for me to hate him," Cooper says from his seat next to me.

I turn to face him, and he's close. Closer than I thought. All either of us would have to do is lean in just a fraction, and we'd be kissing. Something I'll never experience again, but also something I'll never forget as long as I live, is the feel of his lips pressed against mine.

"What are you talking about?" I ask. Neither one of us makes an effort to move out of the other's space.

"Hunter. That message. It makes it hard for me to hate him."

"Why do you want to hate him, Coop?"

His brown eyes hold mine. He leans in a little closer, and his voice is low and gruff. "Because he has you."

Before I can ask him what he means by that, his agent appears, placing his hand on Cooper's shoulder and effectively pulling his attention from me. My hands grip my phone as his words replay in my head. *Because he has you.* What does that mean? I thought he didn't want me? Did he change his mind?

A million questions bounce around in my head, but I don't have time to process them. Cheers erupt as the night begins. I try to clear my mind and focus on the here and now. This night, Cooper's future. However, I can't help but wonder what role I'll be playing in that future.

"Honey, I'm so proud of you. No matter what happens." His mom smiles at him. His dad and my parents both say similar things and offer him wide smiles.

Then he turns to look at me.

"You've got this, Coop."

He reaches under the table and slides his hand in mine, resting them on my lap. "I'm glad you're here for this, Reese. I couldn't imagine being here without you."

"Ladies and gentlemen." The announcer's voice echoes throughout the room. There are large screens placed around so we can watch what's going on behind the curtains. "The Houston Tigers announce their first-round draft pick, quarterback Trey Anderson."

I turn to look over my shoulder, where Trey sits with his family, and he has a shocked expression on his face. He's also speechless. I don't know that I've ever seen Trey speechless. Cooper stands, pulling me with him as we make our way to Trey's table. The three of us hug, and I'm squished between the two of them.

"You did it, man," Cooper cheers.

"Trey, we need you on stage." His agent pulls him away. His family is all smiles and tears as he accepts his Houston Tigers jersey on stage. We're all watching on the screens, and my smile is so big my face hurts.

"For the second pick of the first round, the Indianapolis Defenders pick running back Cooper Reeves."

I freeze. Cooper's hand that's still holding mine squeezes painfully. "Coop!" I scream and launch myself at him. We were so close to our seats that a chair gets knocked over in the process, but I couldn't care less.

He did it.

My best friend is a professional football player.

"Second pick of the first round. Hell yes," I cheer. He hugs me tightly, and when he pulls away, he kisses me. Right on the lips. There are cameras all around us, and I'm sure that will be shown on national television, but I don't care.

He did it!

I try to pull away as his parents, and then mine, hug him, and just like Trey, his agent pulls him away from us. I stand, riveted in the place where he set my feet back on the floor and watch as he places a Defenders hat on his head and holds up his new jersey. I feel arms wrap around me from either side. Looking over each shoulder, I see Nixon and Hank. We stay huddled together, and with their hold on me, and my arms around their waists, I'm unable to wipe the tears from my face. After what seems like an eternity, Cooper comes back into the room, and he hugs his parents, then mine. Trey gets him next, then Nixon and Hank, and Tessa, who I didn't even see beside us. Then his eyes land on me. In one large step, he's standing before me. Hands on my hips, he lifts me in the air and spins me around.

We're all laughing by the time he stops spinning us in circles. We're led to a different room, leaving Hank and Nixon behind. I know this is Cooper's journey, but it feels like mine as well. I know how hard he worked to be here. I've been to the games, stayed after for the practices, and watched as he fought the grueling classwork, practice, and game schedule in college. I'm so incredibly proud of him.

My phone vibrates in my pocket. I pull it out and check the screen. It's a message from Hunter.

Hunter: Second overall pick. Tell Cooper congrats.

Me: Thank you. I'll tell him.

Hunter: Is there something going on with the two of you?

I look around to see if anyone is standing close and reading over my shoulder. Cooper does this a lot. With our height differences, it's easy for him.

Me: What? Why would you ask me that?

He replies with a screenshot of Cooper and me on his TV screen, and it's the exact moment he pressed his lips to mine. It was mere seconds, but the fact remains that we kissed.

On national television.

Shit.

Me: He was caught up in the moment. We're just friends.

Hunter: Okay.

That's it. Just okay. I was expecting a fight, but it appears as though Hunter isn't into that. We're still learning each other, so I don't really know what his one-word answer means.

"Reese, you coming?" I look up to find my dad waiting with his hand out for me. I nod and slide my phone back into my pocket. I'll call Hunter later and explain.

The next two hours, we watch and listen as the draft moves on. All four of my guys went in the first round. All. Four.

Cooper is going to Indianapolis, Nixon to Louisiana and is taking Tessa with him. Trey is going to Houston, and Hank is heading to Atlanta. My friends, my people are going to spread out all over. And me, I'll still be here in Ohio. Sure, Cooper is just a three-hour drive from me. That's wonderful, and can be an easy weekend trip. But he's not going to have time for that until after the season is over. Between training camp and the season starting, he's going to be engrossed in all things Defenders. He's not going to have time for random visits from me. However, if I'm wrong, it will be easy to get to him.

I hope I'm wrong.

After congratulations are said, and hugs are passed around, we leave the hotel as a party of six. Two rows, three wide, leading us back to our hotel. We decided to eat there. It's late, and although Vegas never sleeps, we do. Cooper insisted we all get some rest; he slept like shit last night—his words not mine—and he's exhausted. I don't think he's going to do much better tonight. I'm sure the excitement will keep him wired.

"Thanks again, Reese, for being here," he says, walking me to my room.

"I wouldn't have missed it. I'm so excited for you, Cooper."

"Thanks." He reaches out and tucks a stray hair behind my ear. "Tomorrow, we're sight-seeing all day. If the parents don't want to go, we'll leave them here. But you and me, we're painting this town."

I laugh. "Sounds like a plan to me. Night, Coop."

He leans in, and my heart skips a beat thinking he's going to kiss me, but at the last minute, his lips veer and press to my cheek. "Night, Reese."

Chapter 21

COOPER

This is the last night in the house. The guys and I are all moving away. We're going home to spend some time with our families before we have to report to training camp. We also need to find places to live in our respective new cities. So, that means tonight we're having a party. Not your typical party. No, this one is more low-key. Now that we have four professional league contracts to maintain, we don't need any crazy shit happening. We sure as hell don't need any fucking cleat chasers. They've been following all four of us all over campus. Hell, graduation last week was a nightmare. No, tonight is just going to be our core group of friends. One last hurrah, if you will, before we all go our separate ways.

"I'm going out to get the alcohol. What does Reese want?"

"She said she would bring her own."

"You sure?" Dustin asks.

"Go ahead and grab her some White Claw." I reach into my pocket and pull out some money and hand it to him.

"Nix said that Tess and Reese are making dinner. We need anything else?"

"No," Tessa says, walking into the room. We're all set. Reese is just waiting on Hunter to get to her place, and they're heading over."

Fucking Hunter. I want to hate the guy, but from what I can tell, he's good to her. He's not jealous of our relationship. Not that he should be. Hell, I feel as though I've barely seen her these past few weeks. Life is passing by at a rapid rate. I was hoping he wasn't coming with her. I just wanted a night to chill with my best friend, and our other best friends, before I leave and life gets even crazier.

"All right, well, if that changes, just text me," Dustin tells her. Out of the five of us that live here, he's the only one that didn't declare for the draft. He's always said that wasn't his end game. Turns out, it's nice to be able to send him on runs. Sure, the cleat chasers try to latch on, hoping to get an invite, but Dustin is a big dude, and he can be scary as hell if you don't know him. He doesn't get approached nearly as often as we do.

It's just here on campus and around town where we're noticed all the time. I'm sure when I head to my parents' tomorrow, it will be that way with people that recognize me, but when I get to Indy, I'll just be me— Cooper Reeves, running back for the Indianapolis Defenders.

I still can't fucking believe it.

"You going to behave tonight?" Tessa asks me.

"What?"

"You heard me, Reeves." She plants her hands on her hips and gives me her best "mom" look.

"I don't know what you're talking about." I do, but I'm not going to admit that to her.

"Hunter," she sighs. "You need to be good."

"Aren't I always?"

"No. You're an idiot most days. You let the best thing that ever happened to you slip from your fingers because of fear."

"You don't know what you're talking about." I stand from the couch to head to my room to finish packing.

"I do know what I'm talking about. You might have everyone else fooled… hell, you even have her fooled, but I see you, Cooper. I see the way you watch her. The way no other woman gets your attention. Just her."

"You have my attention," I counter lamely.

"I do. Because I'm talking about her."

"No. It's because you are my best friend's fiancée and my other best friend's best friend." Yeah, it's a complicated mess. "For that, you have my respect and my attention."

"Well then, since I have your full attention, let me tell you this. One day, Cooper Reeves, you're going to wake up and realize that she's gone. You're going to regret your choice to push her away."

"I didn't push her away."

She gives a "don't lie to me" look. "I want you to promise me something." She waits for me to agree, but I don't. Instead, I just stare at her. "When that day finally arrives and you pull your head out of your ass, if she's happy, you need to promise me you will let her be happy."

"That's all I want for her. I want her to be happy."

Again, she hits me with a look that tells me she doesn't believe me. "Cooper." Her tone is a warning.

"Babe, have you seen my shoes?" Nixon calls down the steps.

"Be right there," Tessa calls back. She turns back to me. "You're a great guy, Cooper. You might not agree to it now, but I know you'll do the right thing." With that, she walks away from me.

I plop back down on the couch and think about what she said. I just want Reese to be happy. She deserves to be treated right, and no matter how badly I wish I was the man, I just can't do it. I knew the consequences of my actions. I knew stopping us that night was my one and only shot. I passed. It was the right thing to do.

Two hours later, we're all sitting around with our stomachs full and drinking a few beers. Reese and Tessa made pulled chicken tacos, and there's not even the smallest shred of chicken left. We devoured it.

"Thanks, ladies," I tell them. "Dinner was great."

"That's probably one of the biggest things I'm going to miss about college. Reese and Tessa's brownies," Trey comments.

"Don't worry, Trey. I'll send you some brownies. Not that you need me to. You can afford a chef."

"Not yet I can't, but that's the plan. I'm going to invest first, spend later."

"Me too," the three of us all say at the same time. Trey, Hank, Nixon, and I have talked about this many times. We want a stable future, and with the professional league, you never know where you're going to end up or if your contract is going to get renewed. You never know when or if you're going to get injured. It's the nature of the beast. While we all have degrees to fall back on, we all strive for financial security as well.

"If you need any help with that, I'm happy to guide you." Hunter jumps into the conversation.

"Hunter's an actuary. So he contemplates risks for investments and things like that," Reese explains.

Hunter reaches over and places his hand on her thigh. I stare at it, willing him to move, but he must not get the memo. No, he doesn't move it. Instead, he begins to draw lazy circles with his thumb. I grip my bottle tighter, so tight in fact, I'm worried I might shatter the glass. Not wanting to cause a scene, I drain the bottle and place it on the table next to me.

"Might just take you up on that," Trey tells him. "That gives me an excuse to come back and see our girl anyway."

Hunter doesn't seem the least bit fazed that Trey said "our girl." He should be. He really should be. I mean come on, if Reese were mine, no way would I let another man have a claim to her.

"Sure. I'm happy to help," Hunter replies.

"You staying in town?" Nixon asks him.

"Yes. I have a job at Southern and Hampton. It's the top accounting firm here in the city. I did my internship with them."

"They hired him without question," Reese fills in for him.

"Good for you, man. I'm glad," Hank says. "We were worried about leaving our Reese here all alone."

I watch him and nothing. No flinch. No fisting his hands. Not one little move to show he's uncomfortable with their claim to her. Is this guy for real?

"Yes. I'm glad too." He gives Reese a smile, which she returns. It's not her "I'm happy" smile, or even her "excited" smile. It's just... a smile. A kind one. Not the kind she should be giving the love of her life.

Is Hunter the love of her life?

No. He can't be.

Can he?

I need another beer.

The night moves on. The alcohol is flowing, and there are a lot of laughs. I'm really going to miss this. Miss these people. "Guys," I say, slightly slurring my words. "We have to do this as often as we can. I know it might have to be in the off-season, but this—" I lazily wave my hand around the room. "We must keep doing this."

The room erupts with murmurs of agreement as we hold up our beers for a salute to our new pact. I just hope that when we're sober in the light of day, and as life begins to take us in different directions, that we remember this day. That we remember to make time for those who are important to us. Like Reese.

I'll always make time for Reese.

We tell stories about our shenanigans while at CU and our time on the field. Tessa and Reese were there for all of it. Hunter wasn't, but he sits and listens, laughing and chiming in where he can. All the while, his hand is on her thigh or holding hers, or around her shoulders. He's always fucking touching her.

It's just after one in the morning when Tessa bows out. "It's been fun, but we still have some packing to do tomorrow before we hit the road." She stands, and Nixon follows her. She gives Reese a hug and waves to us as they head upstairs.

"You ready?" Reese asks Hunter.

"Wait. Where are you going?"

"Home."

"You're not staying here?" Through my alcohol-fogged brain, I know that I already knew that she wouldn't be in my bed, not with Hunter by her side. I guess I had hoped that he would leave and she would stay. Like old times.

"No." Her reply is soft, and is that regret I hear?

"You've been drinking."

"She has. I haven't. No way I would risk her or me, or anyone else for that matter," Hunter says. His voice is calm with his reply, but it screams sincerity.

"I'm leaving in the morning."

"I know." Reese looks down at her lap.

"Will I see you before I go?" This is fucked up. Her boyfriend is standing here, and I'm pleading with her, but I can't seem to help myself.

"What time are you leaving?"

"Sometime before noon. Maybe we can get breakfast. You know, just the two of us for old times' sake?" I toss that out there. I don't want my last minutes with her to be filled with Hunter's hands all over her.

"Sure. I'll text you."

"Just come by. When you're up and ready, I'll be ready."

"You sure about that?" She gives me a teasing look to match her tone.

"I'm positive." No matter the alcohol coursing through my veins, my mind still knows that I'm leaving her tomorrow. Every trip I've ever made home since we came to CU, she's been with me. Life is changing rapidly, and I hate it. I just… need some time with her before I go. I need to make sure we're on the same page. That no matter the distance, she's still my best friend and the most important person in my life. I've let this divide between us take root, but I'm fucking chopping that shit down. It ends now.

"Okay. See you tomorrow, Coop." She stands, as does Hunter. With a wave to the room, they leave quietly.

"You good?" Dustin asks.

"Nope," I admit. I'm sure if I weren't buzzed, I would never have spoken the truth, but I can't seem to fight it right now.

"Didn't think so." Dustin empties off his beer and sets the bottle on the table. "Want to talk about it?"

"Nope."

"Didn't think so." He stands and stretches. "When you do, you know how to reach me. I'll see you before you leave tomorrow?"

"Yeah, I'll make sure I say goodbye."

"Good." He claps me on the shoulder as he passes by me to head to his room in the basement.

I sit here for hours, just staring off into the distance. This is supposed to be the happiest time of my life. Tonight was supposed to be a celebration. It was, but it was also a huge reality check for me. I'm leaving her. I knew this day was coming, but it's just finally hit me. I can't call her and ask her to lunch. I won't get to see her every day in the flesh. I knew it was going to be hard, but this... this vise squeezing my chest. I didn't expect that.

I slept like hell. As soon as the sun began to peek through the blinds, I was up and moving. I downed two bottles of water, and some Tylenol, took a shower, and finished packing my shit. I'm grumpy as hell, and there is no need for me to try and figure out why. I know why.

Just after ten, the front door opens. I turn to see Reese walking in. "Hey, you." She smiles, and it's her happy smile.

"Hi. You hungry?"

"Starving, actually. I slept in a little."

Did he stay with her? I mean, of course he did, right? She's his girlfriend and she's Reese. She's a fucking knockout. Of course he stayed over. I clench my fists. "I'm ready when you are." I stand and shove my hands in my pockets.

"You driving?" she asks, tossing her keys in the air toward me.

I have to scramble to pull my hands from my pockets to catch them. "You know it." In two steps, I'm standing next to her. I place my hand on the small of her back and lead her out to her car. "I was thinking we could go to that little diner the next town over? Maybe hopefully try to avoid being recognized." I don't want to be recognized, but also, I don't want any of our friends or her boyfriend crashing our time together. This is it for a while, and I need my Reese time.

"Sure. I've got nothing going on today."

"You plan on coming home to visit your parents anytime soon?" Like before I leave for Indy.

"No. I start my new job next week. I might make it up there for a weekend visit. They talked about coming up here to stay with me for the weekend. Now that I have an extra room and all. I just need to get a bed for it."

"Are you excited about your new job?" I ask, pulling out onto the road.

"Yes. I already know everyone from my internship, so that's helpful, and I'm excited to make a difference. It might be a small one, but that's why I chose social work. It doesn't matter how small the difference, just that I'm making one."

"You're going to do great."

"Thanks. It's surreal that this is all happening. Look at us, college graduates about to be thrust into the world of adulting."

I laugh. "We've been adults since we left for college. Technically," I add.

"You know what I mean." She swats playfully at my shoulder. "What about you? Are you ready for everything headed your way? Fortune, fame, playing football with the big boys."

"I'm ready."

"So confident."

"I'm good at what I do." I shrug. "No shame in knowing that, or admitting it."

"I can see it now. Cooper Reeves, the guy I knew when. Soon you're going to be this big hot-shot professional football player. Women are going to be throwing panties at you left and right and you'll forget about all the little people."

She's teasing, but her words hit home. "It won't be like that."

"Sure," she says. I can hear the smile in her voice.

"I could never forget you, Reese. You know that, right?" I wish I wasn't driving so I could look her in the eye. In fact, glancing in my rearview mirror, I signal to move her car to the side of the road. I hit the button to engage the flashers and turn in my seat as much as the seat belt will allow and face her.

"What are you doing?" She raises her eyebrows in question.

"I need you to see me when I tell you this. I need you to look me in the eye and hear what I'm saying."

"O-kay," she replies hesitantly.

"Never. *Never* will I ever forget about you. You will never be anything less than my favorite person on this entire planet."

"Just earth?" she asks. There's a sparkle in her green eyes.

"Reese. No matter the time or distance, you will always be my best friend. I'm not going to be here, we're not going to get to see each other every day, and that's killing me. I need you to tell me that you understand that me leaving for my job, to follow my dream, that changes nothing between us."

She nods, and her eyes well with tears. "I'm really going to miss you, Coop." Her voice cracks on my name, and so does a little piece of my heart. I hate I'm the reason for her tears.

"You have no idea, Reese's Pieces. You have no idea." Turning back to face the road, I check my mirrors, turn off the hazards, and pull back onto the road once it's clear.

"When you get to Indy, I'm going to need you to send me some Defenders gear," she says after several long minutes of silence.

"You gonna watch my games?"

"What kind of crazy question is that?"

"How will Hunter feel about that?" I hate bringing him up during my time with her, but he's always there lingering in the back of my mind.

"Hunter knows how close we are. He's good with it. Trust me."

"You're going to come to a couple home games, right? And training camp?"

"Depends on my work scheduled for camp. That's during the week, so I doubt I can make it."

"There are weekend days for fans and family to attend."

"I'll just have to see what work is like. And as far as home games, not all of them, but I definitely want to see you out on that field in your Defenders gear. You'll know I'm there. I'll be cheering the loudest. I have to make sure I'm living up to my title of Cooper Reeves's number one fan."

"You've proven that to me hundreds of times. But I'm not going to turn down your cheers or you being in the stands. The first home game I need you there. Will you come?"

"Yes. I'll work it out, and I'll be there. I wouldn't miss it for the world," she says as we pull into the diner.

For the next two hours, we sit and talk and laugh, and we're just... us. Just Reese and Cooper. Two best friends enjoying time together. It's been too damn long since it's been like this, just the two of us. There is always someone tagging along, and I didn't realize how much I missed time with her. How much I miss her. Miss us.

Mentally I'm kicking myself in the ass for not doing more of this sooner. Now, I'm leaving. The new tenants are taking over the house tomorrow. We all have to be out of there today. My life is about to flip upside down, and she's not going to be there.

"You need help packing?" Reese asks when we pull back into the house.

"No. I'm all set. I do have a bag for you, though. You want to come in while I get it?"

"Sure." Together, we exit her car and head into the house. "I'll just wait here," she tells me. I nod and race up the stairs taking them two at a time.

My room is packed, the bed is stripped, and most of the boxes are already loaded into my Jeep. Grabbing the CU backpack off the bed, I throw it over my shoulder and head back downstairs.

"Here. This has all of your stuff from my room."

"Thanks." She takes the bag and places it on her shoulder. "Why does this feel like we're breaking up?" she asks. She's looking at the floor, and I see her wipe her eyes.

"Come here, Reese." I don't give her a chance not to. I step into her space and wrap my arms around her. "This is not a breakup. This is a see you soon. This is not goodbye. You are my best friend, and I don't care what I have to do, I will be seeing you. I'll spend every dime of my contract to make it happen."

"You can't do that. You have a plan, both professional and financial. You have to stick to it."

"There is nothing that could keep me away from you. You know that, right?"

"I do." She lifts her head, and her green eyes are swimming with tears. "I'm going to miss you so much."

My chest heaves as I fight back my emotions. "I'll call you when I get there. I'm leaving as soon as I round up the guys to say goodbye. Maybe you can come home, or I can come back for a weekend before I move?"

"We'll figure it out. You need to go be the incredible running back that you are. Show those Defenders that you're money well spent."

I smile at her. "You're going to have to drive up to help me decorate my new place."

"I can definitely make that happen. We both know you need my help."

I pull her back into my chest for one more tight hug. "Promise me if you need me, you call me day or night. I don't care if you need to tell me that you stubbed your toe. You call me. No matter what."

"Come on, Coop. You're going to have better things to worry about."

"Never anything more important than you." I realize as I say the words, that it's the truest statement I've ever spoken.

"I should go, so you can get on the road." She pulls away and wipes at her cheeks. "Bye, Coop."

"Bye, Reese." With my hands fisted at my sides, I watch her walk out the door. I rush to the window and stare after her until I can no longer see her car. I've never been in a relationship to experience heartbreak, but if it's anything like this, I don't plan on finding out anytime soon. There is one word that can describe this moment.

Agony.

REESE

It's hard to believe that it's been three weeks since everyone left. Work keeps me busy during the day, and at night, Hunter and I usually have dinner and hang out. The more time we spend together, the more he cements how great of a guy he is. He sent me flowers on my first day on the job as an official employee. He brings dinner and gives the best foot massages.

"So, what do you think?" Hunter asks from his seat beside me. It's Friday night, and we decided to order Chinese food and hang out. Our bellies are full, and we're lounging on the couch.

"I don't know. You don't think it's too soon?" I ask him.

"Reese, we've been dating for months. I really want you to meet my family."

"What if they hate me?" I'm not just being coy; I'm being real here. I've never really dated. Not a serious relationship like this one. I've never had to meet the family, and I'm stressing the hell out about it.

"They're going to love you just like I do."

I freeze. He cups my face in the palm of his hands. "I'm crazy about you, Reese Latham. You have to know that." His thumb gently slides back and forth across my cheek. "I'm in love with you. I know you're not there yet, but that doesn't change how I feel about you. Please, come home with me over the holiday weekend. Meet my family."

I nod. "Okay."

He leans in and presses his lips to mine. "Thank you."

I'm nervous as hell, but he's right. We've been dating for months, and it's not that I don't want to meet them. I'm just afraid they won't like me or think that Hunter can do better. I know that's just my nerves talking, and he'll be there with me every step of the way.

"What are we going to watch?" I ask, handing him the remote while covering a yawn.

"Tired?"

"Yes, but I want to watch a movie with you."

He kicks off his shoes and leans back on the couch, propping his feet up on the coffee table. "Come here." He pats his lap, and I waste no time pulling the blanket from the back of the couch and using him as my pillow. He pulls up an episode of *Good Girls* and hits Play. We've been binging this series, and only after a few episodes, I'm addicted.

"Reese." Hunter's whispered voice wakes me. I peel open my eyes and look up at him. "Let's get you to bed."

"What time is it?"

"Just after midnight. We both fell asleep."

I stand and stretch. "You can stay if you want." This would be the first time he's ever slept over. We've kissed, but that's pretty much as far as we've taken things.

"Reese, I think there's something that you should know."

"What's that?"

"This is embarrassing to talk about, and I should have told you by now, but it's never been brought up, and this, tonight, if I stay here, well, I think you need to know."

"Are you married? Seeing someone else?"

"No. Never. No, Reese. It's just you. But, I'm—" He rubs the back of his head with his hand. "There is no other way to say this than to just spit it out."

I nod. "Say it." I have no idea what he's about to say, but the words that come out of his mouth are not at all what I was expecting.

"I'm saving myself, you know, until marriage."

Holy shit. Is this real? Hunter is a good-looking guy. Tall, brown hair, blue eyes, lean and fit, how is it he's still a virgin? "You're a virgin?" I wince as the words leave my mouth. "I'm sorry," I rush to say. That was insensitive of me.

"No. It's okay. Yes, I am. My decision is a big part of who I am, and I know we've never talked about this. I should have brought it up sooner, but I didn't know how. I wasn't sure where we were headed. Now, here I am. I fell in love with you, and I needed you to know."

Wow. This is a big deal, and not at all what I was expecting. "Hunter, I'm not a virgin." I feel like we need to be transparent with one another. If he's hoping I too have been saving myself, he's going to be disappointed. Although my one encounter in high school isn't exactly much to write home about, the fact remains that I indeed have had sex. Just not in a very, very long time. I was holding out hope for me and Cooper, and well, we all know how that turned out. Then Hunter happened, and here we are.

"I don't expect you to be. I just needed you to know that I plan to wait. When I get married, I want my wife to know that she has every part of me. It's not a decision based on religious beliefs, but personal ones."

"Wow," I breathe.

"So... where does that leave us?"

"What do you mean?" I ask, confused.

"Is this a deal breaker for you? Sex?"

Is it? I've never really thought about it. It's not like I'm seasoned in the act myself. My prom-night blunder isn't exactly screaming sex goddess. "No," I answer him. "It's not a deal breaker for me. I respect your decision, and I'm glad that you told me."

"You're not breaking up with me?"

"No. However, I have wondered a few times why you were so patient with me not moving things forward."

"Trust me, Reese. You have been the test to my vow." His eyes heat as they rake over my body. "You don't know how many times I've imagined us together."

"Is your family going to hate me because I'm not… you know, pure?"

"No. I don't even know if they know about my vow. Like I said it has nothing to do with religious beliefs. It's just something I promised myself, and if you can't keep promises made to yourself, what kind of man are you?"

I take a seat back on the couch and curl up under the blanket. "What made you decide?"

"When I was ten, my older brother Jacob was sixteen. I heard him and his girlfriend at the time in his room one night. He was trying to break up with her; she'd gotten clingy, at least that's what he told her. She started to cry and told him that she was pregnant. The room got quiet, and when my brother spoke again, I could hear the fear in his voice. I slipped back into my room and kept my mouth shut. Fast-forward a few weeks, and they told her parents and mine. They were disappointed because they were so young, but taking it one day at a time. We're a family, and we'll get through this. I remember those were my mother's words the day that she found out. My father, he just nodded his agreement. They were on board to help any way that they could."

"They sound great. Your parents." Makes me less fearful to meet them next week.

"Yeah, they really are," he says, taking a seat next to me on the couch. "Anyway, they went to the doctor for her first visit, and there was no baby. Tracy, his girlfriend, said she must have lost it. The doctor told her that's not how it happens. Anyway, long story short, she lied. She wasn't pregnant. She made it all up to keep Jacob from breaking up with her."

"That's terrible. How could anyone do that?"

"I don't know. What I do know is that I never want to be in that position. That day, the way my brother mourned the loss of a child he had grown to love the idea of, the one that didn't exist, I vowed to wait. I want to know that when I'm being told that I'm going to be a father, that it's the real deal. I want to know that I love that woman without a shadow of a doubt, and creating a family with her will be an honor. So, yeah, that's what made my decision for me."

"And your brother?"

"He's married. No kids yet. He didn't have sex again until his wedding night. Hell…" He rakes his hands over his face. "Maybe it's just me wanting to be like my big brother, but really it's to avoid going through what he went through."

"Hey." I reach out and place my hand on his leg. "I respect your choices, Hunter. Thank you for explaining them to me when you didn't have to."

"I did have to. I've never felt like this for anyone. I've felt attraction, have been tempted, but I've never had my heart feel like it's melting just by hearing a name or seeing you walk into a room. I'm in love with you, Reese."

I can't say it back. I'm not there. I care about him, but I'm not in love with him. I don't know if my heart will ever love again. I don't know if I'm capable of giving it to someone else. I'm not sure that I was able to gather all of the pieces when they shattered that night in Cooper's room. What I do know is that Hunter is a great guy, even more than I ever imagined, and I enjoy spending time with him. He's my boyfriend, and just with this conversation, I already feel closer to him. All we can do is take it one day at a time and see where it leads us. Tossing off the cover, I stand from the couch and hold out my hand. "Come on. Let's go to bed." The smile he gives me warms me all over. He really thought I would kick him to the curb for saving himself for his future wife? Hunter Applegate is a unicorn in a sexy man's body.

Without question, he takes my hand. I turn off the lights and lead him down the hall to my bedroom. "I'm going to change," I tell him as I grab some clothes to sleep in. "I have some things of Cooper's still here, if you want to change into something else." I cringe as I say it. It sounds bad, offering your boyfriend another man's clothes to sleep in. It sounds bad, but Cooper and I are just friends. He knows that, and my heart remembers it. Painfully so.

"I can just strip down to my underwear, unless that would make you uncomfortable?"

"No. Cooper did that more often than not too. I'll be right back." I rush out of my room and to the bathroom, quickly slipping inside. I need to stop bringing Cooper up so often. I miss him like crazy, that has to be why I can't shut up about him tonight. Quickly, I change and toss my dirty clothes into the hamper, and head back to my room. When I push open the door, Hunter is standing next to the bed in a pair of black boxer briefs that fit him like a second skin. I rake my eyes over his body for the first time. I skim over his boxers and then back again when my mind registers that he's hard.

"Reese," he groans. "This is going to be hard enough as it is. No pun intended. I need you to not look at me like that."

"Like what?" I ask, licking my lips.

"That. You can't do that. You can't lick those soft as hell kissable lips while staring at my dick. This was a bad idea. I should just go home." He turns to grab his clothes, and I rush toward him to stop him.

"No. We can do this, Hunter. I'm sorry. I know your vow and won't test it. I promise."

"Not possible," he mutters under his breath.

"Let's just go to bed." I move to climb under the covers and scoot over, making room for him. He turns off the light and I feel the bed dip. He slides under the covers, and the only sound is our breathing. This takes me back to all the nights Coop and I slept in the same bed. He used to let me use him as my pillow. I miss him so much, but there is a man, a very good-looking, honorable, kind man sharing my bed. A man who's not my best friend; he's my boyfriend. I should be able to use him as my pillow.

I whisper his name into the darkness, "Hunter."

"Yeah."

"Is cuddling against the rules?"

"No, Reese. Cuddling is definitely not against the rules. Come here." I feel the blanket lift and move over to rest my head on his chest. He wraps his arms around me and sighs. "I could get used to this."

"Yeah," I agree. Not because I could get used to it. I was used to it. Just not with him. Only with Cooper.

I've been lying here awake for I don't know how long. Hunter has his front to my back and is sleeping peacefully. I can't find it in myself to move, partly because I feel guilty. When I woke up, I thought he was Cooper. Just for a fleeting moment… until last night came crashing back to me. I'm terrible, but not because I thought it was Cooper. That's the only guy I've slept in the same bed with, that's a normal reaction. No, the horrible part is, for a split second, a tiny minute slither of time, I wanted it to be Cooper. That's why I'm going to hell. That's why I'm lying still in Hunter's arms, not disturbing him, even though my bladder is screaming for relief.

"Morning." Hunter's groggy voice greets me.

"Morning. I'll be right back." I wiggle out of his arms and slide out of bed.

"Where are you going, Reese?" he asks, his voice more alert.

"I have to pee," I call out as I rush to the bathroom. I take care of business, brush my teeth, and leave out one of the extra toothbrushes I get from the dentist on the sink for Hunter to use. When I open the bathroom door, he's standing there. "Hey, there's a toothbrush on the counter for you.'"

"Thank you." He bends to kiss my cheek and slides past me and closes the bathroom door.

Not really knowing what to do with myself, I head back to my bedroom. It's not even seven in the morning. It's way too early to be awake on a Saturday. I climb back in bed, and pull the covers up to my chin to ward off the chill of the air conditioning. Not two minutes later, Hunter is sliding in next to me. He pulls me into his arms and presses his lips against mine.

"I think I could get used to this."

"Kisses in the morning."

"Well, that too. I was meaning you. Waking up with you." He kisses me again.

"You think so? I mean, you didn't get a whiff of my morning breath," I tease.

"What are we doing today?" he asks, avoiding my question.

"I was thinking about a couple of more hours of sleep."

"Yeah?" he asks, sliding his hand over my hip. We're on our sides facing each other. "Sleep is what you want?" he says, his voice husky.

"Umm… were you not here for last night's conversation?" I ask.

"I said I wasn't having sex until I was married, not that I wasn't ever going to touch a woman's body," he explains as his hand slides under my shirt. The feel of his warm skin on my back causes a shiver to race up my spine.

I mimic him and slide my hand over his chest. "Who would have known you were hiding all of this underneath your clothes," I say teasingly. But for real, he's toned. Not that I thought he wasn't in shape, but I guess he never talks about working out or anything, so I just didn't know what to expect.

His reply is to press his lips against mine. All talking ceases as we explore one another. This is a new concept for me. I'm not exactly the most experienced, and I admit, it's nice to know that sex isn't the end game with us. That we're just learning each other and taking our time. There's no pressure. I'm not ready to take that step with anyone. Not right now. That ship sailed a few months ago when pieces of my heart were thrown overboard.

"I need to go home and shower," Hunter says a few hours later. We're sitting on my couch eating cereal. "What do you want to do today?"

"I was thinking about going to the outlet malls. I need some new clothes."

He points to my room. "You mean all the clothes that are stuffed into your closet aren't enough?" He grins, letting me know he's teasing.

"Fine, I want new clothes."

He chuckles. "I'll go with you. Why don't you get ready, then we'll swing by my place so I can shower and then we'll go?"

"You want to go shopping with me?"

"Sure, why not?"

"I don't know. I mean, the only guy that's ever done that is Coop."

"Well, now you can add me to the list of guys who want to see you happy." Something passes in his eyes, but it's gone before I can define it.

My phone rings, and Hunter reaches out for it where it sits on the table and hands it to me. Cooper's smiling face greets me. I rush to hit the answer button. "Hey, you," I greet him.

"It's so damn good to hear your voice."

I smile. "You just talked to me, what, two days ago?"

"Two days too long. How are you?"

"Good. Hunter and I are getting ready to go shopping," I tell him, smiling at Hunter.

"How'd you con him into that?"

"I didn't. He volunteered." He's quiet so I change the subject. "How's the new condo?"

"Good. I need some furniture still, but it works. That's actually why I'm calling. I'm having some guys from the team over on The Fourth. I was hoping you could come up? Dustin is coming, and Nix and Tessa are going to try to make it as well. I know she'd love to see you."

"Aw, really? I'm sorry. I already have plans."

"Plans? Cancel them."

Oh, how I wish he would have called twenty-four hours sooner. "I'm going with Hunter to his parents' house in Florida."

"You're meeting the parents?" he asks.

"Yes." I laugh nervously. *I am, and I was good with it, but now I want to come and see you instead.*

"Reese, I miss you."

"I know. It's been too long. I'll come visit before training camp starts."

"That's like three weeks from now."

"Okay."

"It's been months since I've seen you, Reese." I can hear the sadness in his voice.

"It's been three weeks, Coop."

"Three weeks that feels like three years."

"I thought you said months?" I laugh.

"With each minute, the time grows farther away."

"Stop it. You're too much. I'll be there to visit the week before training camp. How's that?"

"Fine," he grumbles. "Just you?"

"What do you mean?"

"Are you bringing him with you?"

"I don't know."

"I prefer you didn't. I need my Reese time."

"I'll see what I can do."

"I miss you, Reese."

"Me too," I say. I feel uncomfortable telling him that I miss him in front of my boyfriend. I shouldn't, but my heart still remembers, and that causes me guilt. I miss my best friend, but I also miss him, and the thought of what I hoped we would one day be.

"Talk to you soon."

"Bye, Coop."

"Everything okay?" Hunter asks.

"Oh, yeah, it's fine. He's having a few people over to his new condo and wanted me to come. Tessa is going to be there."

"Oh." The nice guy in him wants to tell me it's okay. I can see it on his face.

"We have plans. There will be other get-togethers." His shoulders visibly relax.

"Good. Go get ready so we can go."

He grabs his phone and begins to scroll, completely unaware of the fact that my heart is racing and feels as though my chest might explode. He doesn't know that my palms are sweaty or that when I stand from my place on the couch, that my knees are weak. I want to go see Cooper. It took everything in me to tell him no. I miss him something fierce. I know I did the right thing, but my heart, well, my heart just doesn't understand.

Chapter 23

COOPER

My new condo has food covering every surface in the kitchen, and it's filled with bodies. Some of the guys from my new team, Dustin and a girl he's been dating, as well as Nixon and Tessa are here. It's good to see my friends, but they're not Reese.

I fucking miss her. More than I ever thought that I would. I can't tell you how many times throughout the day I want to call her just to tell her what I did or show her something I bought for the condo. Then I remember that she's at work. And at night, when we FaceTime, sometimes he's there. I hate it. No, I fucking loathe it, but there is nothing I can do about it. She has to live her life, like I'm living mine. If you call what I'm doing living.

My parents helped me move into my condo that's just a few miles from the stadium. I've had countless meetings with my agent and financial planners and coaching staff. It's not that I'm not staying busy. I am. It's just that everything in my life, circles back around to Reese. Something she would find funny or food she would love, or a story that I need to tell her. I don't know how to stop it. I don't know how to not need her in every facet of my life.

"Nice place," Nixon says, joining me on the patio. "Have you talked to her?"

I pretend I don't know who he's talking about, and we both know I'm full of shit. "Who?"

"You're sulking. This is your party and you're sulking."

"I'm not sulking."

"You are. What happened? Did the two of you have a fight?"

"Like you don't already know. I know she and Tessa still talk every day."

"Maybe." He grins behind the Solo cup that he brings to his lips. "But I want to hear it from you."

"She's meeting the parents," I say sarcastically.

He nods. "And you're sulking."

"No, I'm not."

"And now we sound like toddlers." He laughs.

"I'm just disappointed. I haven't seen her other than through the screen of my phone in a month. That's a long damn time when I'm used to laying my eyes on her every day."

"Did you tell her that?"

"What's with all the questions? You're a Badger now, so you gotta take that shit to heart?"

"Fuck you." His words have no heat behind them. "I refuse to apologize for trying to help you see that you fucked up."

"What?" I whip my head around to look at him. "How did I fuck up? I didn't tell her to go and get a boyfriend and meet his parents."

"No, you didn't. But you did tell her that you were better off as friends."

"We are friends," I say through gritted teeth.

"All right." He holds his hands up in the air in defeat. "So, you ready for training camp?" he asks.

"Yeah, you?"

"Yes and no. I'm not looking forward to being away from Tessa that long, but that's the career we chose. She's supportive and knows that there's no one in my life for me but her."

"Yeah? When's the big day?"

"She's planning it. Probably next spring, after the season ends."

"You making Tess do all the work?"

"I want it to be everything she's ever dreamed of. I don't care when, where, or how. I just want her to be my wife."

"Look at you, all sappy and shit," I say, moving to grab another beer out of the fridge.

"Takes one to know one."

I roll my eyes. He's never going to give up on this crusade he's been on for years that Reese and I are more. He just doesn't understand our connection. Lifelong friends, and then to be torn apart. Anyone would be saddened by that.

"Hey." Tessa comes into the kitchen and gives me a hug before Nixon pulls her into his arms. "I just talked to Reese. She said she texted you but didn't get an answer."

Setting my beer on the counter, I pat down my pockets to find my phone. I turn to look and see it on the counter. Picking it up, sure enough, I have a missed text from Reese. "I don't know how I missed it," I tell her, swiping my finger across the screen.

"Could be that when I found you in here all alone, you looked like your mind was a thousand miles away," Nixon comments.

Not a thousand. Only about two hundred, give or take. I block him out and look at the message.

Reese: Hey. Sorry I can't be there today. I miss you.

She misses me. The last two times I've spoken to her, he's been there, and all I got was a "me too." It's not the same as hearing her sweet voice tell me, but I'll take it.

Me: I miss you too. I can't wait to see you.

Reese: Tessa tracked you down I see.

Me: Yeah. Sorry, my phone was on the counter and I didn't hear it.

Reese: How's the party?

Me: Not the same without you. How about yours? Meet the parents yet?

Reese: Yes, actually, and they're very nice.

Me: We still on for your visit in a couple of weeks?

Reese: Definitely.

Me: You coming alone?

Reese: That's the plan.

Me: Good.

Reese: I gotta go. We're up for cornhole. I can't wait to see you!

Gazing out the window, I see one of the guys on the team and his wife, or fiancée. Though I think they're married. Anyway, the two of them are playing cornhole with Dustin and his date. I hate that she's not here. She should be playing cornhole in my yard. Not his. These next two and a half weeks are going to drag by. I knew I was going to miss her, but I never knew it would feel like this. Like there is a vise around my chest, squeezing painfully. It's as if a piece of myself is missing, and I don't for the life of me know how to get it back.

Gripping my phone in my hands, I want to call her. To hear her voice. See her smile. But she's with him. The boyfriend, who seems like a decent guy, but I'm not there to make sure he treats her right. This is supposed to be an epic time for me. I'm a fucking professional football player. My first year in the league. This is what I've always wanted, but somehow, without Reese here with me, it just doesn't feel as exciting as I thought it would be.

Four days. Four more days until I get to see Reese. I'm going to hug the hell out of her, so I should probably warn her. It's been too damn long. As the days drag by, I get even more excited. I don't know how I've survived this long without seeing her. I've been surviving on phone calls, video chats, and text messages. That's not enough. Not for me.

"Cooper, are you even listening to me?" my agent, Jarvis, asks.

I've been listening to him for the last hour. We've been over all of this hundreds of times. "Yeah," I say when we both know I'm obviously not.

"No, you aren't. Do I have your attention now? I don't want to have to say this a million times."

"Yes. I'm listening." I roll my eyes even though he can't see me. Jarvis is notorious for repeating himself. I think the guy just likes to hear himself talk. That aside, he's a great agent and works his ass off. No way would I have received the contract that I did without him.

"As I was saying, the Defenders coaching staff has decided to bring all the rookies in sooner than usual. You have to report to camp tomorrow."

"What?" Now he really has my attention. "No. It was supposed to be Monday." This is not happening. I'm so close to seeing her. Just four short days.

"It was, but things have changed. They want some time to acclimate the rookies to the stadium and go through some basic PR information before camp starts."

"But we're already reporting early." Why do things keep happening to keep me away from her?

"Well, now you report earlier," he replies, his tone flat.

"Is there any way to get out of this?" I can't believe those words just came out of my mouth. This is my dream, all I've ever wanted, but here I sit on my couch, practically begging my agent to push it all back a week so I can spend some long-overdue time with my best friend.

"No, Cooper. There is no getting out of this," he says, exasperated.

"Okay." I'm defeated. For some fucking reason, the universe is working against me. Now, it's going to be August before I can see her. She's coming down for family day, but that's going to be with our parents, and all the other friends and family. I just want a Reese day. Just the two of us.

"You have to report to the stadium at seven in the morning."

Son of a bitch. "Yeah, okay. I'll be there."

"I'm working on some endorsement deals, but nothing concrete at the moment. I'll keep you posted as soon as I have more details."

"Thanks, Jarvis."

"See you tomorrow."

"You're going to be there?" I ask, surprised.

"Damnit, Cooper, did you hear anything I just told you? Never mind. Don't answer that. I'll email it over to you, so you have it to reference. Let me know if you have any questions and don't be late." With that, he ends the call.

"Fuck!" I scream and toss my phone onto the couch. Bending over, I rest my elbows on my knees and dig my fingers into my hair. I can't fucking believe this. My throat feels tight at the thought of calling her and telling her that I won't be here. I hate that I'm going to miss out on my time with her.

This fucking blows.

Knowing I need to call her and tell her so that I can pack, I reach for my phone and send her a text.

> **Me:** Hey, change of plans. Text me when you get home and we can video chat.

Her reply is immediate.

> **Reese:** I'm home now. I had an offsite meeting and then they told me to go home for the day.

Here goes nothing. I hit her contact and wait for the video call to connect. "Hey, Co—Oh no, what's wrong?" she asks when she sees the expression on my face.

"I have some bad news." Fucking terrible, tragic news. Sure, I'm being dramatic, but that's how much I miss her.

"What? Is it your parents? My parents?"

"No. Nothing like that," I reassure her. "I just talked to my agent."

"Okay?" Her brow furrows, and I know she's trying to figure out where I'm going with this.

"I have to report to training camp early." I grimace when I say the words because they hurt. Not physically, but my heart, well, it misses my best friend.

"Oh." Her face falls, her beautiful smile disappearing. "So that means?"

"That I won't be home this weekend. I have to report tomorrow. I just got off the phone with my agent. Something about PR training for the rookies."

"I understand," she says, but I can tell she's disappointed too.

I nod. My throat is tight with the emotions not seeing her evokes in me. I was really looking forward to this trip. "I'm sorry." I push the words past my lips.

"It's okay. This is your job, Coop. There will be other weekends."

"I wanted to see you." I need to see her to keep my sanity. Missing her is all I can think about.

"I know. I wanted to see you too." She tries to smile, but it doesn't reach her eyes. She might be able to pull that shit with Hunter. Not with me.

"Don't. Don't pretend this doesn't suck."

She chuckles softly. "Fine. It sucks. But this is how things are going to be from now on. You have a career that is going to pull you away more often than not. You knew that. *We* knew that. We knew this was how it was going to be."

"No." I shake my head. "I didn't know this is how it was going to be. I didn't—" I stop, debating on what to say, and decide to just throw it out there. She's my best fucking friend, and I can tell her anything. "I didn't know I would miss you this much. I mean, I knew I would miss you, but this…" I rub my chest, over my heart. "It's more than I thought, Reese."

"So, it's not just me?"

"No. It's not just you."

"Okay. Well, I guess family day of training camp is when I'll see you."

"That's like three more weeks." I'm whining and don't give a fuck.

"I know." Her reply is soft, and sadness hangs in her voice.

"I have to be on during camp. I need to focus, and you've always been good at helping me do that."

"Well then, we better make tonight count. We're going to both order pizza, the same kind, and do you have a TV and Netflix at this fancy new pad of yours?" she teases.

"That's about it, but yeah."

"Good. Then grab your cell phone charger; it's going to be a long night."

"What?" Is she saying what I think she is?

"You and me, we're hanging out tonight. Dinner and a movie. It's the next best thing to being there."

"Don't you have plans with Hunter?" I try hard not to grimace when I say his name.

"I'm texting him now and telling him I have to cancel. Tonight, it's just you and me, Coop."

I should feel like a dick that she's canceling on her boyfriend for me, but I can't seem to find it in me to care. I want this time with her. No, I need this time with her. "Deal."

"I'm going to take a shower and change into some other clothes, and order my pizza. Call you back in thirty minutes?"

Is it wrong that I almost ask her to take me with her? "Sure. Thirty minutes," I say instead. Doesn't matter, though. Images of her naked body are already front and center in my mind. Who am I kidding? That's pretty much where they stay. And the distance, well, that doesn't help matters any.

"Deal. Get ready. I'm picking a chic flick," she teases.

"We could watch paint dry and I'd be good with it. Now, go get ready so we can get to it."

She smiles, waves, and ends the call. While it's not her here where my arms can wrap around her in a hug, she's right. This is the next best thing. I'll take what I can get when it comes to Reese.

REESE

This year is flying by. It seems like graduation was just last week. How it's already Thanksgiving, I have no idea. The summer seemed to drag on, but then work got busier and busier as more cases were assigned to me, and bam, it's already November. Hunter and I are going to my parents' for Thanksgiving, and it's going to be weird not having Cooper and his family there. They won't even be next door. The Defenders play today, so instead of him sitting at the table with us, we're going to be watching him on TV. It's surreal to think that not only us, but millions of people will be watching him. I'm so proud of him and all the hard work he's put in to get to this place in his life.

Speaking of Cooper. My phone rings. I glance over at Hunter and show him the screen before standing from the couch and disappearing down the hall to my childhood room. "Hey," I greet him.

"Reese." His tone is full of relief.

"Coop? What's wrong?"

"I wish you and your parents would have let me fly you out here."

"Cooper, we've been over this. You can't spend your money on flying us to see you every single game."

"It's my money. I can do what I want with it," he grumbles.

"Invest and save. Think about your future."

"All I can think about is how long it's been since I've seen you." He heaves a heavy sigh into the phone.

He's not the only one. I went to the family day at training camp with his parents and mine. I got a few hugs and "how have you beens," but there was so much chaos that we didn't really get to chat. I haven't seen him since. Not in person. Video chats, text messages, and phone calls sum up the relationship I have with my best friend.

"We knew it would be like this," I remind him. I've been saying that a lot lately. I think it's a reminder to both of us. I did know, and I knew it would be hard, but some days it's harder than others.

"Yeah," he agrees, but his one-word reply isn't convincing.

"What are you doing calling me anyway? Don't you play in like an hour?" I look around my room until my eyes land on an alarm clock. Sure enough, game time for the Defenders is less than an hour.

"Are you going to be watching?"

"Of course, I am. What kind of question is that? We're all watching. Me, Mom, Dad, and Hunter. We just finished dinner and are waiting for when the game starts to eat dessert."

"Good."

"Did you really think I wouldn't watch you? You know I watch all of your games."

"Not all of them," he mutters under his breath.

"One time, Cooper Reeves. That was one time and I recorded it. I can't help it that Hunter's parents decided to drop in on Thursday night."

"Yeah." Again with the one-word answers that are not convincing.

"Good luck today, Coop."

"Thanks, Reese's Pieces. I'll call you after."

"You don't have to. I know your parents are there and you'll be celebrating a win."

"You think we're going to win?"

"You're on fire, Coop."

"I spend a lot of time on the field, staying after practice, things like that."

"Why? Is your coach suggesting you do that?"

"No. Keeps my mind busy."

"Well, don't overdo it. Don't make me come up there and kick your ass."

"In that case, I'm going to sleep on the field. When can you be there? I'll fly home tomorrow."

"I was kidding."

"Just my luck," he teases.

"Stop. Go do your thing, Reeves. I'll be sitting on the couch cheering you on."

"I needed to hear that. I'll call you after."

I don't bother to tell him not to again. Cooper has a mind of his own. "Sounds good."

The call ends, and I take a minute to myself. My heart still aches for him, but with each passing day, I also fall a little more for Hunter. He's incredible. He never questions my relationship with Cooper, not that he needs to. We're just friends, and he accepts that. He's supportive of my work, and we have fun together. He's told me he loves me so many times I've lost count, and if I take the time to look past Cooper and what I thought would be our future, I can admit that I love him too. It's not the all-consuming love that I have for Cooper. I'm not sure I'll ever be able to love that deeply ever again. However, I do care for him, love him in a different way.

Opening my bedroom door, I run into Hunter. "Hey," I say, my hands resting on his chest. His arms wrap around my waist.

"Everything all right?"

"Yes. Cooper was just saying Happy Thanksgiving."

He nods. "Your mom is slicing up pie." He grins.

"I swear you and my mother's apple pie."

"What? It's the best I've ever had."

"I'm going to tell your mother you said that."

"Go ahead. She already knows." He leans in and presses a soft kiss to my lips. "Come on, you. You're going to miss the game."

I'm not. We still have plenty of time, but I pull out of his embrace and lace my fingers through his, allowing him to guide me back out to the living room. Mom already has four pie plates of her homemade apple pie sitting on a tray on the coffee table.

"Dig in," she says, handing Dad a plate and then one to Hunter.

The four of us get settled and enjoy our pie while we wait for the game to start. When Cooper takes the field, my eyes are glued to the screen. Luckily, my love for the sport hides the fact that it's Cooper who holds my attention. Will it ever not be like this? Will there ever be a time I'll just say, "Oh, there's my best friend?" Will my heart ever stop aching for him?

I guess only time will tell.

"I'm glad we decided to spend the night instead of driving home," I tell Hunter. We've just got back to our hotel room.

"It's what, an hour and a half? We could have done it, but I'll never pass up a chance to stay in a hotel with you." He wags his eyebrows. He's a flirt, and while sex is off the table, there is lots of touching and kissing and more kissing.

"I know, but I knew it would be a long day after staying for the game and hello, turkey coma," I say, rubbing my belly that's way too full. "I ate way too much."

"You and me both. And to think we have another dinner on Sunday."

"Does your mom and dad go all-out like mine?"

"Yep. And my grandparents and aunts and uncles and cousins… everyone will be there."

"Really? You didn't tell me that."

"Why? Is that a problem? You've met a lot of them already."

"I know, but a little warning would have been nice."

"I'm sorry." He's quick to say. "Next time I'll give you lots of warning."

"Thank you." I smile sweetly, exaggerating it and making him laugh. "I'm going to go change." I grab my clothes and disappear into the bathroom. I don't know why, but I still don't change in front of him.

He's seen me, obviously, but I just… don't do it. He's never mentioned it, and honestly, I've never really thought about how it might appear to be odd until this very moment.

Shaking out of my thoughts, I wash my face, brush my teeth, and change into my pajamas. We could have stayed at my parents'—they offered—but it feels weird sleeping in the same bed as Hunter under my parents' roof. So, yeah, we opted for a hotel.

Opening the bathroom door, I see Hunter sitting on the edge of the bed with a phone pressed to his ear. My phone. He turns to look at me when he hears the door. "Hey, she just came out. Here she is." He stands and walks toward me, handing me the phone. "It's Cooper." He leans in and kisses me. "Be right back."

"Okay." I nod and place the phone to my ear. "Hey, Coop."

"Did he have to let me hear him kissing you?" he says hotly.

"I'm good. Thanks for asking," I bite back. "Good game."

"Thanks." He exhales loudly. "I'm sorry. It's still hard for me to get used to the two of you."

"It's been almost a year, Cooper." Sure, in only about nine months or so in reality, but close enough to a year that Cooper should be thoroughly desensitized to the fact that I have a boyfriend who, yes, kisses me. The horror!

He's quiet on the other end of the line, and I hate it. I hate there seems to be this divide between us, and for the life of me, I don't know how to fix it. I guess the theory that nothing ever stays the same is true. I never thought there would be a day there was silence between Cooper and me, yet here we are.

"You had a good game," I finally say to break the awkward silence.

"I knew you were watching."

Woah. That's… not what I expected him to say. "I always watch your games."

"Yeah. I know you do, Reese. It motivates me to play better."

"Really? Well, you can tell your coach I said you're welcome," I tease, trying to lighten things up between us.

"Hey." Hunter's whispered voice greets me. "I'm going to go grab some ice. You need anything?" He holds up the empty ice bucket.

"Yes. Some Reese's Pieces." I smile, and he returns his.

"Got it." He leans in and kisses me, grabs the hotel key, and walks out of the room.

"Where are you?"

"A hotel."

"A hotel?" he repeats, choking on the words. "I thought you were at your parents' place?"

"We were, but we left after the game, and we're staying here tonight and driving back in the morning."

"You're staying in a hotel with him?" he asks again, repeating what I just said.

"Yes."

He mutters something that I can't understand. "I need to go," he says abruptly.

"O-kay."

"I just wanted to talk to you. Tell you Happy Thanksgiving. I forgot to do that earlier."

"Happy Thanksgiving, Coop."

"I miss you, Reese."

"I know. I miss you too."

"I-I gotta go. I'll talk to you soon," he says, and the line goes dead before I even have the chance to say goodbye. Before I can think too much about his change in demeanor, the door to our room opens, and Hunter comes in carrying a bucket full of ice, a couple bottles of root beer, a bottle of water, and several packages of candy from the vending machine. Among them a pack of Reese's Pieces. My heart stutters in my chest. This is what Cooper would be doing if he were here with me. The only difference is that he never would have had to ask what I wanted. He would have just known.

Chapter 25

COOPER

This week's game is a home game, and my family will be here. Reese will be here. Finally, I get to wrap my arms around her. This has been the longest six months of my life. The longest. I talked to her last night, and she said that she and Hunter were riding up with her parents to watch the game. I hate that he's coming with her. However, I'm not going to let that stop me from hugging the shit out of my best friend. Boyfriend be damned. It's going to happen.

This week is also Christmas. Well, the week before but close enough. If we win today, we play next week in the playoffs. I'm glad to be able to spend a few days with my parents. They're staying until Tuesday. Reese and her parents and the boyfriend are all driving back to her parents' place tonight. I'm going to get a few hours with her at best, but at this point, I'm going to take what I can get and cherish every fucking second. Fuck, I've missed her. I had no idea it would be this bad.

At least we have the early timeslot today. We're all going to dinner after. My parents are staying with me, and I offered the other spare room to Garrett and Eve. I figured Reese could room with me like old times, but then she threw Hunter into the mix. He can take the couch as far as I'm concerned. Of course, I kept that to myself. I had to bite my tongue when she told me they were heading back home tonight. Apparently, all four of them have to work tomorrow. I get it, but I don't like it. My phone vibrates, pulling me out of my thoughts. Grabbing it from the bench beside me, I see a message from Reese.

> **Reese:** Hey! Just got to the stadium. Can't wait to see you out there.

> **Me:** I'm glad you're here.

> **Reese:** Aw, are you missing me, Reeves?

> **Me:** Yes.

More than you know.

The distance my career has put between us weighs heavily on me. So much, in fact, it has me wondering if pushing her away was the right move. I thought it was what was best for her, but then if I hadn't, she would be here with me. I would have made certain she was by my side. I let my mind wander back to that night in my room. She wanted me. Fuck, I wanted her, but I stopped us. I was scared to death it would ruin our friendship. I had no idea the divide, or hell, even the void I would feel without her every day. It's not something I was prepared for. It's not something I know how to handle. I keep thinking that I need to get some time with her in person. Sure, I love our nights we hang out and watch the same movie, and eat the same food, but it's not the same thing. I just need some time with my best friend for everything to feel right. To feel normal again.

> **Reese:** I missed you too, Cooper.

Her reply has my chest inflating. Reese has always been able to make me feel as though I'm ten feet tall. Knowing she's here, not just at home on the couch, that gives me drive. It motivates me to kick some ass and takes some names. It's always been like that, though. If she's here in the crowd, my game is on point. My missing piece is in the stands, and I'm not about to disappoint her. The agony of not seeing her, not feeling that connection we've always shared, loosens its grip around my heart. Today, I get to lay my eyes on her in the flesh. But first, I need to win this game.

"Reeves!" Coach Freeland calls after me as I'm jogging to the locker room. I stop to look over my shoulder, and he's waving off a reporter and headed my way. When he reaches me, he snakes his arm around my neck and pulls me into him. "Damn fine playing out there, son. Six touchdowns! I don't know what got into you, but keep it coming." He releases me and jogs off down the hall toward the locker room.

I smile after him. I was on fire tonight. My hands like glue every time the ball came my way. With every catch, after every play, I would look up in the stands where I knew she was sitting. I couldn't always make her out in the crowd with no time to sit and stare up in the stands, but I knew she was there. I could feel her. It makes me sound crazy as fuck, but it's the truth. It's like she was out there on that field with me today.

My teammates rush past me, clapping me on the back, and I join in the masses, putting one foot in front of the other. I need to shower and get the hell out of here.

Twenty minutes later, after a speech from Coach, and the fastest shower ever, I've got my bag over my shoulder as I hustle to my Jeep. I'm meeting everyone at the hotel just down from my house. I made reservations for a private dining room. I didn't want to waste time cooking or dealing with fans when all I want to do is spend time with my family. Don't get me wrong, I'm grateful for my fans, but tonight, I just need to not be Cooper Reeves the running back for the Defenders. I just want to be Cooper.

The drive to the hotel ends up taking twice as long with all of the game-day traffic. I would have thought it would have been cleared out by now, but no such luck. Grabbing my phone, and making sure I have my wallet, I lock my truck and rush inside. A few people call out to me. I give them a wave and otherwise keep my attention on the hostess, who is leading me back to the private dining room.

"What would you like to drink?" she asks me as we step into the room.

"Water is fine, thank you," I say without looking at her. No, my eyes are locked on Reese. My parents stand and greet me with hugs.

"I've missed you so much," Mom says, wiping her eyes.

"Mom, it's no different than college."

"I missed you then too." She smiles through her tears.

They take a step back as Garrett and Eve stand, waiting to greet me.

Agony | 215

Garrett shakes my hand, and like my mother, Eve hugs me tightly. "Good game, Cooper."

"Thanks." I kiss her cheek and step out of her hold. My eyes find Reese as she slowly stands from the table and walks toward me. I keep my feet planted on the floor, afraid my knees that are weak from the sight of her might give out on me. When she's within reaching distance, I snake my arm around her waist and pull her into my chest. Both of my arms wrap around her like a vise, and I feel emotion clog my throat. It's been too fucking long since I've held her. I bury my face in her neck and breathe her in. The scent of her favorite perfume invades my senses.

My Reese.

"I fucking missed you," I say, not bothering to lower my voice. I don't give a fuck who hears me, not even her boyfriend.

She pulls back and wipes at her eyes. "I missed you too." She steps back out of my hold and turns to look over her shoulder. "You remember, Hunter," she says as he stands and walks toward us. He stops behind her, placing one hand on her waist and the other reaches out to shake my hand.

"Good to see you again, Cooper."

"Yeah, you too." I have to force the words as I accept his handshake. I watch him closely as I squeeze with everything that I have. His eyes widen, but other than that, nothing. When I drop his hand, he places it on her waist as well. My eyes are glued to how intimately he holds her. I fucking hate it. I hate that he's here. I hate that she's his.

"Let's sit," Mom suggests. She loops her arm through mine and leads me to the table.

I pull her chair out for her and take the one next to her, Dad sits on my other side. Across the table, Reese is in front of me. Hunter is next to her. I watch as he leans in and kisses her cheek before whispering in her ear. I reach for my glass of water for something to do. I avert my gaze, staring down at my plate. I can't watch this. I can't watch them together.

Mom and Dad start talking about the game, with Garrett and Eve chiming in. I answer their questions and do my best to join the conversation without looking at Reese and Hunter. When she giggles, I look up to find him smiling at her. The lovesick look on his face should make me happy that she found someone who seems to worship her.

Instead, it does nothing but piss me off. I've waited for this day for months. Months. And he's monopolizing all of her time. This was supposed to be my time with her. I'm aware that my inner self sounds like a five-year-old child throwing a fit, but dammit, I fucking miss her.

All through dinner, he's touching her. His arm on the back of her chair, pushing her hair out of her eyes, wiping the corner of her mouth. He's attentive, and in any other circumstance with any other girl, I'd commend the guy, but she's not just any girl. She's Reese. My Reese. And he's hoarding my chance to spend time with her. I just need a minute or two with her, just us before she leaves. Dinner has long since been cleared, and the dessert plates are empty. It's now or never.

"Reese." I hate the crack in my voice as I say her name. I take a sip of water and try again. "Take a walk with me?" It's a dick move, pulling her from our family and Hunter, but fuck it. I need time with her.

She looks at Hunter, and he nods as if giving her permission, and that pisses me off. She's a grown-ass woman and can do whatever the fuck she wants. She stands, and I rush to do the same, offering her my arm as we leave the room.

"Where are we going?" she asks, looking up at me.

"I'm not sure," I admit. "I just needed some time with you."

Her gaze softens when she looks up at me, a gentle smile on her lips. "You missing me that much?"

"Like a fucking limb." Her eyes widen at my confession. She opens her mouth to reply, but nothing comes out.

I walk down a dark hall until I find a room marked supply closet. This will have to do. Testing the knob, the door opens. I hold it open for her, feeling along the wall for the light switch. The lighting is dim, and we're surrounded by takeout containers and other supplies.

"Are we going to get into trouble for being in here?" she asks, looking around the room.

"No." I'm not certain we won't, but I'll use my spot on the Defenders to get out of it if I have to. I'm not usually one to pull clout, but desperate times call for desperate measures. "Come here." I open my arms and love that she doesn't hesitate to walk into them. I wrap them around her and hold her close. "I've missed you so much," I whisper, my voice thick.

"I've missed you too. It's been… harder than I thought it would be."

"I'm glad it's not just me." I hold her a little tighter, because she's here and I can. My heart is racing, and my palms are sweaty. I wish I understood what was going on, why I feel this need to keep her close to me, and never let her go.

I don't know how long we stand here, locked in each other's embrace. But the ringing of my cell phone has her pulling away. Reaching into my pocket, I pull it out to see my dad's name. "Hello."

"Cooper," he says in his "dad" voice.

"Yeah."

"Bring her back." That's all he says before he hangs up.

"I guess we should get back," Reese says.

"Yeah, that was Dad. They're ready to go. Thank you, Reese. For coming today. It meant the world to me. I missed you." I reach out and tuck a loose strand of hair out of her eyes, tucking it behind her ear. Similar to what Hunter did earlier tonight.

She turns and opens the door, and panic sets in. I don't want her to leave. I can't lose her again. I can't go months without seeing her. I just… can't. I force my feet to follow her. One foot in front of the other, we make our way back to the private dining room. Hunter eyes us, but he's nothing but smiles as Reese goes to him, and he wraps his arms around her. I have to fist my hands at my sides to keep from pulling her away from him.

"Have a safe trip," my mom says, leaning into me. She looks up at me and subtly motions her head toward Reese and her parents.

"Thanks for coming," I say, my voice tight. "Merry Christmas."

"You know we love watching you play," Eve says, coming over to give me a hug. On autopilot, I wrap my arms around her. "Follow your heart, Cooper," she whispers before pulling back.

"Cooper." Garrett holds his hand out for me. "It's an honor to watch you play, son." He shakes my hand, and there is something in his eyes, but he moves away before I can describe it.

Then there she is. Reese is standing in front of me, Hunter beside her. "Great game, Coop." Standing on her tiptoes, she hugs me. I close my eyes and memorize this moment. I don't know how long it will be before I get to hug her again.

"Thank you," I choke out.

"Good to see you again, Cooper." Hunter sticks his hand out for me to shake. I stare at his offered hand for several heartbeats. It's not until Reese clears her throat that I push my hand toward his and accept the shake.

"Yeah, you too," I say, and the words feel like sandpaper in my mouth. With another round of waves and promises to see each other soon, the four of them disappear, leaving just me and my parents.

"Cooper." My dad's deep voice pulls me from staring at the closed door. I turn to face him. "When are you going to man up and face the facts?"

"What?" I shake my head. "What are you talking about?"

"You're in love with her."

"Who?"

"Reese," Mom says, laying her head against Dad's shoulder. "You're in love with her. We can all see it."

"She's my best friend."

"Your mother is mine." He gives me a pointed look.

"You guys ready to head out?" I ask, ignoring him.

"I'm going to run to the restroom before we go." Mom gives my arm a soft squeeze as she passes me.

"I've watched you with her for years," Dad says. "We all have. Your mom and I as well as Garrett and Eve. The four of us always hoped the two of you would end up together."

"What? We're best friends. It's never been like that between us." Except that one night in my room. The one night I've replayed a million times since.

"You can be more than that, Cooper. You're miserable, and, son, I hate to see you like this."

"I just missed her, that's all."

"If you say so. Just think about this. How are you going to feel when he's more than just her boyfriend? You can't go pulling her out of the room and disappear with her. You need to listen to your heart. Decide what you want and go after it. I never want you to have any regrets."

"It's fine, Dad. It's just been so long since I've seen her. I wanted a minute with her."

"You keep telling yourself that, and your fists might explode." He motions to my hands, and I look down to see them tightly gripped at my sides. I release them and stretch out my fingers.

"Ready," Mom says cheerfully.

"Let's go home. I'm beat." I lead them out of the hotel and to my Jeep. The drive to my place is quiet while I think about everything he said. I've had people tell us for years they thought we were more. We spent just as much time defending our friendship as we did actually having one. However, it's never been our families. I've never heard my parents talk about Reese and I like that. And Dad telling me they all wanted us to end up together. Have I been wrong all this time? I mean I overheard our mothers a few times. But this... this is different. My heart rate accelerates as I let my mind drift to a dream of living the rest of my life with Reese by my side. She's all I've ever wanted. I always knew, but living without her, well that makes you realize that she's more than just my best friend. She's my heart.

At my condo, I say goodnight and disappear into my room. I stare at the ceiling for hours, as thoughts of my time with Reese is on a loop. Every moment I'm dissecting and looking at it from a new angle. I know that I love her, she's always been special to me. Could we be more than just friends? Grabbing my phone, I flip through pictures of us, and my heart begins to gallop in my chest. Is it finally time for me to admit that I'm in love with my best friend?

Chapter 26

REESE

It's Super Bowl Sunday and the Defenders are playing. I'm bursting with pride for Cooper and his team. They've fought hard this season, and they deserve to play this game. They're playing the Georgia Panthers. Both teams have gone undefeated this year, and it all comes down to tonight's game. I called Cooper earlier to wish him good luck, but he didn't answer. That's why I'm packing my phone like a pistol waiting for him to call me back.

"Waiting on a call?" Hunter asks.

We're sitting in my parents' basement with Cooper's parents and mine, waiting to watch the game. There are a few other friends of our parents who are here as well. The small kitchenette is covered with food and flows over to a small folding table. There are coolers full of beer and any other drink you can think of. My mom and Ann really went all-out to celebrate Cooper's first Super Bowl. "Yeah, I called Coop, but he didn't answer. Just wanted to wish him good luck, you know?" I say, smiling up at him.

"I'm sure he'll call." He presses a soft kiss to my lips and goes off to talk with Dad and Cooper's.

Glancing at my phone, willing it to ring, I sigh and slide it in my pocket, but as soon as I do, it vibrates. I can't contain my smile when I see it's him. "Hey, you. I was a little worried I wouldn't get to wish you good luck."

"Nah, we had a team meeting. You should know I never miss a chance to talk to my good luck charm."

"You ready for today?"

"Yeah. I wish you were here, and my parents, but I'm ready."

"I know. You should see my parents' basement. Our moms went all-out."

"I wish my parents could have been here."

"I know your mom was really upset that they couldn't make it either. They wanted to be there… but your grandma."

"Yeah, I know. They're where they need to be. Close to her. How is she? Have you heard today?"

"Yeah, I went to visit her at the hospital with your mom. There's no change, really. She's pretty much out of it. I'm not sure she even realizes that we're there."

He sucks in a deep breath and slowly exhales. "Thank you for going with her. I'm going to catch a flight this week and come out to visit. Will you be there?" There's hope in his voice.

"No. I have to go back to work on Tuesday. Hunter and I both took tomorrow off. We knew we would be here late."

"Hunter's there?"

"He is." Silence greets me. "Good luck today, Coop. Not that you need it. You all have kicked ass all season."

"Thank you. The season's over, so we need to plan some time to visit. Maybe a long weekend or something."

"Sure, we can probably make that happen. I have to give two weeks' notice for time off at the office, but that shouldn't be an issue."

"Reese, I—" He stops. "There are a lot of things that I need to say."

"Everything all right?"

"Yeah, I'm fine. Just a few things I need to get off my chest."

"Sure, I'm all ears. Kick ass out there. I'll talk to you after?"

"Definitely."

"Bye, Coop."

"Bye." He sounds subdued. I don't know what's bothering him, but whatever it is, I'll be there to help him work it out. I'm sure this year has been full of changes and he just needs to talk about them. I mean, he's in the freaking Super Bowl. He's living his dream, and I'm sure that comes with a whole host of emotions.

"Hell yes!" Trevor, Cooper's dad yells as he stands from the couch as we watch Cooper run in his fifth touchdown of the game. With twenty seconds left on the clock, this run secures the win for the Defenders. My best friend is a freaking Super Bowl Champion.

The basement erupts in cheers, and we're all being so loud I'm surprised it's not rocking the foundation of the house. He did it. The Defenders did it! Gah! I can't wait to hug him and tell him how fucking proud of him I am.

"Can you believe it? He won!" I cheer, leaping into Hunter's arms. He catches me easily and spins me around.

"Like there was ever any doubt," he says, smiling down at me.

"You're incredible, you know that? You support me, no matter what."

He bends down and presses his forehead to mine. "That's why you love me."

"That's one of the reasons," I admit.

"Yeah? You have a list?" he inquires.

"We don't have enough time," I counter, making him smile. Hunter is a great guy. He's supportive in all aspects of my life, from work to spending time with my family, and even Cooper and his family. He never questions how close we are. He just accepts it.

"Try me." His grin is wide.

"Let's see. You're handsome, smart, caring. You support me, stand beside me always."

"Not bad," he says, nodding. "Can I try?"

"Oh, sure, I mean, if you think you can do better," I tease.

He smiles. "You're beautiful inside and out." He cradles my face in his hands. "You never cease to make me smile, and waking up next to you is something I want to do every day for the rest of my life." He pulls away and drops to one knee.

"Oh my God. Hunter, wh-what are you doing?" I ask, rattled. My eyes dart around the room, and I see that we now have everyone's attention. "Reese Latham. You are the love of my life. Will you do me the incredible honor of becoming my wife?"

I hear a gasp and look over to find my mom and Ann, their arms locked and tears in their eyes. I look back down at Hunter, and he's holding up a round solitaire diamond ring. "Reese, I've been carrying this ring with me for weeks, waiting for the right time to ask you. This moment, it felt right. I love you now and will love you always. Marry me?"

My heart is pounding so hard, I'm sure he can hear it. Hell, I think everyone in the room can hear it. Hunter is a good man, and I'd be lucky to call him my husband. I love him, maybe not like I love Cooper, but he and I don't have that history. In time, we'll get there. We have a lifetime to figure that out.

"Answer the man," someone calls out.

I feel my phone ringing in my pocket, but it's going to have to wait. "Yes," I whisper.

"Yes?" he asks, almost sounding surprised.

I nod. "Yes."

He slides the ring on my finger, then stands and kisses me. Not just a peck. No, he bends me over and kisses me long and hard. In front of everyone. When he stands me back up, he whispers in my ear, "I love you, Reese."

I smile up at him. "I love you too."

"Oh, it's Cooper." I hear Ann say. The room quiets a bit, but it's still loud with everyone telling us congratulations. And there's a noisemaker. I'm not sure where that came from, but Cliff, one of the guys my dad works with, places it to his lips, and the sound echoes throughout the room.

"Reese!" Ann calls out. She raises her phone in the air and motions for me to come to her. Hunter kisses my temple and releases me. "It's Cooper." Ann gives me a sad smile.

I take the phone from her and take the steps two at a time to get upstairs where it's quiet, and I can hear him. "You did it," I say once I reach the top step.

"You're getting married?" he asks.

I look down at the ring on my left hand. "Yeah. Hunter just proposed."

"Son of a bitch," he mutters.

"Coop? Everything okay?"

"Yeah," he clips. "I guess congratulations are in order." His tone sounds anything but congratulatory.

"Gee, thanks," I say sarcastically.

"What am I supposed to say, Reese? Huh?"

"Nothing, Cooper. You're not supposed to say anything."

"Look, I need to go. Tell Mom I'll call her later. I have interviews and press and all kinds of other shit I need to get to. I just wanted—It doesn't matter. Just tell Mom I'll call her," he says, and the line goes dead.

Tears burn my eyes, and I try to fight against them. Why can't he just be happy for me? Support me? I've always been there for him. No matter what the choice, I've supported him with my whole heart. I don't understand. He's mad that I'm engaged? He doesn't want me, but he doesn't want anyone else to have me either. That's not how life works. I've moved on to a man who is good to me. Is it too much to ask that he be happy for me?

Sitting on the couch, I bury my face in my hands. The ring on my left hand feels foreign. This is supposed to be a fun night. A night of celebrations, his and mine. Why is he acting like I just kicked his puppy?

"Reese?" I look up to find Ann standing next to me. "Everything okay?"

"Yes," I choke out and hold her phone out to her.

She takes a seat next to me. "You want to try that again?"

"He's mad. Cooper. He's mad at me."

"Why?"

"Because I agreed to marry Hunter. He doesn't want me, yet he

Agony | 225

doesn't want anyone else to have me either." I slap my hand over my mouth, regretting my word vomit as soon as it spews from my mouth. "I'm sorry. Please forget I said that."

"Come here." She pulls me into a hug. "I don't know what's going on, and it's not my place. What I do know is that you've always been special to my son."

"He's my best friend," I say through tears.

"I know, sweet girl. He's just having a hard time adjusting to missing all the important things in your life, and you his. You two have always been attached at the hip."

"I don't think that's it. He was upset. I just… I don't know what to do. I don't want to lose him in my life, but I feel him slipping further and further away." I can't tell her that it started the night I offered myself to him and he refused me. I keep that to myself. It's been a downhill spiral with us ever since. We've both been distant, but I never would have imagined he would act this way at my news. He's always said he wanted me to find someone who was good to me. Hunter is that man.

"Come on. Your fiancé is waiting, and your dad wants to make a toast." She hands me the box of tissues to dry my face. Once I'm all cleaned up, we make our way downstairs. Hunter is at my side immediately.

"You all right?" he asks softly.

"Yeah, just a lot of emotions, us and Coop winning. It just kind of all came at me at once."

"We don't have to rush," he tells me. "Take all the time you need. I just needed to know that you'll always be mine."

"No." I shake my head. "There's no point in waiting. We're in this together, right? Are you having second thoughts?" I ask Hunter when I should be asking myself. I don't know why I have the sudden urge to get married. It wasn't even on my radar until he asked me. Now, I guess it's just the next step. It's the next part of moving on with my life. I want to feel settled. It's been too long since I've felt that.

"Never."

"Good. Then I say a small ceremony, maybe here in my hometown?"

"Whatever you want."

"What about your parents?"

"They love you as much as I do. As long as it's what we want, they'll support us."

I pull my phone out of my back pocket and scroll through the calendar. "How's the end of March?"

"Reese, that's next month."

"Too soon?"

"No. Not for me, but are you sure? You have a huge wedding or small, it doesn't matter to me as long as you're the one standing next to me."

"Let me make some calls. There are a few venues here in town. I'll see which one can get us in and we'll go from there. How's that?"

"Perfect. Just tell me when and where, and I'll be there."

"Come over here, you two. We have some celebrating to do," my dad calls out.

We make our way to the circle of people I've grown up with and raise our glasses. Dad makes a sappy toast about his baby girl growing up and getting married, and that he couldn't think of a better man to ask for my hand. I once thought he would be saying those words with Cooper standing next to me. Just goes to show you how life changes when you don't expect it to. What you wish for isn't always the way things turn out.

Chapter 27

COOPER

I've been sitting outside of the banquet hall for about an hour. The rehearsal is supposed to start any minute, but for the life of me, I can't make myself get out of my Jeep. I grip the wheel tighter and glance over at the seat at her wedding invitation. My best friend, the love of my life, is getting married, but she's not marrying me.

I'm too late.

I wasted so much time on the fear of what-if. I was too damn blind and fucking stubborn to open my eyes and see what I had right in front of me. It didn't matter who tried to make me see it. I pushed all possibilities that she could be mine way down deep. So deep that it wasn't until she was no longer a part of my daily life after the draft and I moved, that those feelings started to rise up. Missing her made me realize that yes, she's my best friend, but she's also my fucking heart. I didn't know that I needed her to breathe until I could no longer see her smile in the flesh every single day.

Now, though, now I know what this tightness in my chest is every time I think about her, or her name gets mentioned. I know why all I can think about is wrapping my arms around her and never letting go.

I'm in love with her.

Not just the "she's been my best friend since I was eight, and we have so much history" kind of love. Although that rings true, that's not all. No, it's the "can't eat, can't sleep, can't think of anything but her" kind of love. It's imagining our future together where I'm the one who gets to change her last name. A future where we build a family, and I get to make love to her every damn night before we fall asleep exhausted, just to wake up and do it all again the next day.

It's the forever kind of love. I know this because there has never been a woman who can hold a candle to Reese in my eyes. I always thought I was just being picky, but after my dad called me out at dinner that night a few months ago, I really started to think. Think about my feelings for her, and what I want out of life. It didn't take me long. Just one long sleepless night to determine that everything in my life pointed back to her. Back to Reese. She is who I want. She's the missing link to my happiness.

I was going to tell her. I had it all planned out. I had to do my job first, though. Just one more game—the game of all games for a professional football player. I made up my mind that after the big game, we were going to talk. I even told her there were some things I needed to get off my chest. I had a job to do, but after the Super Bowl, I had planned to head back to Ohio, to Columbus specifically, and lay my heart out on the table for her. I was going to peel back all of the layers and tell her exactly what she means to me. What I didn't plan on was Hunter proposing that very night.

Also, something I never expected was to receive a wedding invitation in the mail for a wedding that was happening just one month later. Again, my eyes travel to the passenger seat, where the invitation lies crinkled. I might have wadded it up when I read it. I also might have thrown the wadded-up paper across the room, only to stalk across the room five minutes later and pick it up. I unfolded it as best as I could and hung it on the refrigerator. I used a magnet of the two of us from our family vacation to the beach our junior year of high school.

So, here I am, sitting in the parking lot like the love-sick fool that I am, trying to find the strength to go in there and watch her practice to give herself to another man. I like to think of myself as a man's man. I don't show my emotions often, and I can handle just about anything that comes my way. I'm also man enough to admit that I can't handle this. I don't know how I'm going to survive these next two days.

A knock on my window startles me. Turning, I see Nixon and Tessa. Taking in a slow, deep breath, I hit the button to roll the window down.

"What are you doing sitting out here?" Nixon asks.

"I can't go in there."

"What? Of course, you can. Reese is getting married. She expects you to be there," Tessa says, sassy as ever.

"I can't do it, Tess. I can't watch her marry him." I throw the words out into the universe. Speaking them out loud feels good. I've been keeping this bottled inside for far too long.

"What do you mean?" Her voice is soft now, and the look on her face tells me she knows exactly what I mean.

"I'm in love with her. I was going to tell her. I told her that we needed to talk, and then I called her after the game." I swallow hard. "And she didn't answer, so I called my mom, and she told me that he proposed." I shake my head to ward off the hurt that I still feel from that night. It should have been one of the best nights of my life, a highlight of my career for sure, but instead, I was miserable, angry, and pissed off, mostly at myself for keeping my head in the sand for far too long.

"Fuck," Nixon murmurs. "I told you, Reeves. I told you this would happen." He shakes his head in disappointment.

"I know. Fuck, I know, okay. I just… I can't watch her marry him. I don't know what to do." I sound pathetic, but I truly need some guidance here. I can't sit there and watch the love of my life marry another man like it doesn't bother me. That's not who I am, not when it comes to Reese and how I feel about her. Now that I can finally admit it to myself, I want to shout it to the world.

"I can tell you what you're going to do." This from Tessa. "You're going to climb your ass out of this Jeep, and you're going to go in there and put a smile on your face, and you're going to support her with this."

"I don't think I can do that, Tess." I look at Nixon. "Fuck, I can't do this."

"You have to. What can we do to help? I have to be up there with her. Nix, stay with him. Don't let him leave your sight. If it gets to where you need to leave, the two of you go together. Make it a deal about an agent or football or some other excuse. You will not ruin this for her."

"Do you think…?" I ask, letting my words trail off.

Tessa closes her eyes and exhales. "Yeah, Cooper, I do think."

"What are the two of you talking about?" Nixon asks.

"I have to tell her, Tessa. I can't let her marry him thinking that I don't love her. I have to tell her." I feel my resolve strengthening as I say the words.

"You have shit timing, Reeves."

"Better late than never, right?" I ask, and even I can hear the hope in my voice.

"Didn't Shrek say that?" Nixon asks.

"Focus, Nix. He's going to tell her."

"Wait. What? You can't do that. Not today of all days." Nixon is shaking his head and giving me a look that tells me he thinks I've lost my mind.

I have for her.

For Reese.

"What I think is that I'm crazy for even letting you entertain this, but I think you're right. She needs to know. Give her the information and let her decide. That's all you can do," Tessa says.

"Come on then, Romeo. Let's get this shitshow started." Nixon pulls open my door. I reach over and roll up the window, grabbing my keys and phone, and climb out. I follow them to the doors, and as soon as they open, my throat closes up.

I'm scared out of my mind that telling her will make me lose her for good. However, I've already lost her. If she marries him, I'll have already lost her. My eyes scan the room in search of her, but I don't see her anywhere. Hunter is standing at the end of an aisle talking to two older gentlemen. I'm so focused on looking for her that I run into the back of Tessa and Nixon when they stop walking. "Sorry," I mumble.

"She's in the bride wing." Tessa holds up her phone to show me a text message from Reese. "The time got pushed back, so you have an hour to lay your heart out on the rug." She points behind me and to the right.

"Thank you." I nod and turn on my heel in search of Reese.

"Cooper." Eve, Reese's mom, spots me. "I didn't know you were here yet. How are you?" she asks.

Oh, you know, fine. Just getting ready to tell your daughter I'm in love with her.

"Good, Eve. I was hoping to get to see Reese before this thing gets started."

"She'd like that. She's down this hall. Last door on the right. I just left her."

"Is she alone? You know, I don't want to walk in on anything." I smile. It's forced, but I don't think she notices.

"Yes. She's alone. She needed a few minutes, but I'm sure she'll be glad to see you." She pats my arm and moves on down the hall.

I take long strides until I reach the last door on the right. My hand poised to knock, I suck in a deep breath and slowly exhale. This is it. This is my one and only chance to tell her how I feel about her. To tell her she should be marrying me. My hand raps on the door three times, and I shove it into my pocket, waiting for her to answer.

"Coming!" she calls out. My knees threaten to give out as she pulls open the door. "Cooper." She whispers my name, almost as if she wished for me, and she can't believe I'm really here.

"Hey, Reese. Got a minute."

"Uh, sure, yeah, come in." She steps back and allows me to enter the room. She shuts the door behind her and takes a seat on the couch. "I wasn't sure you would be here."

"Honestly, I wasn't sure I would be here either. Well, I knew I would be here. I just didn't know if I could come inside. I sat in the parking lot for an hour before Nixon and Tessa forced me inside with them." I walk to the door and turn the lock. We don't need any interruptions while I'm pouring my heart out.

"What are you doing? And why did you need to be forced to be here? If you don't want to be here, Cooper, just leave." I can hear the hurt in her voice.

"Th-That's not what I meant." I close my eyes and try to compose my thoughts. "I want to be here for you. Always for you."

"Then why?" Her brow is furrowed as she tries to figure out why in the hell I'm talking in riddles.

Taking a seat on the couch next to her, I turn to face her. "I have so much that I want to say to you. So much that I had planned to say, and then it all got messed up. I lost my chance, and then this, here this

Agony | 233

weekend, I feel as though this is my last opportunity to tell you everything."

"Are you okay?" She leans into me, her hand landing on my forearm. It's like a shot of electricity just from one small touch of her skin to mine. *I've fucking missed her.*

"No." I shake my head. "I'm not okay."

"Talk to me, Cooper."

I don't have a speech prepared. Hell, I didn't even know I would be sitting next to her, just the two of us, giving me the opportunity to tell her what's in my heart. "I love you."

Her eyes soften. "I love you too."

"No." I shake my head. "I mean, I'm in love with you."

She freezes. "What?"

"Reese, I've always loved you. I just fought it. I was afraid that I would lose you in my life, and that if things didn't work out between us, I wouldn't have you, but yet here I am, and I've lost you anyway. To Hunter. No matter how hard we tried or how bad we wanted things to stay the same, they just didn't."

"I-I don't understand," she murmurs with tears in her eyes.

"Don't marry him. Please, Reese, don't marry him," I plead with her.

"Are you kidding me right now? This is low, Cooper. You don't want me, but you don't want anyone else to have me either. That's not fair." She chokes on a sob.

"No, baby. I do want you. I want all of you." I place my hands on her cheeks and wait for her to look at me. "I love you, Reese. Not just because I don't want you to marry him, but because I want you to marry me."

Her eyes widen at my confession. "Why are you doing this? Today of all days, why are you doing this? You've known I was getting married for weeks. Why now? Huh? Why today at my fucking wedding rehearsal? Why today, Cooper?"

"Because the thought of you marrying anyone but me makes me sick to my stomach. The thought of anyone else making babies with you has me seeing red. Because I could never live with myself if I didn't at least try."

"Try?" she asks. "Try? Really, Cooper? Trying is when I threw myself at you, and you turned me away. Trying is calling me to talk to me before this day ever happened. Trying is knowing that I've been in love with you for longer than I can remember."

"You love me?" I ask, my voice hoarse.

"Of course I do. You're my best friend."

"No." I shake my head. "That's not what you said, Reese. You said that you've been in love with me longer than you can remember."

"Fine!" she screams. "You want to lay all of our cards out on the table? Fine. I was in love with you. But you broke me, Cooper. Shattered my heart into a million tiny pieces, and some of them are still missing. Some of them are still gone. There's a gaping Cooper-sized hole in my heart that I know will be there until the day I die." Her chest is heaving as tears spill across her cheeks.

Did you hear that? That's the sound of my heart cracking open, knowing that I hurt her. I wipe at her cheeks with my thumbs. "I'm sorry. I never meant to hurt you, and I promise you I will spend the rest of my life making it up to you. Please, Reese, don't marry him."

"You want what you think you can't have. That's what this is about, isn't it? You don't want me with anyone else, so this is your last-ditch effort."

"You're right. I don't want you with anyone else. I want you with me." I beat my hands across my chest. "Me, Reese. I want you with me. Not just as my best friend, but as the most important person in my life. I want you as my lover. I want you as my wife and the mother of our kids. I want you for me. All of you and all of me."

She stands, and my hands drop to my lap. She wipes at her face as she begins to pace. Suddenly, she stops and turns to look at me. I can't describe the look. Fear, sadness, anger, and something else I can't name. "Get out, Cooper."

"Reese, please. I love you so much. Please just... don't do this. Not yet. Call it off. Give us some time. Let me have the chance to show you that you're it for me."

"You had your chance, Cooper. I can't believe you did this today of all days. How am I supposed to go out there like this? Please, just leave." She turns her back to me, and I hear her sniff.

Standing, I go to her, wrapping my arms around her from behind. I bury my face in her neck and breathe her in. We're shaking, and I'm not sure if it's her or it's me. My guess a combination of both. "I love you, Reese. I love your smile and your laugh. The way your nose scrunches up when you're laughing hard. I love that you get freaked out at scary movies but always want to watch them. I love your heart. The way you always want to help make the world a better place. You make me a better man. You make me whole, Reese. I'm not me without you."

"Cooper." Her voice breaks. "Please, don't do this. Please just go."

My heart sinks. I've lost her.

I hold onto her a little longer needing to memorize the feel of her in my arms, for what I know will be the last time. "I love you so fucking much," I say, choking on the words.

"I love you too, Cooper. A part of me always will." She turns in my arms and stares up at me with those beautiful green eyes of hers. "Do me a favor?"

"Anything."

"Stay. I don't know what brought all of this on, and I don't know what to believe. What I do know is that I'm getting married tomorrow, and I need to know that my best friend is here with me."

I shake my head. "I don't think I can do that, Reese. I can't watch you vow to love him, not when my heart aches for you. I-I don't think I can."

She nods. "You should go," she says, turning to look out the window. "I need a few minutes. If you could just tell everyone that I'll be right out."

"Reese."

"Just go, Cooper." Her voice cracks. "You said what you needed to say. You broke me years ago. To me, you're still my best friend. I pushed past the pain because I needed you in my life. If you can't be here, fine. Just go."

My feet carry me to her, and I kiss her temple. "I will always love you, Reese Latham. I will always be in your corner, and if you ever need me, I don't care how much time has passed, you call me. Do you understand me? I will never love anyone the way that I love you." It's going to fucking kill me, but I'm staying for her. Who knows, maybe it will do me some good to see her marry him. Maybe then my heart will get the message that she's not ours.

A sob escapes her and I want nothing more than to pull her into my arms and hold her tight. I want to tell her that everything will work out as it should, but she doesn't want me. I pushed her away when I should have been pulling her close. I did this to us.

"I love you." I kiss her temple one more time before my feet that feel like lead slowly carry me to the door. I pause, looking over my shoulder, hoping to find her watching me, but she's still got her back to me.

I refuse to say goodbye. I will always be here for her, no matter what. Instead, I force myself to turn around and walk out the door.

Chapter 28

REESE

I'm still wide awake when my alarm goes off at six. I didn't sleep at all. Instead, I stared at the shadows on the wall, my mind racing. No matter what I did, I couldn't shut it off. Cooper showing up yesterday, the things he said, it threw me for a loop. I was slowly rebuilding my heart and one conversation with him, the pieces began to once again crumble.

I don't know what to believe. Cooper has never lied to me, but he's never wanted me with anyone, Hunter included. He had his chance to have me, and he pushed me away. Now he tells me he was wrong? How do I know that it's his true heart talking and not just the fear of losing his best friend? My head is scrambled and my heart, well, like I told him last night, there is always going to be a huge void that only he can fill. That doesn't mean I should just call off my wedding. I love Hunter; he's a great guy. He's good to me.

"Gah!" I scream into the quiet room. I hate him just a little for doing this to me. My phone alerts me to a message, and then another. Reaching for it, I see both Hunter and Cooper's names. I read Hunter's first.

Hunter: Morning, future Mrs. Applegate. I can't wait to marry you today.

See? He's so sweet and considerate.

Me: I'll meet you at the altar.

My thumb hovers over Cooper's message. Part of me just wants to leave it unread. He said his piece, and that's that, but this is Cooper we're talking about, and no matter how mad at him I am about last night, I still want to see what he has to say. Maybe he changed his mind? Things can go back to how they were before he came barging into the bridal suite last night.

> **Cooper:** I laid awake all night wishing you were here with me. What I wouldn't give to sleep next to you every night and hold you in my arms. Pushing you away that night is my biggest regret. I would give up anything and everything to take my actions back. I wanted you, Reese. I wanted you more than my next breath, but I thought I couldn't have you. I know now that I should have just been honest with you. Then today, I would be the one you walk down the aisle to. I would be the man who gets to change your last name and live the rest of his life showing you how much I love you. I want to be that man, Reese. No matter what happens today, or twenty years from now, you will always be the love of my life. The owner of my heart. I love you, Reese Latham. Please, baby, don't marry him.

Tears race down my cheeks, and my chest is tight. I place my hand over my heart and rub, trying to dull the pain. It's no use, nothing can take the pain away. Cooper is finally saying everything I've longed for him to say, but it's just not the right time.

Wiping at my tears, I dial Tessa and place the phone to my ear. "You're getting married today," she sing-songs.

"Tess." My voice cracks.

"Oh, Reese. I'm almost there. I was on my way to drive you to breakfast. Give me five minutes."

"O-Okay." I end the call. After throwing the covers off, I go to unlock the front door. Tessa still has a key from when she lived here with me, but I don't know if she carries it. Curling up on the couch, I let the tears fall. I don't bother trying to wipe them away; they're falling too fast for me to make a difference.

"I'm here," Tess says a few minutes later. She drops her purse and keys to the floor and comes to sit with me on the couch. "What's going on?"

Knowing that if I speak, I'll sound like a blubbering fool, I pull up his message and hand her my phone. I close my eyes, not wanting to see her reaction when she reads it.

"He told you," she says softly.

Her words have my eyes popping open as my mouth falls open, and I gape at her. "What do you mean, he told me?" I wipe at my cheeks with the backs of my hands.

"Last night, we found him sitting in his Jeep in the parking lot. He was a mess, Reese. He blurted out that he loved you. Not that that's news." She shrugs.

"What? Of course it's news." How could she think it's not?

"No, really, it's not. Anyone who knows the two of you can see it. I've seen it for years. I stopped mentioning it because you didn't believe it or were in denial or whatever. Nix has actually called Cooper out on it a few times over the years."

"You didn't think you should have told me?"

"Why? You were finally moving on with your life. I didn't want to see you miserable, waiting around on him forever."

"So, now, here I am." I laugh humorlessly. "The day of my wedding and I've not slept in over twenty-four hours, and all I can think about is the look on his face last night. The pain in his eyes when I told him to leave."

"Why did you tell him to leave?"

"How can you even ask me that? Why are you asking me that?" Am I suddenly living in some kind of alternate universe?

"Just answer me honestly. Why did you ask him to leave, Reese?"

"Because I couldn't listen to him any longer. He wants what he can't have. He's always been protective of me. He will never think that anyone is good enough for me. So he's using the one thing he knows will get to me. Telling me that he loves me."

"I think you're wrong. In fact, I know you are."

"How? How could you possibly know that?"

"I know because I've seen the way he looks at you. I know because anytime we see him or talk to him, all he wants to talk about is you."

"Why didn't you tell me?"

"You were happy, Reese. At least I thought you were. These tears are telling me another version of the story."

"I am happy. Hunter is great."

"But?"

"No." I shake my head. "No buts. Cooper had his chance, and he rejected it. Rejected me."

"Did you ask him why?"

"He said he didn't want to lose me, but now he's lost me anyway, or something like that. I don't know. It's all starting to run together in one giant loop in my mind. I didn't sleep at all last night. I'm sure my eyes are red and swollen, and I *have* to get married in a few hours."

"You don't have to do anything."

"What?"

She gives me a sad smile. "You said that you *have* to get married. You should want to get married because you can't imagine your life without him, not because you feel like it's the right thing or the next step."

"I love Hunter."

She nods. "I'm not saying that you don't love him. Do me a favor. Close your eyes."

"I don't have time to play games, Tessa. My life is falling apart here."

"Trust me, Reese. Just close your eyes."

"Fine." I do as she asks and close my eyes.

"Now, I don't want you to say a word. I don't want to know what you see unless you want to tell me. I'm going to ask you a few questions, and you need to let your heart give you the answers. Not your head. Got it."

"This is crazy."

"Maybe, but humor me anyway."

"Okay. My eyes are closed," I say, even though I know that she can see me.

"Think about your wedding day. Who do you see waiting for you?"

My eyes pop open. "Come on, Tessa. This is crazy. I'm marrying Hunter in a matter of hours."

"Close your eyes." She points her index finger at me. "You agreed to cooperate," she reminds me.

"Fine." I again close my eyes.

"Now, when you think about your wedding day, who do you see waiting for you? Don't tell me, I mean, unless you want to, but this is just for you. Just think about it. Let your heart lead your mind."

With my eyes closed, I think about my wedding day. The one I had secretly always planned. It was always Cooper who was my groom. Standing at the altar, waiting to start our lives together. It was a fantasy, a dream I knew would never come true, but my heart knows that's always been the plan.

Cooper was my plan.

I squeeze my eyes tight, warding off the tears. "Okay, now think beyond the wedding. Who do you see living each day with? Who makes you smile and laugh? Who makes you go weak in the knees?"

This isn't what I need right now. I open my eyes to find her watching me intently. "This isn't helping, Tessa. I'm getting married today. I need to figure out how to hide that I've had zero sleep and to take the redness out of my eyes."

"Is that what you want?"

"It's what's happening."

"Okay." She stands to grab her purse from where she dropped it on the floor. She digs around until she pulls out a bottle of eye drops. "Here. Put a few drops in each eye. Lie down for a few minutes. We still have an hour before we have to be there. I'll wake you if you fall asleep."

"I won't sleep." I'm certain of that.

Taking the eyedrops, I lie back on the couch and drop about five drops in each eye. I'm not sure if that's the right amount, but that's what I'm going with. Closing my eyes, I try to ward off the chaos that is my mind, but nothing works. My phone pings with a message. Reaching behind me, I feel around for it. I don't open my eyes until I have it in my hands and in front of me.

Cooper.

> **Cooper:** I don't know how I'm going to do it, Reese. I don't know how I'm going to be able to sit there and watch you marry him. It's going to take more effort than I think that I have to not stand up and object. I do, Reese. I object. You're mine. You were always meant to be mine. I was just too damn stubborn to see it. Please, baby. Please don't do this.

I bite down hard on my lip, fighting back the sob that wants to break free from my chest. I read over his earlier message and then this one, twice more. My heart physically hurts to read his words.

"Reese?" I look up to find Tessa sitting in the recliner watching me. "You okay?"

"No," I say, even though I nod. My phone pings with another message.

> **Cooper:** You will always be my best friend, Reese. No matter what you choose to do today, nothing will change that. You should also know that I'll never stop loving you. I can say that with complete certainty. My heart belongs to you. I love you now and I'll love you always.

"Oh, God," I say, sobbing. Tessa stands and takes my phone from me.

"Wow. Who knew Cooper had this in him?" She smiles, trying to lighten the mood. "Are you going to reply to him?"

"I don't know what to say," I admit.

"Is he coming?"

"I don't know. I told him that I wanted him there."

"Ask him." She hands me back my phone.

"No. I can't ask him that. I already told him that I wanted him there. I can't get married without him. He's my best friend. Well, he was my best friend. I don't know if he is still or if he ever will be again. I don't know if we can come back from this."

"I wish I could tell you that everything is going to be fine. That Cooper just needs some time to adjust, but I don't know if that's the case. He was really torn up last night. If it helps, I think he's telling you the truth. He loves you, Reese."

"I know he does. Just not the way he thinks he does."

"We need to get going." She stands and offers me her hand, helping me from the couch.

I head back to my room to wash my face and brush my teeth. Today is supposed to be one of the happiest days of my life. I need to put this mess with Cooper out of my mind and try to enjoy the day.

"Reese, it's time," my mom says with tears in her eyes. "Honey, you look so beautiful." She leans in and kisses my cheek. "I always imagined your wedding being a big affair. Are you sure this is what you want?" she asks.

"Thanks, Mom. Yes, this is what I want. I'll see you out there," I tell her. She nods, uncertainty still etched on her face, kisses her fingertips, and presses them to my cheek before turning and leaving the room.

"Just me and you," Tessa says, grabbing our bouquets.

"Let's do this." I nod, and together, we make our way from the bridal suite and down the hallway. We stop at the double doors that lead us into where the ceremony is taking place.

"Reese," she whispers. I look over to find her holding up a set of keys. "I have these if you need them. No questions asked. You just say the word, and they're yours."

"What are you talking about?"

"It's not too late to change your mind, Reese." I open my mouth to speak, but she raises her hands, stopping me. "Listen," she whispers. "If you love Hunter and this is what you want, I am your biggest cheerleader. If you're not ready, or if he's not who you want, no one would fault you for walking away." She places her hand over her heart. "Follow your heart, Reese. Every past has a future. You have to be the one to decide what that future looks like."

I take a deep breath to keep the tears at bay. She dangles the keys again and winks. "I love you, Tessa. Thank you for always being there for me."

"I love you too, and don't worry, you're going to pay me back with my wedding this summer."

"Reese." I hear my dad's voice filled with awe. He stops to stand next to me. "You look beautiful," he says, blinking hard a few times, battling his own tears.

"Thanks, Dad."

"Tessa, won't be long and this will be you."

"I can't wait." She grins at him.

"You ready to do this?" Dad asks.

"Yes." I nod and slip my hand through his offered arm.

"I'll see you down there," Tessa says, pushing open the double doors. She begins her slow trek down the aisle.

My eyes scan the room, taking it all in. They land on a figure in the back row on the left-hand side of the room. The bride's side. *Cooper.* His eyes lock on mine, and I can see the pain and sorrow written all over his face. He mouths, "I love you," and I feel a slight tremble in my knees. I will never forget my best friend sitting in the back row of my wedding, looking as though he's at a funeral. The look on his face will forever haunt me.

Agony.

Thank you for taking the time to read

Agony

Want to know how Reese and Cooper's story ends?
Pre-order your copy of Bliss now.

Never miss a new release:
http://bit.ly/2UW5Xzm

More about Kaylee's books:
http://bit.ly/2CV3hLx

Contact
KAYLEE RYAN

Facebook:

http://bit.ly/2C5DgdF

Instagram:

http://bit.ly/2reBkrV

Reader Group:

http://bit.ly/2o0yWDx

Goodreads:

http://bit.ly/2HodJvx

BookBub:

http://bit.ly/2KulVvH

Website:

www.kayleeryan.com

Other works by KAYLEE RYAN

With You Series:
Anywhere With You | More With You | Everything With You

Soul Serenade Series:
Emphatic | Assured | Definite | Insistent

Southern Heart Series:
Southern Pleasure | Southern Desire | Southern Attraction | Southern Devotion

Unexpected Arrivals Series:
Unexpected Reality | Unexpected Fight
Unexpected Fall | Unexpected Bond | Unexpected Odds

Standalone Titles:
Tempting Tatum | Unwrapping Tatum | Levitate
Just Say When | I Just Want You
Reminding Avery | Hey, Whiskey | When Sparks Collide
Pull You Through | Beyond the Bases
Remedy | The Difference
Trust the Push

Co-written with Lacey Black:
It's Not Over | Just Getting Started | Can't Fight It

Cocky Hero Club:
Lucky Bastard

Acknowledgements

To my readers:

Thank you! You have been with me every step of the way, and I cannot thank you enough for taking this ride with me. I never imagined with I hit publish for the first time almost seven years ago that this is where I would be. You helped me get here and for that I will forever be grateful.

To my family:

Thank you for being by my side through all of this. I could not do this without your support. I love you.

Braadyn Pendrod:

I gave you a concept, and titles that's all you had to go off of and you nailed it! Thank you so much for the images for both Agony and Bliss. You captured Reese and Cooper perfectly.

Tami Integrity Formatting:

Thank you for making the paperbacks beautiful. You're amazing and I cannot thank you enough for all that you do.

Sommer Stein:

Time and time again, you wow me with your talent. Thank you for another amazing cover.

Lacey Black:

You are my sounding board, and I value that so very much. Thank you for always being there, talking me off the ledge and helping me jump from it when necessary.

My beta team:

Jamie, Stacy, Lauren, Erica, and Franci I would be lost without you. You read my words as much as I do, and I can't tell you what your input and all the time you give means to me. Countless messages and bouncing idea, you ladies keep me sane when the characters are being anything but. Thank you from the bottom of my heart for taking this wild ride with me.

Give Me Books:

With every release, your team works diligently to get my book in the hands of bloggers. I cannot tell you how thankful I am for your services.

Tempting Illustrations:

Thank you for everything. I would be lost without you.

Julie Deaton:

Thank you for giving this book a set of fresh final eyes.

Becky Johnson:

I could not do this without you. Thank you for pushing me, and making me work for it.

Marisa Corvisiero:

Thank you for all that you do. I know I'm not the easiest client. I'm blessed to have you on this journey with me.

Kimberly Ann:

Thank you for organizing and tracking the ARC team. I couldn't do it without you.

Bloggers:

Thank you, doesn't seem like enough. You don't get paid to do what you do. It's from the kindness of your heart and your love of reading that fuels you. Without you, without your pages, your voice, your reviews, spreading the word it would be so much harder if not impossible to get my words in reader's hands. I can't tell you how much your never-ending support means to me. Thank you for being you, thank you for all that you do.

To my Kick Ass Crew:

The name of the group speaks for itself. You ladies truly do KICK ASS! I'm honored to have you on this journey with me. Thank you for reading, sharing, commenting, suggesting, the teasers, the messages all of it. Thank you from the bottom of my heart for all that you do. Your support is everything!

With Love,

kaylee Ryan
AUTHOR

Made in the USA
Columbia, SC
17 January 2021

31141164R00155